fake it till you make it

leigh donnelly

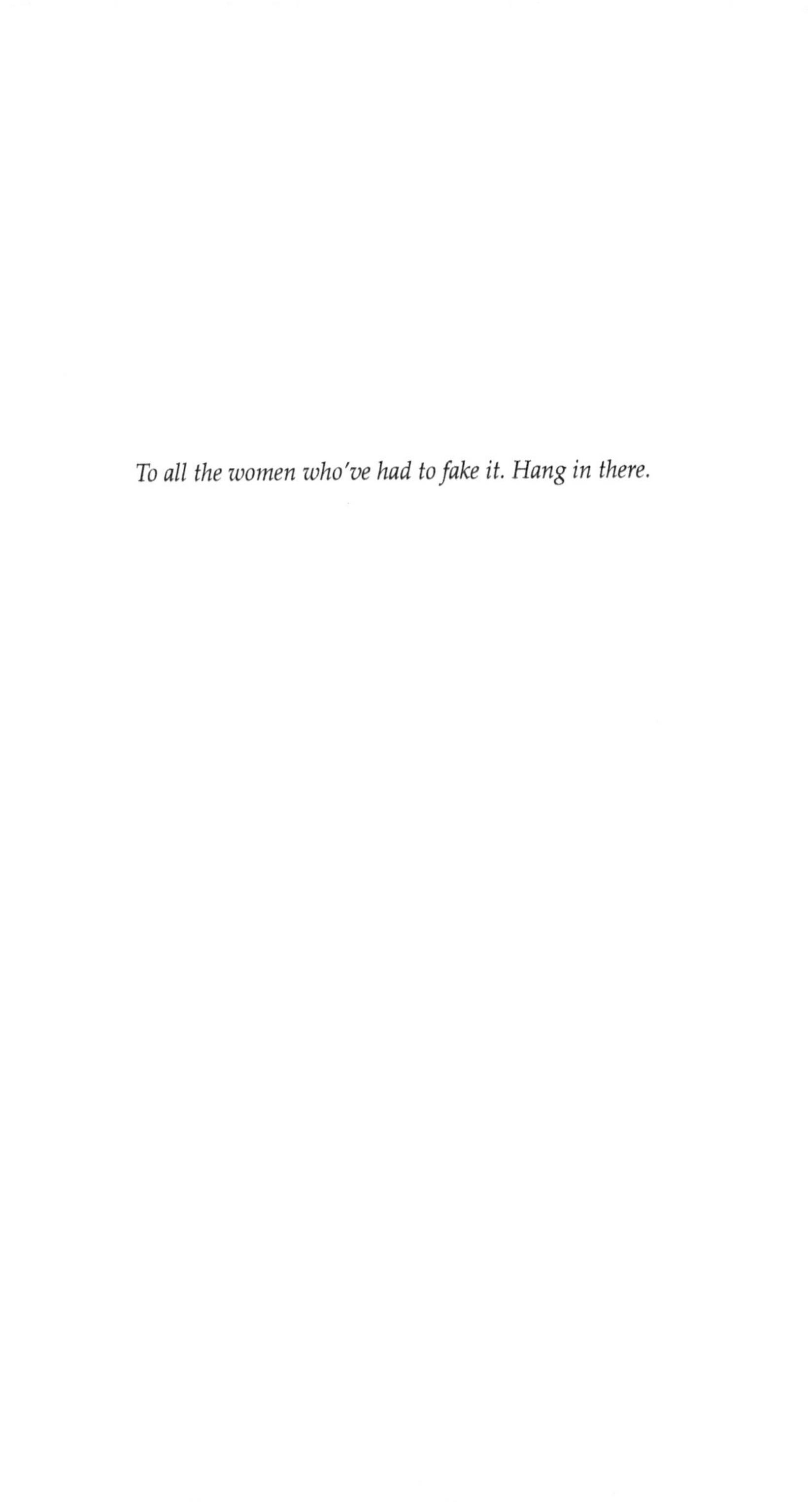

To all the women who've had to fake it. Hang in there.

monday

1

maeve

"Jillian, I can tell you're a wine-tasting kind of gal. Am I right, everyone?" Just as Maeve predicted, the small class of misfit olive oil tasters all pivoted on their stools to look at Jillian; they chuckled as they nodded in agreement.

Just as Maeve knew she would, thanks to a quick social media search the day before, Jillian's back straightened as she announced, "I've been to Napa four times." She even held up four perfectly manicured fingers—including a ring finger with a giant diamond—so anyone struggling to keep up with what the number four meant could understand her comment. How considerate of her.

"I thought so. Now, as we've been swishing around our glasses with one hand cupping the bottom, we've been warming our olive oil and releasing some of the delicious aromas sealed in there with the handy little lid you each got. Jillian, what do you think we'll do next?"

Maeve had done a few classes before where she hadn't laid it on as thick and the customers had stared back at her, dumbfounded. Their faces had screamed, How the fuck should I know? That's why I'm here, to learn what to do!

Not Jillian, though. Sweet, sweet Jillian fell right in line. Her bright red lips formed a broad smile, and she gave the person next to her, her husband of seven years, according to Facebook, a look that said, "See what a star you've married?" Then she explained to Maeve and the rest of the class how they should stick their noses way down into the stemless wine glass, as far as it would go, to pick up the various scents and aromas that had been released.

Once everyone had followed Jillian's expert instructions and identified the different smells of the oil she'd selected for the first round of tasting, Maeve had them to pour it onto the plate in front of them to taste it using the freshly baked gluten-free bread bites that were at the center of each of the high-top barrel tables.

From trial and error, she'd figured out traditional olive oil tasting, the actual swishing and swallowing of olive oil all by its lonesome, was a niche experience few people would pay top dollar to have. Olive oil paired with fresh bread? That was where the money was, even if it didn't follow official tasting protocol.

For the next hour, Maeve played to her audience as she led them through the basic olive oil flavors: fruit, garlic, mushroom, and more. Each round ended with a palate cleanser of green apple which she sliced fresh as they tasted.

Maeve had spent her undergrad years bartending, and she'd perfected the art of matching the right story with her given audience. Through a bit of social media digging prior to the class, and from initial interactions, she pegged the current group as a "live vicariously through her" group—so long as she kept her stories light, they were happy to hear them.

While they dipped and tasted and savored, she filled the silence with history about olive oil and tales about her trip through the Mediterranean where she'd done some tastings of her own to prepare for opening her shop: Olive What She's Having.

Throughout her years in the service industry, she'd found laughter was the key to everything: customers were more forgiving, were willing to leave larger tips, and tended to let down their guard so that they could fully enjoy whatever experience they were engaged in. She was careful to include only the stories that involved humor and happy endings.

This meant she never included the reason she'd taken the trip solo: Jackson, her fiancé at the time, had gotten cold feet. He'd backed out of the trip and their future together at the last minute. Literally. They were supposed to meet at the airport gate and he didn't show. Instead, he'd sent a text message:

This isn't working.

No one wanted to hear the story about her abject dumping, her brief determination to symbolically flip him the bird by taking it on her own, or the drunken mess she'd turned into during the eight-hour flight over. Instead, they were with her to escape their own shitty lives. Together, for one hour, Maeve pretended her life was nothing but silly little misunderstandings that turned into great conversation pieces, and everyone in her class left their troubles at the door as Maeve guided them through a bit of drizzly culinary heaven. A simple thing to do, given their surroundings.

They were in the basement room, a former speakeasy back in the day which in and of itself people wanted to see, with or without the accompanying olive oil tasting. The room had walls of stacked stone that created a large arch along the ceiling down the length of the room. She'd installed outlets and had electricity, but to maintain the ambiance of the historic stonework, she did her best to hide modern technology. She especially loved the candles she'd placed around the perimeter and at the center of each table. It gave 1700s vibes which was what most people were looking for in their travels through the tiny, historical New England towns. Her location in Galway Harbor was the epitome of a pre-revolutionary historical town. The chief attractions were the scattered beaches with crystal clear water, rocky coves covered in granite and river rock, and historic landmarks: sporadic cobblestoned streets and centuries old houses that had somehow survived while time had marched on around them.

Having doled out the latest serving of apples, she looked around and sized up the clientele. She liked to guess what post-class purchases each group would make based on the session and what she'd researched beforehand. There was Jillian and hubby—they looked like they were good for a case or four. Doubtful they'd get through all of it before it went bad, but they were the type that liked everyone to know they had enough money to go to Napa four times and to purchase four cases of flavor-infused olive oil, whether they needed it or not.

With them at their table was a guy named Steve, the only person to show up to the class by himself. She'd immediately clocked that he was a gorgeous specimen of a man, but that was about it. Maeve didn't trust men, and she didn't trust her taste in men after the Jackson debacle. There'd been a few dates here and there since, but those were all blind dates from apps and she'd felt more of a connection with the bacon-wrapped scallops on her dinner plate than with any of the men. Her love of food lasted forever. Men? Not so much.

Steve had a bag full of books about marketing from the indie bookshop a few streets down, and from his online profile she knew he was the owner of a gluten-free food truck. She was counting on him to buy at least a few bottles to test out with his business, maybe more in the future.

For the briefest of moments, she thought about trying to start up some sort of conversation about the food truck industry to see if there was some sort of partnership potential between the two of them. Running a business was no easy task, and it helped to have friends who were local and in a similar industry.

She shot the idea down once she caught herself having indecent thoughts about him: her fingers twisting through that silky dark, almost black hair that was currently in a man bun while her other hand…

No, no way. Terrible idea. She shook her head and cleared her throat as if she could literally shake the thought away. Mixing business with pleasure was a hard no, especially when she had zero interest in men beyond some sort of hook-up.

Galway Harbor was too tiny a town to fill with exes. There would be no escape, just constant reminders of her love life failures. She'd fled her hometown and Jackson, but she was settled now with a career and town she loved. Running away from her problems was no longer a viable solution, it was best to not create any more problems.

Her eyes left Steve's toned upper body and bare ring finger and instead continued on to the next table.

In the middle was a group of older women, reminiscent of *The Golden Girls*. They'd maybe get a bottle each, a little something to liven up their meals. Likely, they'd only signed up for the class for something to do to fill their idle, retired days. Next week, they'd be in some back room learning how to make their own candles or soaps.

The last table was a trio of middle-aged men who were doing an extended food tour of New England. They'd had breakfast in Gloucester before making their way up to Galway Harbor for the night. Olive What She's Having was a way to get in a quick snack between shopping and sight-seeing before grabbing dinner by the water. Given the sole purpose of their trip was to sight-see and eat, Maeve knew she could count on them for at least a few bottles each.

She took a peek at her watch: three on the dot. Holy shit. She impressed even herself with her time management skills. With a clap of her hands, she said, "Okay, everyone. Clearly I've saved the best for last with that bacon olive oil—I saw

Clara over there practically licking her plate—so that concludes today's tasting class. However, the flavor possibilities with olive oil truly are endless and we have an extended variety available upstairs for informal, self-guided tastings as well. Not to mention our fabulous assortment of balsamic vinegars, which are equally delicious. Everything you've tasted is available for purchase by bottle or case, and if you leave us a review on Yelp, we may," Maeve lowered her voice and put a hand to her mouth as if telling a secret, "we absolutely will," before continuing again in her normal teaching voice, "send you an email with a 20% off coupon for your next purchase with us."

After everyone had made their way up the metal spiral staircase to the main retail space above, Maeve reached under the table and pulled out a generously full glass of wine. Being "on" was draining when she wasn't in the right mood for it, so she'd stashed that bad boy under there as part of her prep work for the class. It had called to her throughout the session, encouraging her to continue kicking ass so she could reward herself with the tasty libation right afterwards.

When she'd first opened Olive What She's Having, she'd had such high hopes for what it would do for her life. Mainly that it would fill the hole Jackson had left when he stomped his giant, furrier-than-a-hobbit foot through her chest. There she was three years later with an immensely satisfying career, a cozy little apartment above her store, and an adorable kitten named Hedy who loved her as much as any cat could show love for a human. And yet that hole refused to fill. There was always some feeling of emptiness that would ebb and flow from being an annoying crack to a massive fissure that could swallow her whole.

Each morning she sat at her little breakfast nook, and as the sun rose over the rocky coastline below her, she drank her coffee and read a book. The ball of fur in her lap keeping her company along with the fictional characters in her novels.

What more could she need? Her mind refused to accept the glaringly obvious answer, and instead she'd insist to herself that if only she painted more or read more enlightening books, or traveled more, she wouldn't feel so lonely.

In the cozy basement surrounded by candlelight and the smells of olive oil, bread, and apples, she took a large sip of room temperature wine and pushed the "my life is empty" thoughts from her mind once more. Another one of her strengths aside from successfully opening and running her shop? Running away from things she didn't want to face. So rather than face her feelings of feeling less than satisfied with life, she turned her attention to her glass of wine and her fluffy cat.

Knowing her best friend and employee, Kiki, had everything covered upstairs with the customers, Maeve took her phone out of her work apron and checked her Snapcat app. It soothed her soul to flip through the different video feeds to find her sweet Hedy, named after the kick-ass inventor Hedy Lamarr. A few sips of wine and a look at the black pile of fur sunning on the living room floor actually lifted her shoulders as the emotional weight diminished ever so slightly.

When her phone popped up with a text from Kiki, she immediately tensed up again. Her eyes ran over the text three times, so sure she'd misread it or was missing something.

"No fucking way," she said to no one in particular. Jackson was supposed to be practically married to some woman back in their hometown of Milton, Maryland. So why were they upstairs in her store asking to see her?

2

steve

Steve had big plans for his day off from the truck: guided kayak tour like the tourist he still was, pick up some much-needed reading material on how to market his failing business, and take a course on tasting and using infused olive oil.

He always enjoyed the challenge of switching out menu items while still maintaining the overall feel of the food being exceptional enough that it deserved a spot on the "today's specials" board–hence the name of his food truck: Today's Gluten-Free Special. But he also knew neither the menu nor their cooking was the cause of their financial woes. It was their inability to market themselves, to adequately schedule events for their truck, and to compete for customers in what was steadily becoming an oversaturated market.

The dozenth or so time he saw an ad for the olive oil tasting class pop up on his phone, he finally caved and decided to give a menu revamp another go. Besides, there was something about the owner of the store that drew him in, made him believe that olive oil was the end all be all of cooking, and that he did not know shit about it. A severe problem that only she could solve.

When his business partner Heath suggested they take the day off, not that they'd had anyone begging them to park outside their business or event anyway, it sealed the deal of him booking a last-minute ticket to the class.

Maeve, the owner of Olive What She's Having, reminded him of Heath. She was impressively outgoing as she easily made connections with everyone in the class and created a sort of camaraderie between them. Even more impressive was how she did it without a single ice breaker. All of it had revolved around olive oil and her travels in pursuit of finding the perfect one.

Aside from being an olive oil aficionado, she was also full of random knowledge. As they tasted she talked about her travels and peppered in Mediterranean-related trivia: Turkey's national sport is oil wrestling, they're one of the main grape providers world-wide for wine thanks to their fertile soil, and Shakespeare may not have ever stepped foot in Italy even though *Romeo and Juliet* takes place in fair Verona.

As she talked, Steve daydreamed about the two of them on a couch watching *Jeopardy* together. Both competing to answer before the other and keeping score on some old notepad on the coffee table that was already full of tally marks from previous games.

He'd promptly snapped out of his hypothetical future with Maeve when Jillian accidentally stepped on his foot with her four-inch heel.

The hour flew by and he was mildly disappointed when Maeve signaled the end of the class. There was an advanced tasting that he could have taken as well, but that one involved actually drinking olive oil and he wasn't sure he was that into it, or her. Though in her defense, he'd been captivated enough that he'd left the cellar area without taking along his previously purchased marketing books and had to go back down to retrieve them.

Halfway down the stairs, he noticed her on her phone, fully consumed by some cat videos as she drank a heaping amount of olive oil from one of the tasting cups.

That settled it. He would not be attending the advanced class.

He tried not to disturb her as he tiptoed toward the table and bent down to grab his bag.

"No fucking way," he heard her accuse from behind when his back was to her.

She's an angry olive-oil drunk, he thought before turning to say, "I'm sorry. I just came back to grab my bag." One hand held his bag and the other he held up in front of him in defense.

"What?" She looked up at him with a mixture of confusion and annoyance, though he couldn't tell if the annoyance was aimed at him or not, and then she shook her head. "I... No. Sorry, I didn't even hear you come down. I was..." She sighed, closed her eyes and pressed her lips together, then opened them again as a new person. "It doesn't matter," she said, her voice all flowery again. Just as it had been during the lesson, though now there was a small crease between her eyebrows that betrayed her.

"Got everything this time?" she asked.

"All set. Thanks." He held up his bag again as he hurried for the steps, not wanting to intrude any more than he already had.

He'd almost made it back up when something forced him to take one last glance into the tasting room to check up on her. She'd turned back to her phone again, her face full-on distressed as she turned her glass 180 degrees, desperate to get the remaining drops. He was relieved when he realized Maeve wasn't actually drinking olive oil; it was white wine.

"Everything alright?" he bent down below the ceiling to ask, realizing a touch too late how half-hearted it must have sounded when he was already halfway out of the room.

Her face transformed again, that smile re-emerging as she tucked her red hair behind her ear and cheerfully said, "Absolutely. I'm good."

She wasn't, but she'd made it clear she wasn't about to unload on a random "student" she'd just met. Besides, he had problems of his own to tend to. He was about to leave to get to them when she called out to him.

"Wait. I…" She chewed on her bottom lip. "I might have something small you could help me with, if you don't mind."

Steve turned and walked back down the few steps to the stone floor. He assumed she'd just gotten a text that a last-minute large group was coming through and she needed some help moving tables and stools around. It didn't feel like he did much right lately, but that he could do without mucking it up.

"Sure, I can help. I'm happy to," he said as he rolled up his sleeves.

"I need you to pretend to be my boyfriend," Maeve said quickly, as if ripping off a bandage.

Steve froze. It was so far beyond what he'd expected. His brain couldn't comprehend what she'd said and refused to come up with any sort of response.

"Please, Steve…" Finally, Maeve dropped the fake flowery voice, let her shoulders sag, and let her smile drop away. "My coworker just texted that my ex fiancé is upstairs. I haven't seen him in years. He knows I'm down here finishing up, and he's waiting me out. It sounds petty to want to win after a breakup, but I really want to fucking win, or at the very least, break even. He's with someone new; I need to be with someone new."

Steve didn't have a chance to react before Maeve pressed her lips together again before saying, "I'm so sorry. I usually don't swear in front of customers and I never, ever ask them to be my fake boyfriend. The wine and Jackson are messing with my head. Forget I said anything."

"I don't think—"

"I'll help you with your food truck marketing," Maeve blurted out after she glanced at her phone again, the message still on the screen.

He looked down at his bag, now laying on the floor by the stairs since he thought he was going to do physical heavy lifting. It wasn't hard to guess he was interested in marketing. The translucent material of the bag revealed the covers of his books.

"How did you know I have a food truck?"

"I research all my tasting clients. It's good marketing to know your audience, but let's keep that between us. Some people find it… unnerving."

Steve gave a half smile. That would explain what he'd thought was a random, coincidental comment Maeve had made to the class about how olive oil stores great in cool, dark places, but should not be stored in vehicles or food trucks unless in a climate controlled area. And why she'd had gluten-free bread for their tasting.

"Research. Makes sense, I guess. And you think you can help me with marketing?"

"I regularly convince dozens of people to drink olive oil in my basement and then sell them cases of the stuff. You've seen my packed store in the middle of a weekday."

"Good point."

It was a tempting offer. The books he'd purchased were weighing him down with their physical and metaphorical weight as he imagined how many hours he'd need to devote to reading each one in order to implement the techniques they'd expound. When he realized he'd left the books behind, he was almost certain it had been a desperate attempt by his subconscious to save him from the experience.

And yet he still couldn't allow himself to accept her offer. For one thing, it probably wasn't a good idea to pretend to date someone he actually could see himself dating. Now that he knew she wasn't drinking straight olive oil, his daydreams about them playing *Jeopardy* each evening with a beat up notepad were back in full force.

Unfortunately, what ultimately held him back were the persistent words from his ex reminding and nearly convincing him he was the worst human being on the planet and how all women should steer clear of his many toxic traits. Save some occasional flirting, he hadn't been with anyone since his most recent clusterfuck of a breakup a few months back. The ex's unrelenting voice in his head never allowed it.

"I do all my own marketing," Maeve said as she continued to lure him to the dark side. Her confident, flowery voice was in full effect, giving any listener who tried to resist a run for their money. "What I've done for my store, I can do for Today's Gluten-Free Special."

Steve shifted his weight from one foot to the other. He could head home and dive into his thick, boring books, or he could act like a boyfriend for a few minutes and get some legit one-on-one marketing help from someone whose results he'd already seen in action. He clearly remembered the social media ad she'd created that convinced him to sign up for the tasting that day. Effective indeed.

Maeve stood up and tucked her phone back into her apron. "No, you're right," she said, tucking a rogue section of vibrant, copper-colored hair behind her ear. "That was the wine and the shock talking. It's a stupid idea—"

"I'll do it," he interrupted in a voice louder than what was absolutely necessary given they were in a small, cellar-like room. Apparently, it was Steve's turn to sound desperate.

"Really?"

She was cute when she gave him a genuine smile in return. Hell, it was worth it even for that. Damn, he really was eager to please, and maybe a little too desperate for companionship. Or, maybe there was just something about her situation–the ghosts of relationships past coming back to haunt her when she least expected it–that he knew all too well. Either way, there was some sort of pull and he decided to stop fighting it.

"Yeah, I'm in. I just stand there and look pretty, right? Follow your lead?"

"Exactly. You know next to nothing about me besides my random trip stories, so less is definitely more."

The two spent the next few minutes blowing out all the candles and nailing down the general details about their relationship.

"Since we're keeping it simple, do we stick with the story that we met in your class? I can tell them how I was drawn to your vast knowledge of olive oil and witty anecdotes about traveling around the Mediterranean."

"I don't know about that." Like a reformed nail biter, her thumbnail rested between her teeth, but she didn't bite down. "Is that something someone would do? Ask out their olive oil instructor?"

"It's not as taboo as you think…"

She blushed and gave a soft laugh. "No, not the whole teacher-student thing. It just sounds so lame, meeting and flirting during a sixty-minute session about infused oil."

"Did you not see Clara licking her lips and throwing seductive eyes at Otto? A few more minutes and we'd have had a show; I'm sure of it."

Rightfully so, she wrinkled her nose at the thought of the octogenarians throwing caution to the wind to bump uglies in her tasting cellar and said, "That's not helping your case as much as you think it is."

With all the other candles out, they stood around the last table with the one remaining lit candle between them. Maybe it was the setting, or maybe it was something to do with Clara and Otto's imminent fling. Perhaps it was the way Maeve looked at him with those giant brown eyes, a smile still on her face even though she was clearly not pleased with the ex and his unannounced arrival. Whatever it was, Steve found some of the confidence he'd recently lost and surprised even himself when he said, "Maeve, my love, my one and only. In your wildest dreams, how would we meet? You deserve nothing less, even if it's only for the briefest of moments and only as part of an elaborate ruse."

Witty lines and Casa Nova charms were not his thing, but he'd been watching his ridiculously charismatic roommate lately, so he figured he could just mimic whatever he expected Heath to do in a situation like this one and he laid it on thick.

Without hesitation, she beamed back. "We met at a book-store, the one you got your books from today. I had a stack of books, but when I got to the checkout counter, I realized I forgot my wallet. You were behind me in line and you insisted on paying for my books. All 20 of them."

"You buy that many books at one time?!" The small enclosure of the basement increased the decibel level of his already too loud response and he cleared his throat in some small effort to take back his too shocked response.

"In my wildest dreams? All the time," she said with a wild, vivacious look in her eyes.

"And I offered to buy them all for you?" Never in his own dreams would he ever do something like that. Heath might, but never him. The thought made him feel less deserving of her somehow, and he wished he hadn't questioned it. He sounded like a cheap bastard rather than someone who would never have the guts to make such an offer for someone he didn't know.

"You insisted on buying them," Maeve said. "'Adamant' is probably the best word to use if it comes up. You noticed I had a few of your favorite books and you couldn't bear me missing out on them."

Her energy was infectious, and he was right there with her, longing for it to somehow be their real-life story. This was the version of himself he longed to be. "I like where you're going with this. We could say you had the biography of cod in your stack–"

"Cod?" she asked. "Like the fish?"

"Yeah, cod–"

"And it's a biography?"

He wondered if the soft light from the lone candle was enough for her to notice his face reddening.

"Yes, a biography about cod where Kurlansky, the author, provides a fascinating tour through the history of the fish that changed the world," he said, his voice trailing off at the end as he realized his mistake.

Her eyes narrowed and glanced at the stairs, as if debating if she should make a run for it. Face the ex alone rather than bring up a fake boyfriend who loved biographies about fish.

"I read other stuff, too," he added much too late. In his mind he saw Heath's face contorted with confusion and saying something like 'Bloody hell, Steve. You don't think I'd actually say something as asinine as that to a woman, do you?' His strong British accent came through as it always did when he was indignant about something.

"Stephen King, Allison Feeney, Andy Weir…" Steve listed as he fumbled through his recovery.

"We'll redirect if the titles of the books come up." Maeve looked at her phone. "We should probably get up there. You ready?"

3

maeve

"Jackson, what are you doing in Massachusetts?" Her voice was high pitched, too high pitched, and she felt Steve's warm, soothing hand give hers the slightest squeeze of encouragement. He must have sensed how close she was to losing her shit.

Jackson looked like he'd stepped out of *GQ* magazine. His dark hair was trimmed short and neat, no facial hair, and he was dressed head-to-toe in an outfit that must have come straight off a Helly Hansen mannequin.

Steve was the exact opposite. His long hair was pulled into a tight bun and his clothing was more relaxed with jeans and a flannel that he wore untucked and unbuttoned revealing a Smashing Pumpkins t-shirt underneath.

"Maeve," Jackson said as he took a step away from the blonde beside him to pull her into a bear hug. Her one arm hung limply by her side while the other clung to Steve's and her mind raced.

Instinctively, she closed her eyes and took it all in. He still smelled the same, and the familiar scent transported her to the last time she saw him, when she was picking up her final remaining box of things from the apartment. She'd given him a similar hug as she tried to remind him how much they loved each other and how perfectly their bodies fit together. Could he be trying to do the same in store, in front of his new girlfriend?

"Do you remember Chasity?" Jackson asked as he motioned to the woman next to him who was facing the shelf, engrossed in one of the olive oil labels. When they'd separated, there hadn't been anyone else—as far as she knew.

The blonde, Chasity, turned to face Maeve, and Maeve fought the urge to projectile vomit all the bread, wine, and specially infused olive oil she'd inhaled earlier.

"Maeve!" the blonde cooed as if she'd had no idea Maeve was going to be in the shop that Maeve owned, even though that was clearly why she and Jackson were there to begin with.

"You look great!" she continued as she went in for a hug. Maeve and Chasity had played field hockey together in high school. They weren't best friends, but they had spent a fair amount of time together on the field and on the bus to away games. For the most part, their relationship had been cordial and she couldn't remember disliking Chasity. Though that was before Chasity started sleeping with her ex fiancé.

None of it felt real. She'd so thoroughly created a life up north that was wholly independent of Jackson, that it almost felt like her new life was just a dream. Him with another woman, standing smack in the middle of her devoid-of-Jackson world, was like waking up from the dream by being doused with a bucket of cold water.

"Yeah, and look at you," Maeve said as she took her in and tried to figure out why in the hell Chasity would think Maeve would be excited to see her, the woman about to marry the man she almost married. The man she'd desperately wanted to marry.

Before Maeve could point it out for her, Steve's hand left

hers as he held it out for Jackson and Chasity to shake. "Hi, I'm Steve, Maeve's fiancé."

Woah, Steve for the win with the fiancé improv. She made a mental note to give him a complimentary bottle of her favorite olive oil for that one.

As they did the small introductions, the two women simultaneously eyed each other's ring fingers. Maeve's was bare, obviously, and she couldn't help but notice that Chasity's ring looked eerily similar to the one Jackson had given to her. It clearly wasn't hers since she'd hocked it at a pawn shop in Liguria, Italy, but to say that it had slightly triggered her would be an understatement. She leaned hard into Steve's engagement lie as she held up her hand for Chasity to see.

"It's with the jeweler," she explained. "Steve had it made one-of-a-kind. The only one like it. He's the best in town if you need any work done on yours."

"I'm sure it's beautiful," Jackson said, while his fiancée took a quick glance at her own ring finger, likely questioning how unique her ring was. Jackson cleared his throat. "We're actually in town for a wedding." After the briefest of pauses, he added, "our wedding."

Any other person would have held their head down slightly, sheepishly at such an announcement. Not Jackson. Maeve couldn't tell if it was her eyes playing tricks on her, or if he actually stood up a little straighter when he said it. And were his eyes looking for some negative reaction from her? Before she could over-analyze it any further, Chasity droned on about her upcoming wedding.

"Instead of some big to-do in Maryland," she said, completely ignoring the fact that she was speaking to the woman Jackson almost married, "we decided to come up here for an intimate ceremony with a few select family members and friends."

Maeve's face was frozen in some sort of fake smile that

she usually reserved for disgruntled customers. Galway Harbor was their place. Years ago, on some lovely autumn day, she and Jackson had flipped a coin while standing on a giant map stamped into the concrete at a local park to see where they should go for an extended weekend. The coin first landed in the Atlantic Ocean. Looking back, she could see that was an omen she should have picked up on. The second flip had landed on Galway Harbor. Jackson only knew of the damn place because of that weekend trip with Maeve. Now, he'd brought Chasity—an old classmate and former friend of Maeve's—up to their place to get married with an engagement ring that looked almost identical to the one he'd given her?! The frozen smile remained, but inside she did that thing that happens in cartoons where the top of their head pops off as fire and steam shoots out.

Steve, clearly unable to take the silence that followed and sensing that Maeve needed not only a life saver but an entire damn cruise line to come rescue her, mercifully filled the chasm forming between the couples by offering his congratulations and asking polite questions about the wedding.

Meanwhile, Maeve nodded here and there with her customers-first smile and tried to take in at least some of what they were saying. She was vaguely aware of Steve's hand stroking her back to soothe the beast she was about to become.

"It was nice meeting you, Jackson and Chasity," Steve said with a nudge on Maeve's shoulder.

"Hmm?" Her eyes had been glued to Chasity's ring as her own thumb rubbed the spot on her finger where her ring had been a few years prior. "Oh, right. Have a good," there was another abrupt pause mid-sentence. Then she swallowed down her boiling over emotions and said, "wedding. Have a good wedding."

The three other adults in the conversation circle kindly acted as though that was something people commonly said and proceeded with their own polite goodbyes. Jackson said they should all get together before the wedding, but no one else took him up on it and the suggestion withered up and died without any firm plans being made.

As soon as Jackson and Chasity were out the door, Steve—a complete stranger a little over an hour ago—stepped back out of Maeve's personal space and let his hand drop from her back.

"Thank you for doing that, Steve. Here," she said as she pulled a business card from her apron and handed it to him. "Just shoot me a text so I have your number, and we'll set up a time to talk about marketing."

"Sounds good." Before he turned to leave, he leaned in slightly. "For what it's worth, it was a dick move for him to ambush you like that. I think you dodged a bullet."

"Thanks," she said, disregarding his comments. He was clearly delusional assuming she'd dodged a bullet. She could think of very few women who would see Jackson and Chasity and say, "That poor woman with her handsome and charming fiancé. So sad…"

Once Steve left, her co-worker Kiki locked the door and flipped the "We're Open" sign to "Sorry, We're Closed."

"Come on," she said, grabbing the emergency bottle of red they'd kept under the front counter for the past two years. It had been a gift from the Wine Not wine tasting bar across the street when she'd first opened her olive oil store. Kiki brushed off the dust and snagged two tasting glasses as she led Maeve down into the tasting cellar.

Kiki glanced at her phone. "You have another tasting in less than an hour, but first, we need wine. I have the perfect playlist already queued up, starting with Annana's 'I Really, Really Hope You Die.' I'll light the candles and some incense. We need to get that nasty juju out of here before the next crew comes through."

4

steve

He spent the drive home debating how in the hell he was going to explain to Heath how he'd gotten roped into pretending to date Maeve in exchange for marketing help. As he put the car in park, he was no closer to figuring out the perfect segue into a conversation about his unorthodox quid pro quo, so he settled on his time-honored tradition of avoidance until it was unavoidable. Then he'd just wing it.

Heath was on the couch watching a reality cooking show on some entertainment channel. It was the same spot he'd been in when Steve left the apartment hours earlier, and it was the same show though clearly a season or two later since most of the celebrity judges had had a significant amount of plastic surgery since he'd left that morning.

He was about to rag on Heath about wasting his day watching TV when his past finally resurfaced to bite him in the ass. There, on one of those damn news tickers at the bottom of the screen, was Annana's name listed along with some other random celebrities who were all "spotted" at whatever club they'd been at the night before.

"You're home early," Heath said. He didn't bother turning away from the TV to see who it was. They were both single. They had been when they first started the business, then they continued to be once it took over their lives. Though Heath–with his accent and rugged good looks–frequently had women visiting his bedroom, no one ever made it to girlfriend status.

"It's after three," he said absently as he set the books down on the tiny round dining room table that sat between the living room area and what was considered a kitchen: one wall of cabinets that had a sink, oven, and refrigerator smashed into it.

"Shit. It is. I guess I zoned out for a bit. Did you see that thing about Annana?"

Heath and Steve had waited tables together back in LA. Heath had been the first to migrate out to the East Coast to try his hand at opening a restaurant with the help of an already successful uncle located not too far from Galway Harbor. He'd left right when Steve had started dating Annana and knew nothing of how it ended.

"Yeah. Looks like she's finally made it." He took a breath and then added with a considerable amount of sincerity, "Good for her."

One of the best things about rooming with Heath was that he gave zero fucks about Steve's personal life. Sure, he'd turned to look at Steve and cocked one eyebrow up to show the slightest bit of confusion, but that was it. He wouldn't ask Steve to dive into all the seedy details of why he wasn't more interested in an ex who was sky-rocketing to fame before their very eyes.

Even so, Heath acknowledging that Steve had some connection with Annana and thus with the song that was currently driving her newfound fame was still too much for him. His stomach roiled and he could feel his body tensing–

every muscle seizing as it mistook the emotional stress for actual life-threatening stress and prepared to do physical battle.

Steve had realized Annana wasn't a good fit for him sometime after New Year's, just a few months into their relationship, and had broken up with her not long after because he didn't want her to get the wrong idea about how serious their relationship was.

Based on her reaction, he'd thought their break-up had been mutual; he'd found out he was very, very wrong when in April he'd heard her latest song, "I Really, Really Hope You Die," while he was cruising down the cereal aisle of a grocery store.

The lyrics detailed how some guy named Reeve (how generous of her to change the names to protect the innocent) had callously destroyed her soul with his dismissive break-up before moving on to his next victim almost immediately. Not seeing the connection at first, he actually was on her side wondering what dick she'd dated after him.

Then came the lyrics about how Reeve had kissed her when he had strep a few days before the biggest gig of her career, and dumped her on her birthday at her favorite place in the city, thus tainting all memories of that sacred location. That was when it finally dawned on him: he was the dick. Steve was Reeve. There could be no other explanation.

While he hadn't left her for someone else, most everything else in the song had some truth to it. Steve got strep when they were dating, but he'd been asymptomatic. He hadn't known when he was kissing Annana that he was passing on his strep throat to her. It hadn't been malicious or negligent as her song had accused.

Similarly, he'd dumped her on *a* birthday, but it wasn't *her* birthday, it was her dog's gotcha day and he'd not been privy to that information since they hadn't been dating that long and she'd never brought it up before. To him, she'd seemed mostly indifferent towards the animal.

Still, he couldn't bring himself to explain it all to Heath or anyone else. It always sounded so petty in his mind when he tried to clear up the inaccuracies of the song. He also struggled to reconcile with himself how even though he knew the most hateful parts of the song were only loosely based on his relationship with her, it still hurt his soul to hear teenagers (and sometimes adults) randomly belting out lyrics about dick-head Reeve as they drove through parking lots, it hurt to be in a store and hear the hateful words blaring from ear buds with the volume turned up too high, and it hurt to hear her loathsome lexicon accusing and accosting him in his own car when he turned the key first thing in the morning.

Heath snapped a few times. "You there? I asked about the class and you zoned out on me."

"No, yeah. I'm fine. Class was good." Rather than risk any further conversation about Annana, he pivoted right into his arrangement with Maeve. He pulled her business card out, punched the number into his contacts, and then tossed the card over to Heath.

"What's this?" Heath asked. He paused his show and picked up the card to take a closer look.

"Maeve's business card. She owns Olive What She's Having and does all their marketing. She's going to help us market the truck."

"Yeah?" Heath handed the card back to Steve. While Heath had started out strong with the idea of co-running Today's Gluten-Free Special after the deal with his uncle had fallen through, he'd steadily slid into a bit of a funk as their funds and customers dwindled by the day. "Why's she going to do that?"

Steve sat down on the other side of the couch and shrugged his shoulders. "I did a quick favor for her after the tasting class."

Heath's face contorted. "Gross. We're not that desperate. Not yet." The player of the two scooted away from Steve as if he might catch the clap or a touch of herpes by sharing a tiny corner of a cushion with him.

Ironic, given that when Steve had first moved in, he'd found a calendar hanging in the kitchen marked only with the words "came inside" and "fucking came inside" on various days of the month. Steve had deduced quite quickly that it was regarding Heath's various sexcapades, though he hadn't yet gotten up the nerve to ask him about it.

"No, nothing like that," Steve said. "I pretended to be her boyfriend for a few minutes; her ex ambushed her with another woman."

Heath's expression didn't change. "Still sounds dodgy and completely unprofessional."

"And that sounds hypocritical coming from the guy who's regularly shagging what few customers we have."

Heath tsked as he watched a contestant add more chicken to an already overcrowded pan. "Fine, we're both unprofessional, but I'm not proffering my business expertise to anyone. Is she even qualified?"

Steve clicked off the TV and showed Heath a quick rundown of the online marketing for the shop. He'd done a bit of Facebook stalking on the way to his truck and had a few tabs already queued up on his phone.

"And I have marketing research for us to go through tonight," he said, pointing to the stack of books he'd set on the table. "Between the three of us, we can turn this around before winter."

"Okay. Yeah." Heath sat back up and ran his fingers over the bit of facial hair he'd allowed to come through during his recent bout of laziness. "I didn't get to the store today. Let's order takeout. We'll eat while we work."

A little after six they were surrounded by marketing

books, notebooks full of scribbles and ideas, and empty cartons of food from one of the few gluten-free restaurants in town.

"I don't want to freak you out, but there's something I need to tell you."

Steve leaned back in his chair, bracing himself for whatever horrible news Heath was about to lay on him about their insurance, health inspection, or whatever other administrative nightmare Heath had been handling and shielding him from.

"Marley Mae's went out of business. Closed up for good last Sunday."

Heath's Uncle Marley and Aunt Mae had been successfully running the home-style restaurant for the past three decades. As far as Steve could tell, Heath idolized everything about them, especially the lifestyle they enjoyed as successful restaurant owners: everything on their own terms while they enjoyed the exciting, fast-paced work that was pervasive through most restaurants.

It was like what Heath and Steve had loved that about the service industry: the random, interesting people they'd meet, the camaraderie of the staff, the urgency of the position, but without the life-and-death consequences of working in industries like the medical field since when it came down to it, they were serving food, not saving lives. The allure of running a food truck, which felt like a smaller, more attainable goal than opening their own restaurant, was too much for them to resist.

The past month had more than humbled both of them, but they'd always referred to the lows as rough patches. Something to struggle through with nothing but good times on the other end–at least until the next cycle of rough patches repeated itself.

The shuttering of Marley Mae's doors was too ominous

for their already diminishing optimism. Steve slumped his shoulders, too. What were they thinking assuming that they could run a food truck with their meager experience as wait staff, Steve's degree in kinesiology and Heath's high school social studies teaching certification? How did they overlook that running a business would require some sort of experience or knowledge on how to run a business?

"How are they holding up?" He knew the answer already, but what else was there to say?

Marley and Mae had been out to LA to visit Heath a few times. They had tales about their three vacations each year, the mornings they spent relaxing around the house together or playing on the neighborhood bocce ball team since they didn't have to be at work until later in the day, and their time spent together at work with a staff and large group of regulars who all felt like family. Surely it was a jarring readjustment to start all over again with something new. To start careers or jobs that were nothing like what they were used to and would never again afford them the lifestyle they'd grown accustomed to.

"Devastated. He and Aunt Mae are putting out applications for desk jobs." The absolute contempt in Heath's voice said it all: he feared a similar fate.

"That's not going to be us." Steve straightened his back and put his hands flat on the table, hoping to show even a modicum of authority in a situation he had very little control over. Sheer determination would keep them afloat; it had to. In fact, maybe all of this was a sign, some sort of wake-up call that they'd better start acting and taking risks before they ended up like Uncle Marley and Aunt Mae.

Steve's phone vibrated and flashed Maeve's name, the small illuminated screen acting like a light at the end of a dark and treacherous tunnel.

"It's her," Steve said. "I'll put her on speaker so you can hear, too."

Heath closed his book. Admitting aloud his aunt and uncle had lost the restaurant must have shaken him even further if he was willing to put faith in Maeve, the woman he'd so recently claimed was dodgy and unprofessional.

"Hey—" he said as he hit the green answer button followed by the speaker button.

Suddenly, the apartment reverberated with Maeve's panicky voice. "Steve! Please tell me you aren't busy right now. I really need your help."

Heath rolled his eyes and went back to the books and his notes, once again writing off any ideas of Maeve being the marketing savant Steve claimed she was.

"My help?" Steve got up from the table and walked the two feet into the kitchen, as if that would provide him the privacy he needed.

"Yes," she hissed back in a loud voice.

"Where are you? Are you hurt?" Steve glanced back at the table and caught Heath shaking his head in disgust. Steve turned his back to him and looked at their sad little sink instead.

"I'm at Cuppa Chowda and Jackson just showed up. I can't be here alone."

He had taken her off speaker, but he was sure Heath heard every word given the cramped quarters of their apartment.

"Why are you alone?"

"Monday night is my book club for one: food, wine, and a new book. Very low-key which means I look like shit, and they caught me completely off guard."

"Oh…"

"When they saw me and noticed the one place setting, I could see the pity in their eyes. I swear I saw Chasity's pouty lower lip protrude even further from her mouth if you can believe it."

Steve heard flushing in the background followed by the sound of one of those hurricane-winds air dryers.

"I couldn't handle their pity looks," Maeve semi-yelled into the phone to be heard over the noise in the bathroom she was apparently hiding out in to make her call. "I practically shouted across the restaurant that you were on your way and just running a little late."

"This doesn't sound—" Steve had been more than intrigued by Maeve during her class. Her confidence, her intellect, her humor. She was the first woman to truly catch his attention since the breakup. The woman calling him from a restaurant bathroom sounded like a Maeve imposter.

"Please, Steve. I'm desperate and in a way this is a little, tiny bit your fault, too." The background noise stopped again.

"My fault?"

She detailed out how he'd gone off script with the fiancé comment, but Steve's attention was on Heath, who was suddenly at his side. He put the phone against his chest.

"Do it, but tell her you want TikTok videos through October. A new video for each day," Heath said.

"What? You think she's crazy." Steve held the phone closer to his chest to prevent Maeve from hearing what they were saying. He could feel the soft vibration of the phone as she continued to talk, though the only sound coming from it was muffled mumbles.

"Batshit crazy, and she absolutely is. That doesn't mean she's not good at marketing. Besides, we have nothing to lose. Do you want to make TikTok videos every day for the next sixty days?"

An image of Heath and him trying to perform coordinated dances in front of their food truck flashed through his mind. It was not good. Even in his fantasies they were off beat and clumsy as they tried to execute the most basic of moves. Hands shooting up in the air before slowly making their way back down as they wiggled jazz fingers seemed easy enough, but they would butcher it. He knew it, and so did Heath.

He shot Heath a look he hoped communicated how much

he hated him for extending out the fake fiancé thing beyond the fifteen minutes of that afternoon. Though, oddly enough, he wanted to see her again. The frantic call from the bathroom may have been completely off-putting to Heath, but a tiny part of him found it vulnerable and mildly endearing.

Fuck… Is that my type? Bat-shit crazy? He put the thought from his mind and held the phone back up to his ear as he took a step away from Heath.

"Maeve… Maeve… Maeve!" he finally said with force to pull her out of the spiral she'd gone down. "I'll come to dinner."

"Oh, thank go—"

"But we're going to need more than marketing advice in return."

"Yeah, I heard. TikTok videos. That's fine. I can do that," she said without hesitation.

Just as Maeve had overheard the conversation between him and Heath, Heath overheard everything as well and slapped Steve on the ass as he whispered, "Atta-boy. Way to take one for the team."

Boundaries be damned, Heath invited himself into the bathroom to lecture Steve about flirting while Steve showered before his impromptu date. Just a few minutes in, Heath's patience waned as he found Steve to be hopeless in the romance department.

"Look, if she's trying to make this guy jealous, you need to lay on the charm. Some witty banter, winks, playful jokes, the lot of it. Doesn't matter if the guy can't hear what you're saying, *she* will react to it. She'll blush, smile, laugh—and that he will notice."

"I know how to date. I take women out on dates all the time." Or rather, he did. But no need to mince words when he needed to be out of the shower and out the door as soon as possible.

"Just…" Heath let the word trail off as he searched for

what he was trying to say. "Don't fuck it up. Okay? You woo the marketing chick and I'll cold call for some more events this week." He walked Steve to the front door and practically threw him out. "This will be good. Things are turning around; I can feel it."

5

maeve

She almost didn't have her book-club-for-one Monday night out. That run-in with Jackson and Chasity had spooked her. They were staying in the heart of Galway Harbor, the tiniest little town which was really just a long main street of old repurposed lobsterman shacks and tourist attractions—her olive oil business being one of them. The odds of her running into them over the next week were sky high.

In the end, that was the main reason she risked going out for dinner. Her favorite book club restaurant was on the other side of a neighboring town. A place that mostly locals went to since it didn't have the tourist appeal of the waterfront views Jackson and Chasity would look for during their stay.

And yet, there they were, just five minutes after Maeve was seated. She hadn't even cracked open her newest true-crime novel when she'd spotted them at the hostess stand. They'd both changed clothes for more of an evening-out-on-the-town look while Maeve was still clad in her "cinched at the waist so she didn't look too frumpy at work" flannel, skinny jeans, and brown boots. Typical casual New England attire from what she'd found over the past three years living there.

Even so, she felt like she was the one out of place at the restaurant, not them in their evening attire of a casual suit for him and bright red fuck-me-pumps for her. The feeling had her cracking the spine of her book—something she took great care under normal circumstances to never do—as she hurriedly held it up in front of her face.

It was all for naught. Like a magnet, she could not get away from this couple. They were seated two tables over and had spotted and acknowledged her before they even sat down. In a fight-or-flight reaction gone wrong, she'd announced Steve would arrive any minute for their weekly romantic night out.

Once she was in the bathroom explaining everything to Steve, she realized how irrational it all sounded. No one would have judged her for getting dinner alone and reading a book, and they'd already met Steve and knew she wasn't single. That was all in hindsight. When it happened, having Steve present felt like a non-negotiable and she'd blurted it out.

After getting a confirmation from Steve, she put her phone back in her purse and checked her face in the bathroom mirror to make sure all traces of crazy had left her eyes. She practiced a few flirty smiles she planned to throw Steve's way on the off-chance Jackson noticed, and put on some Chap-Stick–the only thing in her purse that remotely resembled makeup–before confidently heading back to her table to continue reading her book.

"Hi, sweetheart," Steve said as he got to the table. Adorably, he'd taken his hair down from the man bun it had been in earlier and swapped out his flannel for a collared shirt. She appreciated a man that made an effort.

She'd give it right back, of course, with her own efforts on his marketing campaign. She'd already reached out to

Samantha Smith, an old Maryland friend who was currently crushing it on BookTok. Maeve was certain she was one viral video away from paying Steve back tenfold. Not to mention that she'd be buying dinner, too. Well, she'd buy him the one gluten-free entrée they offered.

She stood up to give Steve a hug, tilting her head to the left while his went to the right, and suddenly her lips were on his for the briefest of moments. A quick brush, really, but it left her feeling flushed and all warm inside.

Steve pushed a lock of his dark hair behind his ear, gave a sheepish grin, and took a seat at the table. Still smiling, he asked in a low voice, "Was that me, or you?"

Maeve reached over the table to take his hands in hers. She kept up her smile as well, though behind her fake look of adoration for her fake fiancé, there was nothing but turmoil. Jackson knew her too well. Even after all those years had passed, at the heart of it, she hadn't changed that much. He'd be able to spot their deceit in a heartbeat if they didn't figure out the details, fast. She ignored the voice in her head that asked why she cared what Jackson thought, and why she now wondered how kissing Steve for real would feel.

"I don't even know," she said. "This is all a bit nuts, but thank you for showing up and rolling with it."

Steve gave her hands a squeeze. "Hey, this is going to work out. Okay?"

He said it with such assurance and while his thumb soothingly stroked her palm, that for a split second she allowed herself to believe it was real and that she could get used to having Steve around. She allowed herself to believe having Jackson a few tables over and temporarily in her town was not fucking with her head and heart.

Steve's lips pressed together before licking his lower lip. "Mmmm," he murmured in a way that implied some sort of satisfaction. "Is that cherry ChapStick?"

Her eyes followed his tongue, and she was the tiniest bit

disappointed when it disappeared back into his mouth. Gently, she pulled her hands away and took a very generous sip—nay gulp—of the riesling she'd ordered for herself. She'd expected Jackson to be the sole source of her confusing thoughts that night.

Steve's large, firm hands retreated to his side of the table and he tentatively raised his glass to take a drink himself.

"Whiskey," Maeve offered. It was Jackson's favorite and something she'd seen on TV a million times. Guys liked whiskey on the rocks.

He took the smallest of sips and placed the glass back down on the table. "I'm not much of a drinker, but don't let that stop you. I don't like the taste, but I don't mind other people drinking," he added when Maeve looked guiltily at her half-empty wine glass. It was her third since she'd already had two at work. Unheard of for her, but then again, so was everything else lately.

"Thanks. I'm having a bit of a day."

At that Steve gave a small laugh and Maeve felt herself relax. It was nice being out with a guy and not worrying about what he thought of her. Because even though she felt a tiny smidge of attraction to him, she was not in a good place to be starting anything, and he was seeing her at her absolute worst. No way was Steve interested in the dumpster fire sitting before him.

"I don't even know why I dragged you out here."

"Not interested in winning anymore?" Steve asked as he picked up a menu and casually held it in a way that he could surreptitiously look beyond it at Jackson and Chasity.

"No, I'm not." Maeve reached out and lowered his menu so he'd look back at her. "It was more of a knee-jerk reaction, is all. I've put a considerable amount of effort into distancing myself from Jackson. No stalking on social media; no asking friends who still live in town what he's up to; no wasting my time wondering what life would have been like if he'd shown up for our trip. I was a damned saint with my will-power, but I think it's catching up with me, all that avoidance."

She caught Steve off-guard with the trip comment. He'd spent an hour listening to her stories about her travels around various countries, sipping oils and comfort-eating every bit of food she could get her hands on. Until then, he hadn't known she'd done it all under the shadow of Jackson's sudden abandonment.

There it is, she thought as she watched his expression change to pity and concern.

"Your olive oil trip? He was supposed to go with you?"

She nodded. "We'd been planning it for over a year. I couldn't not go. I was already at the airport and past security. My options were to go on the trip without him or go home and feel pathetic. I couldn't let some guy stand in the way of what I wanted to do. I went anyway, and then I threw myself into the olive oil tasting business as soon as I got back." Her candor deserved a sip of wine, so she took one. "I think that's why I'm losing my mind now. I never fully processed it all, just moved on with my life."

"Seems to me like you're doing fine. You are engaged, after all," he continued with a wink.

The words and his wink caught her off guard, so unlike the reserved and almost shy guy during the class, or the slightly geeky person she'd spoken to about books.

"I'm anything but fine. Not that you would understand. I'm sure you've never been dumped."

"What? Of course I have. Everyone gets dumped at some point."

The server came for their orders and Maeve stole a quick glance at Jackson. She'd overheard him order the crab cocktail, one of his favorites.

"Why would you say that?"

Maeve turned back to Steve. "Say what?"

"That I've never been dumped." He seemed thoroughly amused at her random assessment of him.

"You're really going to make me say it?" She felt a blush creeping across her cheeks.

"Say what?" he asked before taking a sip of his water, a cheap ploy to hide his smile at what he knew he was really asking her.

Maeve rolled her eyes. "You're hot, Steve. You know you are. And occasionally smooth and charismatic, it seems. Don't even pretend you have trouble finding dates." The fact that she herself had begged him to date her was not lost on her.

"What?" he asked in mock surprise, his hand going to his chest for effect. "Me?" He looked over his shoulder as if some other hot guy named Steve would be right behind him, thus solving the mystery of whom Maeve was referring to.

Maeve hadn't been on a suitable date in years, but this was how she imagined it would be. Some awkward pauses, but mostly two people easing into the lifelong journey of learning everything about each other. So far she knew Steve liked to read, had some interest in fishing though she wasn't sure if he fished himself, co-ran a food truck, and he was capable of a secret charm that she liked to think he pulled out only for her.

He chuckled at his own antics and said, "I appreciate the ego boost, Maeve, but being attractive does not prevent someone from being dumped. You got dumped."

"No, don't do that thing where I say you're hot and you feel the need to say it back to me." She looked down at the table.

"Then don't do that thing where someone gives you a compliment and you act like it couldn't possibly be sincere."

Maeve acquiesced with a slight nod. "Fair enough," she said, her eyes meeting his again. "Speaking of fair... Since I already gave you the quick rundown of Jackson's dismissal of me, I think it's only fair you tell me the one time you got dumped."

It was his turn to look anywhere but at her, and Maeve wondered why in the hell she thought transitioning from flirty banter to his previous heartbreak had been a good idea.

6
steve

"You don't want to hear about that. It's complicated." His eyes broke away from hers as he stared down into the glass of water he was swirling. There was a long pause as she munched on what little remained of the bread basket in silence. She was right. He hadn't been dumped yet, but what happened to him felt so much worse, and his inability to discuss it made it difficult to transition to a new topic. He was fucking it up and they couldn't afford for that to happen. The happier Maeve was, the more she'd be willing to go the extra mile with their marketing.

The idea caused a flurry of mental arguments in his mind, mostly stemming from the morally gray areas of, well, everything. But what really bothered him was their strange agreement based on a pretend relationship that had somehow extended to dinner as an engaged couple in exchange for months' worth of marketing material from Maeve. It suddenly felt dirty.

"Listen," he said, when the little voice in his head wouldn't stop accusing him of a being a terrible person who was taking advantage of someone in need, "I know you overheard Heath, my business partner, saying we wanted a bunch of TikTok videos, but that was just him talking out of his ass, or arse as he'd say."

He could already tell that Maeve was an expert at putting on her everything-is-awesome mask and leaving it there in perpetuity, so it was nice to see her genuinely smirk at his comment. He could feel her relaxing back into their previous roles of two people having a chill dinner together while they pretended to be madly in love to deceive an ex-fiancé she didn't even care about anymore. Well, according to her. He wasn't sold on that aspect of it yet. It was the reason he could muster enough confidence to flirt with her: it would never lead to anything, so why not risk making an ass of himself?

She shook her head. "No, it's fine. I figured when I first offered to do your marketing you'd probably want something with TikTok."

"Really? I thought you'd take an hour to put together a few designs in Photoshop or Canva. Show me how to set up the ads on our social media accounts and then disappear forever."

"Disappear? In this tiny town?" she asked. "Impossible. I'm actually surprised we haven't run into each other yet. How long have you lived here?"

"Since May." He could feel his smile falter; he wasn't nearly as good at putting his best face forward as she was.

"Yeah? Where did you come from?" Her eyes widened briefly, and she went pale. "I mean, where did you live before? Before you moved here, where did you live?" She pressed her lips together as if forbidding them to say anything else that might appear racist.

Steve was amused. He was born in Taiwan but adopted as an infant and had lived in LA his whole life. It wasn't the first time someone had asked him where he was from, though he doubted that was what Maeve meant.

"LA, originally."

The color returned to her cheeks. "Sounds nice and warm.

What brought you all the way out here, well above the Mason Dixon line?"

Steve considered her question for a beat, then said, "It's, uh, it's complicated." He cocked his head to the right, as if their previous conversation about his bad relationship was sitting next to him.

He considered coming clean about everything, testing out the waters to see how someone would react to hearing that he was Reeve from "I Really, Really Hope You Die." Too bad he didn't have the guts. He'd made it for so many months now he'd gotten used to the optimist in him who kept insisting no one would ever have to know.

"Right, I understand. Say no more." She took a sip of her drink. "So anyway, about the videos. You really should get in on this whole TikTok craze. At least some of your business thrives on tourists; it can't hurt to have wide publicity. You never know how many random people in Wisconsin are planning some future trip out to this area. You have to play the long game here."

"The long game?"

"The long game. You can't spend an hour on marketing and see results. I mean, that does rarely happen, but usually it takes much longer and it needs to be targeted and unrelenting. Especially if you're going to capitalize on TikTok's current marketing power. That algorithm does not play around. And it changes. Frequently."

It was the business version of Maeve again, and her passion and knowledge entranced him. Marketing was never something he found interesting. Neither was olive oil. And yet he could sit and listen to her talk about either all night long.

He noticed she did this cute thing with her hands where she'd get really into a story or whatever she was saying, and her hands couldn't help but busy themselves, like she had so much pent-up energy and excitement about whatever she discussed that she just had to move her body as well. During the oil tasting, she was in constant motion around the room as she told stories and sliced apples and bread pieces. At dinner, it was the swirling of her straw in her water glass and elaborate gestures.

"If you're not posting daily quality content, people won't see it," she insisted, her swirl movement speeding up at the declaration. "Even if you lay out a decent amount of money to promote your videos or ads on any of the social media outlets, you still need to play to the algorithms."

Steve winced. "That sounds like way too much work for you considering how little I've done on my end." He'd been trying so hard to be the good guy; he didn't want to put her out, even if she was the one who'd come up with the whole scheme and had offered increased marketing in return.

"Seriously? You allowed a random stranger to convince you to lie to other random strangers. You dropped everything tonight to continue my nefarious lie."

"Nefarious?" He asked in a teasing voice. He loved a woman with a strong but not too pretentious lexicon.

"Yes, Steve, nefarious. Downright fucking evil."

Yup, not too pretentious at all.

He almost stopped her there to set the record straight about how little he'd been doing when she'd called an hour earlier, and how little he cared about lying to Jackson and Chasity, but she was on a roll and his mother always said it was rude to interrupt.

"And then, you change your shirt and comb your hair, only to have me accidentally kiss you as soon as you get here."

At the mention of their kiss, Steve involuntarily licked his lips, searching for any remains of her ChapStick as his mind replayed it and his whole body remembered the spark he'd felt deep down in some recently deceased area of his heart when her lips had brushed against his. Not that he'd been in love with Annana–far from it if he was honest with himself–but she'd killed his motivation to meet anyone new or to even feel worthy of someone's love and affection.

Steve shook his head at her nonsense. She clearly didn't know how demanding some of his previous friends and girlfriends had been back in LA. A nice meal with good company was hardly deserving of the excessive payment she was offering in the way of her marketing services.

"Seriously," Maeve said. "I really appreciate you helping me out, and this type of marketing, for me, is not the hardship you're making it out to be. I can make a month's worth of content–that's posting a video or two a day– in a weekend, two max. Besides, I like to be busy, and I like the artistic aspect of it."

"Okay. If you're sure." Not only could he picture them sitting around the table at his apartment, huddled close so they could both see what she was doing on her laptop, he also imagined their truck at events with snaking lines full of hungry customers. No way was he going to keep fighting her offers.

"I'm sure." She stole a glance to her right at Jackson's table. "I'd shake on it with you, but engaged couples rarely do that in the middle of romantic dinners."

"We're still engaged?" he asked as he gave her an "I call bullshit" smirk.

Her hot and cold feelings regarding Jackson were tricky to maneuver, but he understood it. He was running from his own past shit rather than cope with it. There was an appeal to the approach, but it messed with a person's head. Some days he thought the whole thing was behind him and he'd openly flirt like he was with Maeve, and other days he'd feel something akin to a panic attack overhearing Annana's song playing somewhere and he'd shut down again as if it had only just happened the day before, so certain that once a woman got to know him she'd feel the same way Annana did.

Maeve waved to dismiss the whole Jackson thing, as if her magic wand of a hand could undo it all, freeing her up for a future where Jackson was merely a sporadic appearance in a few old photos here and there.

"Seriously. I don't care about him. It's old habits, is all," she said, explaining her lingering feelings and the need to keep the fake fiancé ploy going. "I won't go out of my way anymore—calling people in a panic from the bathroom, for example…"

The assurance left her eyes, and she almost turned to steal a quick glimpse of the ex. With a sigh, she leaned in and said in a low, embarrassed voice, "I'm also not ready for him to know how pathetic I was that I created this whole fake dating thing to begin with, so if we could just finish out the night like this…"

Steve leaned forward as well, as if they were sharing some sexy secret about what they'd do to each other as soon as they got back to their apartment.

"I know you don't believe me, but I do understand." He took her hand in his again and trained his eyes on hers. "We'll play out tonight and then let him go about his business marrying… your old friend?"

"Friend-ish," Maeve corrected. "And yes, please. That sounds good. Maybe it's the wine I've steadily consumed throughout the day, but I feel like I'm just about ready to end this thing once and for all. This will be closure for me."

He highly doubted what she was saying, but he gave her hand an encouraging squeeze in solidarity. Steve couldn't tell if Maeve was picking up on it or not, but there was much, much more to Jackson's sudden reappearance than he was letting on. He'd felt it at Maeve's store but had all but dismissed it based on how little he'd known about the players in the scenario. Getting to know Maeve, and by extension, a little more about Jackson throughout the dinner, had changed his mind.

When Steve had first arrived at Cuppa Chowda, he'd seen everyone through the window of the restaurant. Maeve's head had been buried in some romance novel and beyond her he saw Jackson looking her way while his own date was preoccupied with her phone. Throughout his dinner with Maeve, Steve had locked eyes with Jackson on three separate occasions. Each time it had been after he'd glanced over at Maeve–his gaze moving on to Steve to see if Steve had caught him in the act. Three times. Who knew how many times he hadn't caught him.

Not that Steve could tell Maeve any of it. The woman was working her ass off convincing herself everything was fine and that she was ready to officially say goodbye to any chance of a reconnection or reunion with Jackson.

Rather than reopen the wound that was finally scarring over, Steve picked up his glass of whiskey and once again channeled his charming Heath self.

"To the prettiest woman in the restaurant finding some much-needed closure," he said as he raised his glass to her.

Maeve rolled her eyes while her mouth formed an unwilling smile.

"To closure."

She tapped her wineglass to his. Maeve took a large drink that almost finished the glass, while Steve took the tiniest of sips of whiskey to satisfy the tradition of taking a drink after toasting.

"Now that that's settled," she said, "I have a million questions to ask about your food truck before we get your marketing campaign started."

"Fire away." He leaned back in his seat, not minding in the least that their dinner might take longer than he'd expected.

7

maeve

Before they officially called it a night, Maeve dipped into the women's room one last time.

She took in her appearance in the mirror and saw a change in herself. Nothing she could put her finger on, for sure, but the confident-looking woman looking back at her wasn't the same desperate, jaded woman she'd been earlier that night. She even blushed slightly, thinking about how Steve had called her the prettiest woman in the restaurant.

That fabulous feeling fled as soon as she opened the bathroom door and bumped into Jackson in the back hallway. Their chests collided as his hands went up to her shoulders to keep her steady.

"Maeve, I didn't see you there. Are you okay?"

"I'm fine. Really." Was there anything else to say? Not as far as she was concerned. "Have a nice night," she said automatically before sidestepping to get around him and back to her table.

"Wait, Maeve…" Jackson's arm reached out to stop her from walking away, and to her own surprise, she stopped. What was it about Jackson that she couldn't let go?

"What, Jackson?"

"How are you holding up… With everything…"

The sun had already set. Without its beams streaming into the restaurant's floor-to-ceiling windows, the back hallway with the bathrooms was dark and shadowy. She couldn't be sure if he was actually sincere.

"Fine," she said with the tail end trailing up in pitch, hinting that she wasn't sure what kind of answer he was expecting from her.

"Good," he said. He then repeated the most basic of words with a smidge more confidence before giving a curt nod and heading into the men's room.

"The weirdest thing just happened," Maeve said to Steve as soon as she got back to the table. They'd finished eating and were waiting for their chatty server, Laurence, to return with her credit card. Steve had tried to pay once and then let it go when she'd insisted on buying.

"You mean Jackson cornering you in the back hallway?" Steve asked without missing a beat.

Maeve took a quick look around the restaurant, suddenly feeling as though her every move was being clocked. Her eyes finally landed on Chasity who had her phone up to check her hair and makeup while Jackson was away from the table.

"You saw that?" she asked, turning back to Steve.

"No, you can't see the back hallway from here. Jackson watched you walk back there. He waited a minute or two—he looked nervous; his leg was shaking under the table the entire time—then he excused himself and followed you."

"His leg was probably shaking because he had to pee. I do the same thing when I'm playing bathroom chicken."

"Maybe…"

A pit formed in her stomach. She'd been so close to closure and moving on. She'd literally walked away from Jackson with no intention of looking back.

How was she supposed to do that now when she had so many new questions? What exactly had Jackson been trying to say to her? Had he really planned that accidental encounter in the hallway? And if he had, why was he so nervous about it? And what the fuck was he doing getting married at their spot?

She needed answers.

"I'm sorry, but I have to ask," Laurence said as he set the customer receipt and her credit card down on the table, "do I know you from somewhere? You look so familiar to me."

Maeve's usual server, Don, was out sick and her current server was quite the talker. He'd loudly chatted with all of his tables about football, the leaves, and bands coming into town for concerts; he'd even eavesdropped on their marketing conversation and name-dropped his cousin who was friends with an intern for an advertising firm. Maybe he could get them some sort of family and friends discount.

Maeve opened her mouth to say she was there every week, so that was why she looked familiar, but he wasn't talking to her. He was talking to Steve.

"I run the Today's Gluten-Free Special food truck."

Laurence wasn't convinced. "Yeah, maybe that's it." He turned away and then immediately turned back to their table. "Hold up. You have a food truck? Do you cater? One of my other tables was talking about how the caterer for their wedding on Friday just canceled on them. I bet you could fill in."

What were the odds Laurence was talking about Jackson and Chasity? Very good, apparently, as he turned and pointed to Jackson's still empty seat and Chasity, still on her phone but now tapping away. Possibly looking up local catering services.

Laurence excused himself to help another table as Steve and Maeve eyed each other up, each taking in the new information.

"A wedding," Maeve said, "even whatever small, intimate affair Chasity is planning would be great for your business."

She gave Laurence a fifty percent tip, a type of finder's fee for the invaluable information he'd casually plopped in front of them, then she slid her credit card into her purse. In the back of her mind, a small voice whispered dangerous thoughts like how having Steve and Heath cater the wedding would help to maintain the miniscule connection to Jackson she still craved.

"It would be huge for us," he agreed, his face registering a look of suppressed excitement. "You wouldn't mind?"

"Me?" Her voice had taken on a weird high pitch and she took a quick breath to get it back under control, lest she upset the seeing-eye dog at the table behind her.

"No," she said. "All part of my closure. Would you mind? You'd have to keep up the whole fiancé facade. I never even asked before; you're not dating anyone, are you?"

"Just you." His eyes left hers for a beat, and then they were back with that easy smile of his. "You'd be my one and only from now to Friday."

Maeve took the final swig of her wine and pointed at Steve. "You think you're real charming, don't you?" What she couldn't tell was if he was laying on the charm because he actually enjoyed flirting with her or if he was simply looking for a big payday with the catering gig.

"It's working, right?" He threw out a wink and made her chuckle. "Since we're both in agreement that we don't mind, how do we go about casually offering our services for their wedding?"

"*Our* services?"

"Our services. Heath and I can't handle a last-minute wedding on our own. And there's no way we'd be able to recruit and hire someone else for one night."

There it was, her golden opportunity to prove to herself that she was done with Jackson while still keeping him close.

Even though the ideas sounded contradictory, in her mind they paired as perfectly as tequila, lime, and salt. But was working a food truck for her ex-fiancé's wedding the answer? Sounded crazy. It had to be crazy. She was crazy.

Or was she...

"I've seen you drizzle olive oil; you'll be great," Steve continued, likely aware of the war happening inside her mind and doing his best to help her overcome it while helping himself in the process.

The four-top between them got up and left, leaving the surrounding tables of exes without a proper buffer. Before Maeve and Steve could discuss it further, they overheard their verbose server telling Jackson and Chasity about Steve's food truck and how they should ask Steve to cater their wedding.

Having created a thoroughly awkward situation for the two tables, Laurence then walked away to take a quick, well-deserved smoke break out back.

Everyone spoke at once.

Chasity: "I don't know about–"

Jackson: "That's perfect!"

Maeve: "Well, maybe–"

Steve: "We're wide open–"

The only thing worse than the four of them all speaking at once was when they all stopped and stared silently at one another over the vacant table full of dirty dishes. Each person considered what they should say next and whether it was rude to be the first one to talk again.

Steve did the honors. "Deciding on a caterer for your wedding is a huge decision. Why don't you both talk it over, and if you decide you're interested–"

"We're interested," Jackson insisted. "Chasity's mom has celiac. This is perfect."

"Babe... Miles is already reaching out to his contacts." Chasity put just enough edge in her voice to get his attention back to her.

"He's been making calls all evening and we haven't heard anything back yet," Jackson reminded her, a slight edge to his voice. At that, Chasity softened. "We don't know anyone up here, and half your family has special dietary needs. Besides, Miles found our first caterer and look how that worked out for us."

Maeve and Steve averted their eyes as if that would be enough to give them the privacy they needed.

Chasity said something Maeve couldn't make out. Something that was truly for Jackson's ears only.

"We'll be in touch," Jackson said across the empty table. He glanced back at his lovely fiancé and then added, "Soon. We'll be in touch soon." It was over. Chasity had surrendered. Maeve was sure of it.

"Sounds good," she said as she pushed out her chair and gathered her things. "Hun, we should get going." She almost pulled a business card out, but decided against it. Even if Jackson had deleted her number from his phone, he could stop by the store or find her number on the website. "Nice seeing you both… Again."

"Here's my card," Steve said, handing it to Jackson rather than Chasity. Then his hand fell casually on Maeve's lower back.

8

maeve

"I can't believe on top of everything else you've already done, you had to drive me home. This is mortifying," Maeve said from the passenger seat of Steve's Toyota RAV4. She couldn't tell if she thought his pristine interior was sexy or if she was tipsy enough that she would even consider something so random as a squeaky clean car as a trait she would find sexy.

"Really?" He laughed, shooting a quick glance her way before turning back to the road. "This is the mortifying part of your day? It wasn't propositioning me to be your fake fiancé or begging me to show up at the restaurant tonight? It's this part here? Me driving you home because you're being responsible and overly cautious?"

She drummed her fingers on the center console. "Yup, this is hands down the most embarrassing part. Not the craziest part, of course. That goes to the time I offered to help cater Jackson's wedding on Friday."

Her eyes were trained on the road ahead, but she could feel Steve assessing her from the driver seat. It wasn't altogether unpleasant. Sometimes when she caught Jackson watching her, she got the feeling there was some sort of judgment or criticism beneath the surface of his gaze. Steve's looks always had a curious undertone to them, as if she was some sort of puzzle he was trying to work out.

Keeping up boundaries and maintaining his role as the perfect gentleman, he pulled up to Olive What She's Having and put the car in park without turning off the ignition. She'd be lying if she said it hadn't crossed her mind, the idea that maybe their fake relationship could turn into something real in the bedroom.

That had been before she saw that brief flash of something in Jackson's eyes when they'd had their hallway encounter in Cuppa Chowda. Steve's confirmation that it had been an intentional run-in, and that Jackson had been nervous, only fueled her need to put any potential feelings for Steve to the side while she navigated through whatever was going on with Jackson.

Regardless, it sounded like Steve had his own baggage with whatever ex left him unable to even talk about their breakup. If she'd correctly read his body language, his ex was also the reason he'd moved from one coast to the other.

Besides all of that, they should probably keep it professional since she had a feeling Jackson was going to wear down Chasity and hire Today's Gluten-Free Special for their wedding. Steve would have his hands full planning for how he and Heath would make something like that happen with such short notice, and she would be busy herself, potentially helping in the truck. She wasn't sure if she wanted to laugh or cry at how ludicrous her life had become.

"Do you have a roommate?" he asked, leaning over the center console to look out the passenger window at her apartment above the shop. She closed her eyes and took in the smell of sandalwood.

Even as the scent sent good vibes throughout her body, she was hyper-aware everything about Steve was tied to other variables in her life. She couldn't say if her feelings towards him were genuine or the result of everything else at play: Jackson randomly stopping by and re-igniting long ago feelings, the fake fiancé antics of their touches and their accidental kiss that wasn't actually real, and him smelling identical to her all-time favorite scent.

She opened her eyes again and surreptitiously let out the deep breath she'd taken. She looked up at her place. In the dark of the night, it was easy to see every light in the upstairs apartment was on.

"That's just for Hedy, my cat. She's afraid of the dark; I keep the lights on for her."

"And the woman who's now staring down at us from the window, drinking wine straight from the bottle? Isn't that your employee?"

"Kiki. My accountant, inventory expert, and closest friend." Maeve reached for the door handle. It was time to go. "I'm sure she's dying to hear how this all went. I should get up there."

"Yeah, I should get back to Heath and fill him in, too." Steve sat back in the driver's seat, ready to go. "Thanks for dinner; It was interesting."

"Thank you for saving me. We'll talk soon."

He nodded, and she got out of the car and gave a quick wave goodbye.

"What the hell is he thinking?" Kiki asked once Maeve finished her recap. They were on the couch with Hedy on Maeve's lap, softly purring as she scratched behind her ears, just the way she liked it.

"I don't know, but I'm going to find out."

"Really? Have you forgotten about the aftermath of the last time you and Jackson were together?"

Actually, Maeve had, to a degree, forgotten about that. Or at the very least she'd creatively rewritten her trip and discussed only the happy memories with her olive oil tasting classes so many times over the past few years she almost believed those classroom anecdotes and opening up her shop were the bulk of what had happened in her life post Jackson.

"I know, I know." She didn't, but she didn't want to rehash it with Kiki either. "Let's focus on marketing, please."

Kiki being Kiki, she'd insisted on helping with the truck marketing. While Maeve had the visual aspect of marketing down to a science, she'd wasted more money than she cared to know with her inability to track return on investments with her ads. That was Kiki's speciality. Similar to Maeve, Kiki swore the spreadsheets and barrage of various graphs were soothing to her: a puzzle that had an answer if she only took the time to sort through it. When she did, she swore that cracking the marketing code was a natural high she could ride for a week. Originally hired to help Maeve with the initial set-up of her finances and inventory, Maeve had brought her on full time when she realized what an absolute gem Kiki was.

"Did you see Sam's email?" Maeve had a generic marketing email address that she and Kiki both had access to. She saw the email notification on her phone during dinner and was eager to hear what Samantha had to say since she was the veritable expert on current marketing. Sam's latest TikTok videos averaged tens of thousands of views. It wasn't the same field, but surely she'd have some words of wisdom to get them started.

Kiki's face lit up. "Your friend is a marketing beast. Sam said she recently did a series of videos about books on sexy chefs and books with plots about battling food trucks—an up-and-coming hot topic in the smutty book industry it seems—and she included links to what she called go-to food-industry videos. I've been binging while you were out playing house."

"Funny," Maeve deadpanned. "What's our angle? A bunch of videos showcasing the different dishes? Them making the food? Customers eating it?"

"All the above, but with sex appeal, humor, flawless transitions, the perfect trending sounds, and all the right hashtags." She put up a finger and took out her phone. "Hold on; let me pull one up for you to see."

Hedy grew tired of the two and jumped down from Maeve's lap to nibble on the scraps of food left in her food dish.

"Got it. Slide over here so you can see. This one is from someone who runs an aphrodisiac food truck. Sells nothing but foods that will lead to a lil' hanky-panky." Kiki made an obscene gesture with her hand and tongue to demonstrate a particularly lewd sex act.

Maeve was ready to protest that there was no way a food truck like that actually existed when the screen filled with people that resembled some combination of Chippendale dancers and Victoria's Secret models putting together dishes of oysters and asparagus, each plated in a way that resembled naughty bits. Words popped up on the screen here and there stating where they would be parked in Vegas (of course they were in Vegas) and giving other basic details while Sam Smith's "Unholy" played in the background.

"We can't do anything like that!" Maeve protested while also making a mental note to follow them on TikTok when she got the chance.

"Not that, exactly… But we can show the two hot guys cooking it up in the truck and maybe use music that's playful and flirty—not as on-the-nose as 'Unholy.'"

"Steve already said he doesn't want to be in the videos. At all. Maybe his hands, but that's it."

"Why not?" Kiki's eyes remained glued to the screen which had moved onto the next video. The content was similar, but in this one everyone moved in time to the classic, "Put it in My Mouth" by Akinyele. They certainly had Kiki's almost undivided attention, though it wasn't likely she would ever be an actual customer there since they were thousands of miles away.

"I didn't ask," Maeve admitted. When they'd talked during dinner, Steve vacillated between distinct personalities: dorky, awkward nerd; charismatic charmer; and broken ex-lover. Whenever he slipped into his wounded persona, she couldn't bring herself to ask for details or specifics.

"It sounded like a non-negotiable the way he said it. I didn't push it."

Kiki paused the video and looked back up at Maeve. "Okay. What about the other guy?"

"Not sure. I haven't met him yet."

"Well, let's hope he's hot and isn't camera shy. Most of what Sam sent us confirms the most basic marketing tactic: sex sells."

"It's a gluten-free food truck in a tiny New England fishing town. I don't think that strategy is going to work here."

They spent the next few hours going through various social media pages, noting what worked and which strategies would even be realistic for them to attempt given their limited budget of zero dollars and limited-experience staff which comprised the two of them. Kiki, a master of all things numbers and data, whipped up a generic spreadsheet and took notes as she and Maeve dove deep into the seedy underbelly of FoodTok.

Eager for the distraction from Jackson that a new marketing campaign would bring, Maeve sent Steve a text asking if they could ride along on their next gig, whenever that was. She could either fully immerse herself into work and projects, or obsess about her ex-lover and his impending nuptials.

Maeve's phone vibrated. "It's Steve. Heath got them two gigs for tomorrow. It's short notice, but if we want to tag along for either, we can." There was also a gif of an adorable all-black, Hedy look-alike kitten struggling to hold on to a rope with the words "Hang in there. You've got this!" underneath its kicking back paws.

Her involuntary smile did not go unnoticed. Kiki grabbed the phone and read the message thread. "You little slut… You have Jackson and Steve clamoring to get a taste of that Ginger Snatch you got going on there."

Maeve whacked her shoulder with the back of her hand. "Stop calling my vagina 'Ginger Snatch,'" she said only half seriously. "Jackson isn't clamoring for shit, and Steve is lugging more baggage than I am. He's being friendly."

Maeve watched as Kiki sent a message to Steve about what time they should be there. "Baggage? Do tell…" she said, her attention back on Maeve.

"It's nothing concrete, but when we brought up exes, he said it was complicated and…" She paused, trying to figure out how to put into words the way Steve looked after the mention of his ex. "He just looked so defeated about the whole thing. Like whoever he'd been with before had really done a number on him."

"Huh. That's too bad." She looked back down at Maeve's phone. "He said they can pick us up here at 7 tomorrow morning if we don't mind tagging along to get ingredients, or we can meet them at the business park at 11 for lunch service."

Maeve's brow furrowed. "Think I can get Charles to come in and cover my shift tomorrow?" He was a retired schoolteacher who had originally started working at the shop to ease the boredom of his newfound freedom and maintain an air of productivity.

"Probably. I'll text him for you."

Maeve reached for her phone, but Kiki twisted as she typed, keeping the treasured technology just out of reach of Maeve's half-hearted attempt.

When it was settled that Charles would cover her shift, and after they'd made a rough plan of what videos they'd try to create the next day, Kiki gathered her things. "You going to be okay? I can stay a little longer—can crash on the couch if you wanna do a rom-com movie night."

The offer wasn't unexpected. Three years ago, Maeve had been an absolute wreck when she'd randomly moved up to Galway Harbor and blew her life savings to open an olive oil tasting store of all places. She only made it through her early-mid-life-crisis because Kiki had metaphorically strapped Maeve to her back and carried her through the worst parts.

During their first month working together, Kiki had caught Maeve, her new boss, sobbing as she built display tables and again when she was setting up her back office, but said nothing about it. Instead, knowing what a disaster Maeve was, Keek insisted on Friday night happy hours at the wine tasting bar where they quickly became more than just boss and employee.

Three years later, she was still Maeve's rock.

"Thanks, Keek, but I'm okay. Really."

tuesday

9

steve

"What time did you get up?" Steve asked, his hand doing a mediocre job of rubbing the sleep from his eyes.

"Five. I've been working on a tentative menu for the wedding and outlining a basic quote and contract." He didn't mention it, but judging by the gym bag left next to the front door, he'd also worked out already. All good signs that Heath was getting back to his usual self.

He'd played it cool when Steve came home the night before and told him all about the potential catering gig for Jackson and Chasity. Had literally said, "That's cool," and then called it a night. Now, there were twenty open tabs lining the top of his computer screen and his notebook was splayed out and full of work-related scribbles.

"I really don't think they're going to book us," Steve said with an even tone, not wanting to put down their services but also wanting to keep things realistic. Maeve was Jackson's ex. What were the odds that his new fiancé would be okay with having the old one around serving food at the wedding? But when he said as much to Heath, Heath shrugged it off.

"We should be looking to get more gigs like this, anyway.

If we don't use it this time, we'll be ready for the next one. I already have a database started with a list of contacts in the area for weddings, like Miles, their planner. I sent him a message about where we'd be today and said they should stop by."

"Did you get a response?" He wasn't nearly as optimistic as Heath, but he'd be lying if he said Heath's excitement was at least mildly infectious. Maybe things were turning around for them.

"Nothing yet, but they will. I can feel it. You going to be ready to go soon?"

"Let me get a quick shower, then we can leave." He noted Heath's dark gray polo. "Is that what you're wearing today? For the videos?"

Heath looked down. "Planned to. Solid color, collar to keep it professional looking. Why? What are you wearing?"

He and Heath had been lax about their work dress code while they went back and forth about what style of shirt to get. Heath pushed for the formal look of matching polos with their logo—a more fancy looking gluten-free marking that's typically put on food packages—embroidered on the chest, while Steve wanted the relaxed look of a t-shirt with Today's Gluten-Free Specials printed in large letters on the back. Perhaps with a vintage-looking food truck or menu signage in the background behind their name.

"I dunno." Steve shrugged his shoulders to better sell the lie he was telling. He'd spent thirty minutes picking out his shirt the night before and settled on his favorite tee: a retro print that was actually retro since it belonged to his father. It was one of the very few things he'd ever gotten from him; mom was always the gifter of the two. And while he hated his father 99% of the time, he loved the shirt and it looked good on him. Really good. "I figured I could wear my 'Dad's Grilling' shirt."

Heath glared back at him, and rightfully so. As much as

the color and fit made him look like an Asian god, the worn, faded material had started to make him look like an Asian god dressed like a homeless man. Not a good look for a food truck.

"Fine. My navy polo? Will that please you?"

"Very much. Now hurry. I don't want to be late."

"Morning, loves," Heath said to the women as he laid on his thickest British accent. As planned, his intended audience blushed as they shook his hand and went through introductions. West coast, east coast—it didn't matter; Heath never had trouble attracting the opposite sex with his strong jaw bone, ripped physique, and "adorable" British accent. The "ish" part of British being essential since Heath's natural accent was mostly American at that point. Lucky for Heath, only the true Brits picked up on his hack-job of an accent, and they were few and far between.

Not that Steve was jealous that Heath was catnip for women. Not much, at least. Heath's MO was to date a woman for a few weeks before finding some reason to end things and move on to the next target. He'd been that way back in LA when they'd waited tables together.

Steve couldn't do the whole casual dating thing. That was the sort of behavior that got guys in trouble—though he had yet to see Heath experience anything negative aside from a nasty case of the clap a few years back.

Since Heath was going to be the face of their TikTok videos, Steve drove while the women filled Heath in on what plans they had for the various video clips they wanted to post. They showed him some examples they'd found online and talked about how he could imitate their style while Heath did his best to deliver. Most of the videos seemed silly or downright boring, but the women swore once they added the trending sounds or stitched it to another video, it would be massively entertaining.

Thanks to a bit of cold-calling and sweet-talking from

Heath the day before, they were setting up at a local business park for lunch before changing locations to do dinner outside a hotel on a stretch of beach at the edge of Galway Harbor. A lucky break considering they had nothing lined up for the rest of the week unless they got the wedding gig.

"Is that the spot? Up there?" Kiki asked as they pulled into a large business park not too far from the fish market.

"That's the one," Heath said.

"Perfect. Let me out where you guys are going to park, and then circle the lot so I can get a shot of the truck arriving. I want to mimic that set-up video I showed you."

Kiki had shown the guys a video of someone's food truck service sped up to warp speed. The truck arrived, set up, fed hundreds of people, and then tore down all in a matter of seconds. It was incredibly satisfying to watch. They were limited on phones and stands, so they would only record the truck arriving and their set-up, but the women were certain it would be an easy-enough video to film and one that would provide a decent amount of views in return for the minimal effort.

"Anything for you, love," Heath teased as he eased the truck up to the parking spot, and Steve rolled his eyes for the tenth time that morning.

Maeve had already said she didn't want to be in any of the videos either, even if it was just in the background of Kiki's footage, so she stayed in the tight quarters of the back of the truck with Steve while Heath and Kiki took care of the basics on the outside. All the while, Kiki's phone recorded them working.

The size of the back of the truck reminded Steve of his current tiny kitchen in the apartment. Except unlike their barren space at home, they'd methodically stuffed the truck with everything they'd need to feed hundreds of people. The truck's main service window had a long prep shelf front and center. Behind that, against the back wall, was the grilling station. It was a little off to the right so that whoever was cooking wouldn't constantly bump back against whoever was working the window. On the back wall behind the window was a staging area where meals were plated into to-go containers before sauces and garnishes were added. Above and below the prep shelf was extra storage. Aside from the back door, just about every inch of space was accounted for.

As if on autopilot, Steve grabbed his apron from the side wall and stacked out ingredients onto the prep shelves. When he saw Maeve pull out her phone, his body stiffened like a knee-jerk reaction.

"Just your hands. I promise. Kiki and I did a ton of research. We know all the angles to use and how to keep anything resembling you out of it." Their eyes locked, and she was the only other person on the planet. "Trust me?" she added in a voice that was a tad too breathy for their platonic friendship.

Steve pushed out Annana's whispers about what an ass he was and charged boldly ahead. "Of course I trust my fiancé."

Alone, there was no need to continue with the pretense. He said it because he enjoyed saying that sort of thing to her. Because even though they were pretending, it made him feel all warm inside when he said the words. Based on the sweet smile she gave in return, she didn't mind being on the receiving end of it, either.

"Good answer. Now, ignore me and go about your work like I'm not even here."

"Ignore you? Impossible."

He continued as if he'd said nothing out of the ordinary, but she lowered her phone and gave him a "Did you really just say that cheesy line to me?" look.

"What?" His cheeks flushed red. Flirting did not come easily to him. He struggled to stay on the right side of the fine line between charming (Heath 80% of the time) and sleazy con-artist (Heath the other 20% of the time). "I'd say I'm pretty low-key compared to my business partner out there."

They both looked out the serving window to see Kiki messing with the settings on her phone and Heath practically on top of her as he offered his expertise and assistance. She set the camera up a slight distance away from them to get the entire truck in the shot, so Maeve and Steve couldn't hear what they were saying. Based on their body language, Heath was pulling out every move he had, and she was falling hook, line, and sinker into those dark brown eyes.

"Everyone's low-key compared to Heath," she countered.

"That's true. Speaking of..."

Steve told her about the "came inside" calendar he'd found on the side of the fridge. It was a day or two after he'd moved into the apartment when he'd first spotted it hanging there. It was an old-school one that he'd likely gotten at some sort of community festival since it was all images of Galway Harbor and had a page filled with local businesses and logos.

"He does not have a 'came inside' sex calendar. You're making that up," Maeve laughed in response, her body leaning into his as if they were old friends, or lovers, enjoying some delicious secret together. Without meaning to, he took in the scent of her: vanilla with some sort of sweet, sugary scent on top of it like cookies. He noticed the mention of Heath's calendar made her nose wrinkle and it scrunched all those tiny little freckles in the process.

"Why would I make something like that up? He did. I swear," Steve said. "Granted, he'd been living alone for a few months, so I'm assuming he hadn't expected anyone else to see it."

"No... It must have meant something else. Did he say that's what it was for?"

"No. What other explanation is there? You think those were just all the times he walked inside the kitchen?"

Maeve bit her lip to suppress a devilish grin, so he egged

her on some more, desperate to have her do that thing again where she succumbed to laughter and her body leaned into his for support. It was a terrible idea. The worst, really. But he couldn't stay in hiding for the rest of his life. At some point, he was going to have to take the leap and start dating again. Wouldn't his fake fiancé be a good starting point? Aside from the fact that she was hung up on her ex, but that was all a technicality.

"Then how do you explain the ones marked 'fucking came inside'?" he asked. At that one, her mouth fell open, and she gave him a playful punch to his arm.

"Stop. You're making this up." She looked back outside to Heath and Kiki, then back to Steve.

"Is it still there? In the kitchen?"

They'd huddled together in the already cramped quarters of the truck as they continued their conversation in semi-hushed tones, though it was difficult to keep it down when they were both hysterical with laughter.

"No, sadly. I'm no longer privy to the dates and sizes of Heath's loads–I'm assuming that's what the 'fucking' was for on some entries, to emphasize the size of the came-inside load. I think he may have moved into the 21st century and started a digital calendar."

She suppressed her laughter to take on the tone of someone discussing mortgage lending options. "Hmmm. That's a wise choice. Easier to track long-term that way."

Imitating her business-casual tone, he stifled his laughter as well. "Absolutely. He can track his sperm over decades and retrieve dates in a matter of seconds. Scatter plots, comparison charts, pie graphs… The possibilities are endless."

They were staring into each other's eyes now, and they were way too close for comfort. Or rather, he was way too comfortable given how close they were.

"You're telling me, Steve, that you've never had a 'came inside' calendar?" That mischievous, challenging smile was back, and it almost convinced him she wouldn't have judged him if he had said yes.

"Do you?" he countered, leaning in as part of his interrogation and as part of his ploy to see how far he could push their flirting. Not to mention that he couldn't get enough of her intoxicating scent or that feeling of electricity that coursed through him whenever they touched.

"No," she sighed. "I haven't needed to for quite some time." Her eyes looked down at his lips. Her own bottom lip was caught firmly between her teeth, either in debate or as some sort of preventative action, since they were only supposed to be pretending to date. The sight of that bottom lip being released, only to be smoothed over with her tongue was almost too much to bear. He could feel his skin buzzing with anticipation, demanding that he go to her. Everything about this woman was driving him crazy and somehow, he was having a similar effect on her. He was sure of it.

Just when he raised his hand to brush back her hair and cup her jaw, they heard Heath and Kiki heading back to the truck.

Maeve slid back into her own personal space and picked up her phone again, poised and ready to capture the footage they needed for their marketing campaign. For whatever reason, Kiki and Heath paused, then turned back to the main building, leaving Maeve and Steve alone once again. But the moment was lost, so they carried on with their original plans of making TikTok videos: chopping, cooking, mixing, etc.

Since they were going to use whatever sounds and music were currently trending, they didn't have to worry about their conversations getting caught on film. At one point, Maeve climbed up on a shelf to get an aerial view of whatever Steve was cooking, and he'd started telling her about the time his waterbed had caught fire. Heath always swore that laughter was one of the key ingredients to getting a woman to fall, so Steve was going to give it a go. In the past he'd been thoroughly embarrassed by the waterbed story, but there was something about Maeve that took away that feeling and let him see it for what it was, a funny little anecdote about his past.

"We're still not entirely sure what happened," he said as he chopped vegetables just like the people in the viral videos had, "but there was a spark or something with the electrical warmer part of the bed, and one random evening the far corner of my bed started smoking. Within seconds, there were flames and I was freaking out. My parents were at some fundraiser for the night and teenager me was so sure I could put it out myself." Steve flashed Maeve a cocky smile that only grew when he saw she was taking in every word. Leaning towards him ever so slightly as she waited to hear what came next.

"It was an electrical fire; I knew that much, so I couldn't put it out with water. That's when I noticed a bit of paper sticking out from under the mattress and under the bed, too. I figured it was the main source of kindling for the flames, so I grabbed it as best as I could. When I had it in my hands, now a burning stack of paper that was quickly getting out of control, I looked up and saw my open window. Without another thought–there wasn't time for any other thoughts–I raced over to the window and threw the paper out before going back to the still burning sheets and wood frame."

Maeve nodded her approval at his cat-like reflexes and quick thinking. "Then what? Don't tell me your whole house caught fire."

"No. Worse. I finally put it out a few minutes before my parents got home. Turns out they were home early because my neighbor called them. They said I was in the house playing with fire, and I'd purposely ruined their dinner party with my flagrant display of burning pornography."

Maeve's phone lowered to her lap, and she clapped a hand over her mouth. "Noooo...."

His hands continued on autopilot as he moved from veggie prep to mixing up the dips he'd made a million times before; his mind focused only on Maeve and the delivery of his story. He had two options for how to end it: in one version, he focused on the humorous side of it that would result in Maeve's full-body laugh; in the other version, they'd take their friendship to another level, and he'd mention how his dad had hit and berated him while his mom stood off to the side, unwilling to weigh in one way or the other. He'd tell Maeve how his dad had left just a few short weeks later and never came back.

Her eyes sparkling in anticipation, he kept course with the humorous aspect of it. There'd be time later for the deeply personal stuff.

"That's right," he said, confirming her assumptions. "What paper does a teenage boy keep under his bed? I was sixteen at the time of the fire; I'd completely forgotten that thirteen-year-old me had left them there, and I was so focused on the fire I didn't realize what I was holding. So right in the middle of the Epstein's annual Master Gardener Cocktail Hour in their backyard, I threw flaming, spread-eagle naked women out of my window for all to see. Some of them even fluttered into their yard and singed their prized poppies with their fiery filth. Mrs. Epstein's words, not mine."

Maeve was hysterical over it all. "Stop it! I can't... I'm going to drop my phone in the food," she managed, still perched up on a shelf to film his cooking from a higher angle

Humor had been the right choice. They had a good thing going in the truck that morning. No need to bring it down with the ugly details of his past. Besides, she already knew on some level he'd left it all for a reason.

Unable to cook while he was nervous–and who wouldn't be nervous with the lovely and talented Maeve catching every move on camera–Steve dropped the stories and moved instead to conversation about the various foods and recipes.

Talking not only helped to soothe his nerves, but he also wanted to impress her with his culinary prowess.

"Do you mind if I try a shot where I'm behind you and holding my phone so that it's right in front of your face? Not blocking your view, but sort of showing on the screen exactly what you see when you're looking down?" Maeve asked after she'd exhausted some of the other shot ideas they'd talked about earlier.

"Not at all. Whatever you need to do; I'm in as long as I'm not in it beyond my hands." Not thinking through what the shot would actually entail, Steve tensed for half a second when she lined her body up behind his and moved her arms around him to hold the phone up.

It was immensely sensual for a beat or two and he worried about getting a raging hard-on in the truck: her body against his, her sweet scent lingering. The sound of her breath catching told him she felt it all, too.

His erection worries vanished as the sensual scene quickly turned comical. He chuckled when he looked down to find her fingers floundering about seeking the record button. Even if she'd found it, her footage would be useless. She'd angled the phone more towards the back wall than what he was cooking.

"A little help, please," she said as she laughed at their awkward situation. It was almost too much for him. He felt her shaking with laughter behind him and watched the phone jerk in front of his face. It was his favorite version of Maeve, where she wasn't putting on some face or personality for an audience, and she wasn't lost in her thoughts. This version of Maeve was silly and in the moment and irresistible.

"Okay, Magellan. First of all, your phone's pointed due north. Tilt down about twenty degrees… There. Right there. Now, let's say your left thumb is at the center of a clock. You want to click seven, about half an inch from where yours is right now."

"Right there?"

He could feel her breath on his back. She was a few inches shorter than him, so her mouth ended up between his shoulder blades. Nestled in like that was where it belonged. He allowed himself a quick moment to imagine the same scenario but in a bed. Their bodies flushed together on some cold winter morning before the sun was even up and they would talk about their upcoming day as they lazily laid around, completely content and at ease.

Even though they were fully clothed and his hands were working over the white hot, dangerous stovetop as he cooked, it still had the effect of an intimate moment between the two of them. How long had it been since he'd felt a woman's body against his?

Since Annana. That was how long it had been.

A loud throat clear behind them had Maeve jumping away and Steve almost flinging half-raw halibut across the truck. When he turned around, he found Jackson–one reason he had previously dismissed any hopes of having a chance with Maeve–standing at his truck window with his arms crossed and an unreadable expression on his face.

10

maeve

Maeve briefly reverted to her previous life, where she and Jackson were engaged and madly in love. She took an extra step away from Steve, slamming her back into the handle of the in-truck fridge.

When she noticed Chasity next to Jackson, she was instantly reminded of reality: they'd been broken up for years and she was supposed to be in a fake relationship with Steve.

"Sorry about that." She could feel herself blushing. "We're usually more professional in the truck. We weren't expecting customers yet," she said, trying to smooth over the fact that she had jumped away from her loving fiancé.

Chasity looked at her watch. "It's five after. Miles and your Facebook post said you'd be open at eleven." Chasity and Jackson wore sunglasses, so it was hard to tell if they were there with good news or bad news about the truck catering the wedding. Based on their crossed arms and looks of mild disgust, Maeve expected the worst.

"What?" Steve asked, glancing at his own watch. "Heath should have been in fifteen minutes ago to help with prep." He looked back and forth between the customers and his cooking food. "Maeve, can you take their orders, please, until Heath gets back?"

She nodded as if she always helped with orders. Then she slid her phone in her back pocket and washed her hands as she said, "What can I get you? We have a great menu today." Was that right? She'd never worked in the food industry outside of bartending and her olive oil business.

The videos she and Kiki watched the night before had been zero help in this department. The aphrodisiac truck employees said things like, "Our food is guaranteed to elicit pleasure beyond anything you've ever had in your mouth," and, "Try our moist desserts; you'll practically cum in your pants."

No, none of that would do with the gluten-free truck and her ex and his fiancée for customers.

Chasity's pouty, bright red lips formed into what Maeve guessed was a smile of sorts. "I told Jackson and Miles I'd consider using the truck if we did a tasting beforehand."

Steve chimed in over Maeve's shoulder, "You know, we're not booked for anything tomorrow. We could do a proper tasting–"

"No," Chasity said, cutting him off. "No offense, but I want to experience an authentic meal from you; not something you put together in an actual kitchen, preparing only enough food for one couple. I want what you would serve my wedding guests, and I want to see how you handle a crowd."

On cue, a strong breeze came through and blew a few empty plastic bags around the barren expanse that made up the parking lot surrounding their truck.

It was Steve's turn to clear his throat. "We, um, we pick up as the time passes. No one wants to be the first. Once they see people at the window, they line up. Happens every time."

"Absolutely," Maeve agreed. "Thanks for starting us off, guys!" It came out with the same, too positive voice she occasionally used in tasting classes when she felt like she was losing customers' attention.

More blank expressions from Jackson and Chasity.

"Now, what can I get you?" Maeve asked, powering through the awkward moment as best as she could.

Once they finished ordering, the two walked away from the truck window to have a private side conversation. Maeve was still way too new to everything to even consider helping Steve cook and plate, so she took up her phone again to record Steve working. It probably wouldn't make the cut, though. That charming man who'd almost kissed her wasn't feeling playful and his tension came through on camera.

"Looks like we're throwing you guys off a bit," Maeve said sheepishly. It probably wasn't a coincidence things were going wrong on the day she and Kiki showed up to film.

"It's fine. I just need to finish these orders and get everything set up. I wasn't kidding that once one person lines up, the others will come."

"We're back," Heath announced as he and Kiki climbed into the back. "We ran in real quick to let everyone know we were here and ready for orders."

"That's Jackson out there, isn't it?" Kiki asked, motioning to the couple standing off to the side with their backs to them.

"Sure is," Steve said. "They're doing an unannounced tasting to see if they want us to cater the wedding."

Heath's face fell. "Bloody hell. Sorry, I'm late. We only popped inside for a second." He checked his phone. "A heads-up from Miles would've been helpful."

"I know; it's fine," Steve said again, even though it was clear from his tone it was anything but.

"They must have made that all-call. Here they come." Kiki pointed to the building doors where people trickled out like ants drawn to a sugary treat.

"Steve, stick with the grill so your back's to everyone and you're not in any of the shots," Heath called over his shoulder as he got himself situated at the front window. I'll man the orders and work my British charm on the birds."

Maeve and Kiki had already decided Maeve would film inside the truck, mostly focusing on the cooking and shots looking out, while Kiki would film from outside to get the customer interactions along with candid food and service reviews. Kiki would also be in charge of getting permission from customers to post their images online. Technically, they didn't need to do that, but the last thing they wanted was to generate negative publicity by posting videos against anyone's wishes.

Even though Steve got massive praise for his fish tacos, the biggest winner of the day was undoubtedly Heath. Maeve had seen characters like him in movies, those charming leading men who knew exactly what to say regardless of the situation. To experience it firsthand was surreal, and she mentally apologized for all the times she'd rolled her eyes seeing the unrealistically suave men in rom-com movies.

She didn't have to worry about falling victim to his charm since she was privy to his secret calendar–hands down a huge libido killer. Maeve made an additional mental note to inform Kiki lest she fall prey to the gorgeous, handsome man who was allergic to commitment. Not that commitment mattered to Kiki. She was a female version of Heath.

A group of three women came up to the window and one of them insisted on buying lunch for the other since she had just been dumped by her boyfriend. At this, Heath turned to Maeve and told her to record the interaction. Kiki was busy off to the side recording some customers who'd already gotten their food and were giving reviews.

Maeve gave Heath a nod that she was rolling and Heath dove into his performance.

"What? You were dumped?" Heath said, his tone revealing his indignation at the very thought that the customer at his window could have suffered through such an injustice. "Bollocks! I don't believe it. What's the wanker's name?"

The three women, who all looked to be somewhere in their mid-twenties, looked at each other, unsure of what to say, before turning back to the window and Heath's intense gaze.

"Dereck," the woman muttered. Maeve watched it all through her phone and she could practically feel the contempt the woman had toward the man. She tried to remember if she'd felt that way about Jackson, but before she could search the recesses of her mind, Heath's dramatics brought her back to the present.

"Give me your hand, love, and look me in the eye. Right here, all your focus." Heath leaned out the window so he could hold her hand.

"Stay with me now. Are you with me?"

The hatred melted away, and now the woman was practically swooning as she nodded confirmation. Heath's hand completely enveloped hers; his thumb gently massaging the underside of her wrist over her pulse point.

"Good." His voice was softer, slightly conspiratorial. "What's your name?"

"Bethany."

"Lovely, Bethany, just like you. Now, repeat after me." He paused and didn't continue until he saw the almost imperceptible nod from Bethany. "Dereck is a massive wanker."

epiphany,Bethany's eyes lit up as if she'd had an epiphany and her friends giggled next to her while she repeated the words. "Dereck is a massive wanker."

Caught up in the moment herself, Maeve tried the technique as well. In her mind, she confidently said, "Jackson is a massive wanker."

"Brilliant. Now, here's your next one: I'm a gorgeous, successful woman who is beyond too good for him."

With more authority than before, the woman repeated his

words back. Maeve did likewise in her mind, her eyes darting out into the lot to glance at her intended target as he and Chasity ate and discussed their catering options.

"Perfect; you're a natural, Bethany. I have one more for you now." Throughout it all, Heath's hands continued caressing and massaging; his eyes never left hers. "You ready?" She gave an enthusiastic nod. "Okay, repeat after me: I was the best shag of Dereck's life, and that wanker will never, ever get to experience that again."

At that, her friends squealed with delight and a few cheers and hoots erupted from other customers behind them in line.

Bethany's head started to turn and Heath gave her hand a gentle squeeze to keep her focused on him.

"Bethany, love, I can't let you go until I hear you own those words. You can do it." He gave a quick nod and a wink.

Almost shouting now, Bethany repeated the words and Maeve was right there with her, embracing the crowd's cheers as if they were for her as well.

Heath gave Bethany's hand a quick kiss before releasing it. "Good girl," he said to her before shouting to the rest of the line, "Let's hear it for Bethany, everyone." He called over his shoulder for Steve to throw an extra handful of chips on her order, on the house, then he gave one final wink to Bethany before moving on to the next customer.

Kiki promptly caught Bethany afterwards and got her approval to post the exchange on TikTok. She looked rather pleased at the prospect of Dereck seeing it, and Maeve could understand the feeling all too well.

11
steve

As Heath worked his magic on Bethany, Steve noted Chasity's and Jackson's reactions. Their heads were tilted towards each other, each holding a container of their famous fish tacos in one hand while their other hands pointed this way and that in the truck's direction. The oversized sunglasses were killing him as he tried to gauge their reaction to the food and the shenanigans. If they didn't like Heath hamming it up with the guests, they could always tone it down, but he didn't think it was possible to fix any concerns over the food, at least not between then and Friday.

He also couldn't tell what Maeve was thinking. Not that he had a ton of extra time given how the work lunch rush was a beast since most employees had a set time they needed to be back at their desks. Still, even with the challenge of juggling different orders so they all finished at just the right time (drop the sweet potato wedges into the fryer a little over two minutes before the shrimp, start on the fish before doing any of that since it cooks the longest, and get another batch of prepared wedges out so they'd be ready for the next orders that were sure to come through) he found the odd second or two to notice Maeve glancing out the truck towards the couple as well.

Finally, an hour into their service and long after Chasity and Jackson had finished eating, they sauntered over during a break in the lunch rush. Jackson had what Steve could only describe as a smirk on his face, while Chasity appeared almost neutral and unaffected. He usually relied on people's eyes to help tune him into their emotions if they weren't readily available in the rest of their expression, but the damn sunglasses made it impossible. Every time he looked into them, he only saw himself looking large and slightly distorted.

"The guests of honor. I trust your halibut tacos were nothing short of spectacular," Heath said confidently.

A curt nod from Jackson. "They were good," he conceded.

"Excellent. Would either of you care to sample the other items on our menu? Steve's happy to whip up anything you'd like, on the house, of course," Heath said, as if they were long-lost friends and it was an absolute pleasure to see each other again. From behind, Steve couldn't see his expression, but he could almost guarantee Heath was throwing Chasity, the bride-to-be, a flirty smile. The man was shameless. Though Jackson looked like the type that enjoyed having other men openly gawk at his wife, so he couldn't fault him too much for it.

Either from Heath's charm or from the offer of free food, Chasity finally smiled back at them and said, "I'm dying to try the Spicy Shrimp Bites and the lobster bisque. They look amazing."

"And so you shall. An order of bites and soup, Steve, for the blushing bride," Heath called over his shoulder. He turned back to the couple and made a big to-do about the gluten-free breading they used on the shrimp bites and how it made all the difference.

Steve coated a batch of shrimp with breading and

dropped them into the deep fryer before chopping up a few more green onions to sprinkle on top. Mid chopping onions, he realized Maeve wasn't filming him anymore. At all. After the Bethany video she'd given a little space because they were too busy to film some of the specific shots she'd wanted: him rolling a lime before chopping into it, him stirring a saucepan in just the right way, and him chopping up vegetables with that satisfying sound that comes from exaggerated hits against the cutting board. It had only been a few hours of her hovering over him as he prepped and cooked, but he already missed it. She'd had to back off a little when they were really busy and when she was filming Heath, but he'd figured she would have started up again by now.

With a glance to the back of the truck, he saw her off to the side, almost in a trance as she watched Heath make his sales pitch to Jackson and Chasity during the brief lull they were having.

"Maeve," he said, just loud enough to get her attention. Once those large brown eyes were fixed on him, he gave a quick tilt of his head, beckoning her over to join him at the stove.

"Do you need help? I'll need to wash my hands again," she said, already turning towards the sink in the truck.

"No, no." He raised his hand and was desperate to make some sort of contact with her, but he didn't, and the moment passed, so he put both his hands back to work. "I wanted to give you a final out. It's not too late; they can find someone else."

Her smile dropped, and she shook her head. "You guys need this job; I need closure. Are you sure I can't help?" Of course she wanted to work. That was what he always wanted to do, too, any time life got shitty.

"Actually, we should pick up again any minute. Why don't you wash your hands and I'll walk you through some of the basics of our staple dishes. If you're really okay with this wedding gig..."

He let it trail off, and she nodded her head that she was fine with it.

"And you're still good to help us out Friday night? It's more complicated than it seems and I'm pretty sure I just heard Chasity say their quaint guest list of closest family and friends is at 150."

"Absolutely."

A millisecond too late, she forced a smile. It was a convincing one that helped to light up her face. He would have believed she was done with winning or whatever she was doing regarding Jackson, but that tiny delay said otherwise.

"Okay, wash up and put your phone in the drawer over there with ours."

Once they'd gotten their food, Jackson and Chasity left to run errands. They made plans to meet up with the truck at their beach dinner service to get a contract signed and go over any last details.

The next rush wasn't anything like the first. People trickled in, keeping the work steady but manageable. Maeve was a fast learner, and they quickly moved from positions of teacher and student to two people working side-by-side with occasional direction or reminders from Steve. The benefits of a small menu and a strong prep plan on their part.

"I moved to Massachusetts because of my ex," Steve said, apropos of nothing at all.

It just came out. He was placing another batch of marinated fish on the pan and without thinking, he said it. The fish needed a few minutes on each side and he didn't need to tend to them aside from one flip, but he found himself unable to turn and look at her.

As soon as the words were out there, the basket of shrimp dropped from her hand into the fryer and her head snapped towards him. All attention given to whatever it was he was going to say next.

It felt stupid now to bring up the whole breakup when he didn't know what he was going to say next, but the information, a confession of sorts, was desperate to get out of him and he didn't know any other way or time to do it. Like Maeve, he found purpose in his work in the service industry, even though some people couldn't stand it or looked down on it. He could create something from scratch and then see people enjoy and get value from his creation. That must have been why he said something in the truck while they were cooking. He was in his safe place, and he couldn't stop noticing how Maeve hadn't fully rebounded since Jackson showed up at the truck. Maybe they both needed to talk about it.

"That bad, huh?" she asked when he wouldn't return her gaze or go any further with his explanation. Even though they'd only met the day before, it felt like they were having a much larger unspoken conversation, so much more beyond the few words that were actually being said. Her three words had the subtleties underneath them that said, "I've been through relationship hell, too, so I'm not going to prod for more details if you aren't ready to share them. I'm here for you, though, if you do feel like you're ready to open up."

Just when Steve came to his senses and realized it was utterly impossible for them to have that kind of connection after such a short period of time, he turned to find her expression reiterating everything he'd thought he'd heard her wordlessly say.

Her brown eyes, the ones he'd looked into before but only now noticed they had the tiniest specks of green in them, were large and full of concern. Every ounce of body language said she was right there next to him as they plowed through their lows with a few tons of ex-baggage strapped to their backs.

So as they worked the orders Heath kept sending back, Steve detailed out what the first few weeks with Annana had been like. Nothing too specific, but a general overview of their shared interests and how their personalities seemed to mesh well together: sense of humor, politics, future aspirations, etc. It wasn't an overnight change, but something happened that he couldn't pinpoint exactly. He just knew that it wasn't working after all, and maybe he'd wanted to see connections that had never been there, and wanted to be on the same page so badly that he'd tried to force himself to be there with her, even though it wasn't who he was.

Maeve didn't say a word. She nodded at the right times and made a sympathetic wince right where he'd expected her to, but she didn't move the narrative over to herself or say something she thought was helpful but actually trivialized what he was feeling like, "You're letting this negative energy control you and you need to let it go," the way Annana used to do.

"Anyway, long story short, what I thought was a neutral break-up wasn't, and it felt like the giant city of LA wasn't big enough for the two of us. That, on top of some things going on with my family…"

His stomach tied up in knots. He'd clearly glazed over the most significant part of the story about why the giant city of LA wasn't big enough for two people who barely dated, and it felt akin to lying. At the very least, it fell widely short of the confession he'd meant to make, which left him feeling like a coward. As far as he could tell, Maeve had been painstakingly honest with him: sharing how her fiancé broke up via text before their trip, admitting she wanted to win their break up, calling in desperation from a bathroom.

Once again, Maeve was supportive without prodding, and so his family drama was left as a nebulous gray comment that could mean anything from actual physical abuse to a difference in political views that made family dinners slightly uncomfortable. Officially, he was a massive wuss, undeserving of Maeve.

However, he did find comfort right before dinner service when during his meeting with Jackson and Chasity, it was clear Jackson was one hundred times more undeserving than he was.

Since dinner service was at a local public beach, there were plenty of picnic tables around. Maeve and Kiki stayed in the truck working on their marketing campaigns while Heath and Steve hammered out all the details with the couple and their wedding planner, Miles.

Miles did most of the talking, with Jackson coming in at a close second. Steve had originally pegged her as being shy since during lunch service she said little to Heath, but the real reason for her reserved behavior came out within just minutes of their talking when Jackson turned and shushed her.

Mother. Fucking. Shushed. Her.

Miles didn't flinch, which led to only one reasonable explanation: he'd already witnessed it. This was not a onetime thing. Steve and Heath exchanged quick "what the fuck" glances and Chasity only spoke when spoken to for the rest of the meeting. If Steve didn't hate Jackson before, he did now and the loathsome feelings only grew from there.

Luckily, Heath was the one who'd already done all the legwork that morning coming up with menu options and pricing on the off-chance they actually got the last-minute wedding gig, so he naturally led and Steve didn't need to worry about accidentally calling Jackson a douchebag in the middle of their business meeting. Though he got the sense that all parties present (aside from Jackson) would not have faulted him for it if he had.

As they wrapped things up, Heath asked what they should wear since they didn't have official uniforms yet.

Chasity opened and closed her mouth. Jackson thought for half a beat before the shit-eating grin spread across his

Ken-doll face again. "Chasity's little sister has a Cricut she's obsessed with. Made our groomsmen and bridesmaids matching shirts for the bachelorette and bachelor parties a few months back. I'm sure she can whip some up by Friday."

He looked expectantly to Chasity who gave a nod in return. "Yeah, I can ask her."

Jackson leaned over and put his arm around her, possibly lightly digging his fingers into her side because she bent over slightly and a reluctant smile and laugh escaped her.

"We want everything to be perfect. Right, babe?" He placed a few playful kisses on her head and cheek until she relented with a few giggles and pushed him away.

"It will be."

There was a fine line between a meeting being active, and everyone shutting their brain down and officially moving on to the next task at hand, whatever that may be for everyone. They were right on the verge of crossing that line as everyone gathered folders, papers, and cell phones when Jackson cleared his throat and said, "Is Maeve around? We wanted to talk to her about last-minute wedding favors."

Chasity's mouth twisted ever so slightly and crossed her arms. Miles opened his folder and flipped through the pages, a look of uncertainty on his face.

"You ordered the soundtrack CDs," he said, his voice on the verge of panic. "They arrived two months ago. We can't return them."

Steve was already standing to leave the meeting, and Heath was caught in the middle where his ass was slightly off the bench and his toned thighs and glutes were painstakingly keeping him in place as he decided if this discussion about wedding favors was one he needed to stick around for.

"Maeve's in the truck working on marketing," Steve said. Having responded to their question, Heath took off for the truck himself while Steve stayed put. His interest was too piqued to leave now.

"Jackson thinks a CD along with dancing, dinner, and all the free booze they can drink isn't enough for our guests," Chasity said through gritted teeth.

A look from Jackson stopped her from saying anything more.

"It's going to look lame on the table by itself. You agreed those mini bottles of garlic infused olive oil would be a perfect gift. You said that." It was more of an accusation than a reminder. He shook his head and changed his tone back to conversational as he turned to Steve. "It's fine. We'll catch up with her later."

12

maeve

She'd second-guessed her involvement in Jackson's wedding from the beginning. What kind of nut-job goes from avoiding the man to insisting on working at his wedding? It takes a special kind of person to completely shut down prior memories, but damn if she was the epitome of that kind of person. Within a few weeks of living in Galway Harbor, she'd stopped thinking of it as their place and started thinking of it as her own, completely separate from him.

In less than a month she'd successfully culled her Facebook list of friends to completely remove him from her feed, moved out of their apartment leaving everything that slightly reminded her of him behind, and so thoroughly immersed herself into work and random hobbies that she didn't lie awake in bed at night wondering what she did wrong and where she would be now if they were still together.

So it felt like a tsunami ambushed her from behind when she looked at and really saw Jackson and Chasity at the food truck talking catering details with Heath at the window. Where would she be if she was still with Jackson? Right there. On the outside of this life that she loved, briefly looking in.

There would be no Kiki, there would be no independently run shop where she made every decision and relished in that fact every damn time one had to be made.

She would have been standing on the balcony of their hotel room looking out into the Atlantic Ocean trying to figure out why it felt like she could almost hear the waves calling out to her, beckoning her away from the life she was leading even though the water could only offer a cold, suffocating alternative. Maeve was certain of it; she remembered all too well how that had happened the first time they'd visited though previously she'd forced that memory into the deepest recesses of her mind. It was back now, though. All the memories were floating back up to the surface now that she wasn't actively fighting against them.

No, that life was not what she wanted. Perhaps she didn't have to go through with catering the wedding to get whatever final closure had yet to happen, but she couldn't leave Steve and Heath hanging. She'd pulled them into this thing, and she had an obligation to see it through with them.

The new insight had helped her to see how beyond fucked up it was that Jackson was getting married in the town where she now lived; in a town that had once been one of their special places. It also helped her realize Chasity was not the enemy.

So when Chasity showed up with her newly manicured nails and her engagement ring sparkling in the bright August sunshine, Maeve could genuinely smile back at her. Chasity explained how she'd seen Heath's performance with Bethany, even found it on TikTok, and hoped that he'd do the same with her. Heath was all too willing to shmooze it up again for a TikTok, and Maeve even moved to the other side of Heath, per Chasity's request, in order to get Chasity's good side and the perfect sunset in the background during her order.

Chasity was not the enemy; Maeve did not want the life she had with Jackson back.

Heath laid on all the charm as he made an epically big deal about their upcoming nuptials. Both Chasity and Jackson appeared to be pleased with the public display. Not that Maeve took too much notice of Jackson.

"Chasity, oh, Chasity… Please say it isn't so. You are far too lovely for this bloke next to you." He once again did that thing where he took the customer's hand and held it as if it was the most precious thing he had ever had the pleasure of touching. To his credit, Jackson was a good sport about Heath laying on the charm right in front of him.

"When's the wedding, love?" Heath asked conspiratorially and yet loud enough for the phone's audio to catch.

Chasity giggled and acted as if she couldn't believe Heath was going on and on the way he was. "It's this Friday. We're getting married right over there, on the beach, at sunset."

"Right there? That beach right over there?" A convincing performance given that Heath knew every detail since they'd need to plan accordingly as the caterers for the event.

"Uh, huh. That one."

Heath kept his eyes on Chasity as he called to the back of the truck. "Steve, I need to take off Friday night. I'm crashing Chasity's wedding. I'll show up just as they ask if anyone objects, and I'll publicly declare my love for you. Then we'll run away together. Anywhere you want, love."

One of his hands continued to clutch hers while the other went straight to his heart as if he'd been hit. "No, no. Don't say anything. You'll gut me if you tell me no and I have a long line of people to feed."

"Let go of the customer and grab this order," Steve called from behind him.

"We're like Romeo and Juliet," he whispered just loud enough for Maeve to pick up on her phone. "They want to keep us apart, but we won't let them, will we, Chasity? I'm going to let go now before my mate gives me an earful, but I'll see you on Friday." He gave a quick wink before standing upright again and grabbing their food. As he handed it off to them, he called out to the rest of the line: "Jackson and Chasity are getting married on Friday! Let's hear it for the bride and groom-to-be!"

The crowd cheered just as they had earlier, but this time it sounded louder than before. Maeve lowered her phone and took a peek out the truck window. The line turned and went well down Beach Street towards Main Street. Some were so far off they probably hadn't even heard Heath yelling his congratulations at the end.

"Holy crap," she said when she was upright again in the truck. "You guys have a huge line."

"Shit," Heath said, poking his own head out for a look. "She's right. I'm going to chill with the sweet talking for a bit. Better yet, Maeve, can you take over orders while I help cook?"

Maeve nodded and put away her phone so she could grab the order pad. Thanks to their lunch service earlier, she was more than familiar with their menu and their point of sale system was similar enough to hers that she could figure out the payments without too much help from the guys.

Kiki took a break from recording as she hunkered down off to the side with her phone and computer out. The allure of working to solve the enigma that was social media marketing was too much for her to resist. As soon as they'd posted their first few videos, she'd started monitoring their views, likes, and comments, filling out the spreadsheet she'd created to track which videos worked for them and which didn't.

"D'you think the line's because of the marketing?" Steve asked Maeve.

"No, it couldn't be. I mean, I would love to take credit for this, but it doesn't work that fast," she said between orders. "Majority of the people who saw or liked the video probably weren't even from here. We were mostly just playing around and getting a feel for what we were doing before we tried targeting any specific audience."

"Ask a few people how they heard about us–where the crowd is coming from."

Maeve's first customer responses were vague: one group was walking around and spotted the truck; another couple was visiting the beach and noticed the crowd.

"Everyone's just queuing up. They saw the truck and the line," Maeve said.

The excitement inside the truck was at an all-time high. She remembered when it had happened to her with her shop. There had been this expectation that her customer base would increase at a pace so slow she wouldn't be able to pinpoint when it even happened. That wasn't what happened to her, though. One day she was busy, and it had mostly stayed busy in the years since. Maybe the food truck would be the same. This was the first of many busy days to come.

Not long after she'd stopped asking how people found the truck, the real reason for the line finally made it to the window. A customer called beyond Maeve to the back of the truck and said, "Is that Reeve back there? I'm dying to know, man, what did you really do to piss her off so bad?"

The guy next to him added, "Yeah, we have a bet going. Don't let me down—the pool is up to $130 and I have an overdue electric bill. Tell me you cheated on her with her best friend."

"Are you the best friend?" another customer asked, waggling his eyebrows at Maeve.

"Get the fuck out of here. Now," Steve growled as he nudged Maeve off to the side and took over the window. Silence was all she could manage as a response.

Not that the customers particularly cared. They continued to snicker and antagonize as one said, "Holy shit. No wonder he has a song about him." The man turned towards the crowd of people, many of whom were pulling out their phones to capture whatever was about to go down, and called, "It's him! It's Annana's ex, Reeve!"

Maeve's eyes widened: Steve was Reeve? As in Reeve, the giant dick who'd inspired Annana to write a hit song about what a horrible human being he was? The man a sizable chunk of the population wanted dead?

Fucking A, she thought, *why am I only attracted to toxic men?*

"Bloody hell," Heath muttered as turned off the burners and joined Steve and Maeve at the window. "Sorry, all. Just ran out of every single item on the menu. Try us next time. Cheers." Then he lowered the door to the window, and it was just the three of them in the truck again, minus the audience outside now that they were shut out.

"You shouldn't have closed up; we need the customers."

"Oh, yeah. Brilliant idea, Steve. Or should I say, Reeve. What's going to happen once videos start surfacing of you cussing people out over that song? You think everyone's going to be on your side?" He pulled out his phone. "I'll text Kiki to grab our signs and everything still outside the truck."

"I could have handled it," Steve said.

From outside they could hear a light chanting of "I Really, Really, Hope You Die."

"There's nothing to handle. You don't win in this situation. Do you not hear that angry mob outside? Did you not hear yourself interacting with our customers?" Heath was losing patience and Maeve couldn't fault him for it. What exactly did Steve think he could do to turn the situation around?

"Maeve," Steve said, "you didn't post anything with my face in it, did you?"

"No, nothing." She and Kiki had double checked that the only videos they'd posted earlier were of the food with just his hands making it (the prep videos from before lunch service) and Heath's interaction with the scorned woman. It was only Heath and the woman; they were sure of it. Kiki and

Maeve were extra cautious and had captured it from the side, so Steve cooking in the back hadn't been in the frame.

Steve continued to stare her down as if she had been the one to write and capitalize on the song that dragged him through the mud. It was eerily similar to the looks Jackson would sometimes throw her way.

"I didn't!" she shouted back, years' worth of anger towards Jackson flooding out in her exchange with Steve. "But maybe you could have warned us about your random connection with pop star Annana so we didn't use her song in one of our videos."

Steve squeezed his eyes shut and his hands went to the sides of his head as if his palms were the only thing keeping his head from exploding. "You used 'I Really, Really Hope You Die' in one of our videos?"

"Why wouldn't we? It's a song about a jerk boyfriend and Heath was doing his whole wanker bit with Bethany. It was genius marketing."

"I shouldn't have to tell you not to use a no-talent musician's pop song in your videos about a food truck!"

"Enough!" Heath shouted over them. The inside of the truck became eerily silent. Even the chants from outside had ceased.

"I have some bad news," Kiki said as she climbed into the truck with their things.

13
steve

Steve felt his feet automatically spread ever so slightly, as if he was on some sort of fun-house ride where the floor spun and he needed to accommodate his stance to keep his balance.

"Mix 97 said on-air that you guys are here, and that one of the co-owners, Steve, is Reeve from 'I Really, Really Hope You Die.' They did a whole bit on it and dared their listeners to come see for themselves and then report back on what really happened between you and Annana."

A sheen of sweat covered Steve's face and neck. A small part of him had always known this was inevitable. Secrets never die; they lay in wait for the perfect time to surface—usually at one's highest point so that the fall would be that much sweeter to witness.

Because even knowing the truth about his breakup and relationship, Steve still felt like shit hearing it. It was the ultimate gas-lighting, and it was coming at him from all angles. It affected him enough that he'd said goodbye to LA for good and started his journey towards the East Coast. While he knew music didn't work that way—the song's popularity wasn't something that would stay in LA—he had to do something to ease the feeling of constant asphyxiation he felt every time he left his house in LA.

Since he'd arrived in Galway, he'd been able to breathe easier, but he'd still been a man locked up in a guillotine with Annana's song hanging over his head as he waited for her to cut the rope and break her silence on whom the song was about. Now, with the blade finally released and thoroughly through his neck, he felt both relief and horrific anxiety all at once.

"It was our video. I'm so sorry, Steve," Kiki said as she pulled her phone out. "Those guys told me Annana did a duet with our video where we used her song. I don't know how she knew it was you behind Heath, but she did, and she called you out for using her art in your marketing. Her video went viral, almost instantly."

Steve leaned back against the wall of the truck, suddenly finding it difficult to stand on his own as his world imploded around him. He wasn't just the dickhead ex; he was the dickhead ex who then used her fame for his own gain.

First things first, he needed to get out of there and away from all the random people who had come to their food truck simply to gawk at the instant local celebrity. Except he wasn't famous; he was infamous.

"Did you know the song was about you?" Heath asked in a voice that almost sounded American. When he wasn't putting on a show, Heath reverted to his normal self and Steve was immensely grateful. He needed normalcy.

"Of course I knew it was about me. There's an obvious lack of imagination from Steve to Reeve. And yes, I gave her strep throat and sort of dumped her on a birthday, but it wasn't hers. I knew I was Reeve. Okay? Why else would I be out here with you in this fucking food truck?"

"Right..." Heath stiffened as he took one small step away from Steve, and Steve wondered how much more of an ass he could be. He glanced at Maeve and found her jaw clenched and her eyes boring holes into the ground.

Steve put a hand on Heath's shoulder. "I'm sorry. I didn't mean that. I'm not thinking clearly with everything that's going on."

Heath nodded, and the guys had a quick moment of understanding.

"I knew it was about me," he continued in a lower, more rational voice, "but in a way, I didn't think it was actually about me. Like she started with the very basics of our relationship and twisted and pulled at it until it was something else entirely. Isn't that what artists do? They start with a very general truth and morph it into whatever art they want to create?"

Heath's shoulders went up, and he shook his head slightly to send the nonverbal message of "I have no fucking clue."

"It was such an exaggeration of our time together; in a way, it didn't feel like it was me anymore. I never expected her to publically out me as the inspiration. Who does that? I'll tell you who doesn't do that: Taylor fucking Swift. Why didn't I date Taylor Swift?"

Heath gave a hollow laugh. "That was never going to happen."

Heath had been there the day Steve met Annana. Really, it was supposed to have been Heath caught up in the mess since he was the one who had waited on her table and had been using his excessive charm and strong accent on her and her friends. At the time, Steve thought it was a miracle that she'd noticed him over Heath; had given him and not Heath her number so they could meet up after his shift at some karaoke bar down the road.

"Should have been you…" he reminded Heath.

As if he'd known it was coming, Heath was already shaking his head in disagreement. "Never would have been me. I wouldn't have made it past the first date with that one."

Steve glared at Heath so he could see what a load of shit that was without him having to say so aloud.

"I'm serious! She had this way about her; you could just tell that she was only in it for herself… A whatever-it-takes kinda vibe coming off of her."

Vzzt, vzzt, vzzt.

It was Steve's phone, almost vibrating its way out of the drawer they'd all stored their phones in. He had twenty text messages with more coming in by the minute.

<h1 style="text-align:center">14</h1>

<h1 style="text-align:center">maeve</h1>

Back at Maeve's apartment above the shop, she and Kiki cracked open a few beers and sat on the couch to decompress.

"What the fuck…" Kiki said in between sips of her Sam Adams.

"I know."

"Of all the songs…"

"I know."

"Of all the–"

"I know, Keek. I know…." She pulled out her phone and watched their own video for the hundredth time. They'd watched Annana's duet video only once. They didn't want to add to its viral status—as if their measly views would have any noticeable impact when it was already at a few hundred thousand and steadily climbing.

As she watched, she wondered for the millionth time how many stars had to align so that Annana would find their food truck video out of the other thousands of random TikTokers posting and using that same song. Not only that, but Annana had to randomly notice Steve's name tag on his shirt in the background when he turned to say something to Heath, and

Annana had to catch Steve's face in the customer's sunglasses in the few seconds that it was visible. Her sunglasses!

They'd been so focused on the other aspects of the video—matching the beats of the song to the text they'd included, listing off the best possible hashtags, and picking all the right settings like if they'd allow duets—so many little details that they'd wanted to get right, and they'd overlooked the one thing Steve had begged of them: don't let his face be in any of the videos.

The public was eating it up. There were already extensive Reddit threads about how Annana put it all together and whether she was a genius or if there was something creepy about her ability to spot an ex-boyfriend in the sunglasses' reflection of a customer. The internet was also a breeding ground for Steve/Reeve related memes and parodies. It was downright awe-inspiring how quickly the collective creative public made it their mission to get in on the Steve Reeve hating game.

The song itself was already bad enough with her catchy lyrics:

And just when I was falling, falling

You said that we were stalling, stalling

You were out the door so fast you made the floor shake

Leaving me to pay for dinner and my birthday cake

I used to sit and wonder why

But now I really, really hope you die

They weren't good stylistically, and they really weren't good overall for Steve, but Annana's TikTok duet video on top of it made everything so much worse. She called out Steve, by name, justifying the decision by saying that if he was going to be "dick-head ballsy enough" to use her song to promote his new business, he deserved for everyone to know she wrote it about him.

"I have terrible taste in men." She gave Kiki a half-smile at her self-deprecating comment.

"What?" Kiki responded in a high, off-pitch tone. "You? No way. I don't believe it."

"Jackson was my first serious boyfriend. I almost married him, and he turned out to be a giant ass who gas-lit me to where I would have walked down the aisle with him and thought myself the luckiest woman in the world."

Kiki gave a sympathetic smile but didn't contradict her.

"And now, the first guy that I'm interested in since then, has this crazy past where his ex is accusing him of being just as bad. Maybe even worse." She shook her and dropped her head as she tried to sort her scattered, disconnecting thoughts.

"Did you see the way he looked at me in the back of the truck?" Maeve looked down into her lap. Kiki would never judge her, but it was still hard to get the words out. "Jackson would look at me like that sometimes. Sometimes it was over stupid shit. Other times it was over something serious."

Kiki's mouth twisted in contemplation before she said, "I don't know Steve or Jackson much outside of what you've told me or what I've seen over the past few days... Even so, I'm not sure it's a fair comparison. Jackson was horrible."

"Really?" It was the answer Maeve was desperate to hear, and it was almost word for word what she had told herself a few times since dinner service, but she didn't trust her judgment. Jackson had thoroughly destroyed her confidence in deciphering between a mildly negative trait and a toxic, cancerous one.

"Really. Remember that time we ended up at Bernie's?" Kiki asked. Bernie's was a dive bar down the road where Maeve had gotten so thoroughly smashed that she hadn't found the courage to show her face there ever since.

"Vaguely..." Maeve said, as though the memory of her belting out "Nothing Compares to You" where she inserted Jackson's name every time she was supposed to say "You" wasn't seared into her brain for all of eternity.

Kiki smirked, knowing damn well Maeve knew exactly what she was talking about.

"Yeah, that night. When we were back here and you were puking your liquid dinner into the toilet, you let it all out about Jackson."

That particular detail was news to Maeve. She remembered waking up on the bathroom floor with a towel blanket and the smell of vomit lingering in every room of the apartment, but she hadn't remembered anything beyond the stumble home from the bar where she kept sneaking sips of vodka from a tiny bottle in her purse.

"I know you don't like talking about Jackson, so I didn't bring it up the next day. Acted like nothing had happened," Kiki said after she took in Maeve's slacked jaw and blinking eyes. She shook her head slightly, her black curls bobbing and swaying as she said, "You let loose about the nasty crap Jackson said to you, the outright emotional abuse he put out at you.

"And then, as if he were in the room somehow, you would change your mind and follow it up with something like, 'I'm sure he was just having a bad day,' or 'I can be really difficult to live with sometimes, I know that.'"

Maeve was hot with shame at it all. There was no doubt in her mind it had played out exactly as Kiki described it. She'd spent her first few weeks in Galway going through all the motions of working and grocery shopping and taking a walk, all the while she went back and forth in her mind about the reality versus the fantasy of how she had seen her relationship with Jackson. In the end, she couldn't figure it out and instead pretended none of it happened in the first place as she locked up Jackson and her relationship with him in a tiny little box and literally chucked a symbolic key (a piece of beach glass she'd found on a walk) into the Atlantic.

"This is different," Kiki said, reaching a hand out to give Maeve's arm a light squeeze. "Did Jackson ever apologize to you? Those times he flipped his shit and got raging mad at you?"

"No." Maeve hadn't needed to think about it. She already knew the answer to that one. If anyone had been to blame in her relationship with Jackson, it had always been her, and she'd always apologized.

"Steve apologized to Heath, almost immediately. He probably would have apologized to you, too, but his mind was scattered with the entire country knowing he's the asshole in the song, and with the small crowd of people outside the truck chanting it like it was some sort of anthem."

"Yeah… I might have cracked a bit too if I was in his shoes."

Maeve also had the sinking suspicion that there was more at stake than she and Kiki had realized. The marketing books and the lengths that Steve and Heath were going to to get the wedding gig were all big red arrows pointing to some financial issues. Maeve could relate to that. The first few months of running her shop, she had to force herself to look at her bank statements as she watched her life savings bleeding out and hemorrhaging due to her lack of sales.

Sensing that Maeve could use a little love, Hedy appeared on the back of the couch. She walked along the edge, peered over at Maeve and Kiki, then dropped into Maeve's lap and nuzzled against her.

Kiki shrugged her shoulders and said, "But none of it really matters unless you plan on making some sort of move with Steve." Her eyes were fixed on Maeve's, daring her to deny it, which she couldn't. Kiki knew her too well. It was a slightly high-pitched giggle between lunch and dinner service that had really set it off, though. Kiki's head spun around, and she'd given Maeve the "I told you he wants that Ginger Snatch and you want to give it to him" look.

"Then I guess it doesn't matter."

"Because of the song?"

"The song's not great, obviously, but no. It doesn't matter because it's a bad idea: getting involved with some guy who originally pretended to be my fiancé so I could parade him around my ex-fiancé and win my past breakup. It's a terrible romance origin story."

"People have met under worse circumstances."

Maeve continued to pet Hedy who purred her appreciation as she kneaded Maeve's belly.

"When we were at dinner last night, it felt like we had… Something."

Kiki leaned forward. "Why didn't you mention this last night when we were looking at TikTok food porn?"

"I don't know how to explain it. Nothing about my personality yesterday was in any way attractive. He saw me freaking out about Jackson and asking a total stranger, him, to pretend to date me. I literally told Steve I wanted to win my breakup. Not sexy. Then I was a hysterical mess and called him from a restaurant bathroom and begged him to come to dinner with me so I could continue to lie to my ex."

"Not sexy," Kiki agreed, before Maeve could say it herself.

"No, not sexy at all. I would have cringed and flat-out refused if a guy had done that with me. And then I would have texted you asking why only damaged guys are attracted to me."

"Same."

"Right?"

"Right."

"So, back to the something with Steve. Even with all the craziness of the past few days, and Jackson screwing with, well, everything, I can't stop thinking about Steve."

"Obviously. The man is gorgeous, motivated, usually pretty level-headed, and he knows his way around a kitchen."

Maeve's eyes flickered over to the sandalwood candle she'd picked up from the store because it smelled like Steve.

No reason to tell Kiki about that and reveal how far in over her head she already was.

"But in my mind, I'd already blown it because I was such a dumpster fire all day yesterday."

"A blazing *hot* dumpster fire, you mean."

Maeve's deadpan expression had Kiki defending her comment.

"Okay, fine. You weren't particularly hot or sexy. Don't give me that look. The pun was there for the taking."

"Since he'd already seen me at my absolute worst, I didn't bother trying to impress him at dinner and we had a great time together."

"You think he felt it, too?"

Maeve shrugged even though she was fairly certain she knew the answer to that question. "There was a subtle amount of flirting going back and forth over the table. And when he first got there, we accidentally kissed." Maeve's fingers went up to her lips as she tried to land on a final decision on if it had been an accidental lip bump or if either (maybe both?) had reacted to it. "It felt like there was something today, too, when we were prepping for lunch."

Kiki was a grinning fool as she loudly proclaimed, "One: holy crap, you actually like this guy. You should see your face right now. And two: could you ever date the really, really hope you die guy?"

"Someone has to…"

A line formed between Kiki's brows and her head tilted ever so slightly to the side.

"That came out wrong," Maeve conceded. "I meant that people don't stop dating altogether after one awful experience. Look at Dave Coulier and Alanis Morrisett. How many women belted out 'You Oughta Know' with an excessive amount of passion and hatred? It was a collective 'fuck you' to sweet Uncle Joey that lives on to this day. But he still got married to someone else. There was a woman out there who dated and promised to love forever the guy from the 'You Oughta Know' song.

Kiki shook her head.

"What do you mean, no?"

"The song wasn't about Coulier. Morrisett confirmed it in 2021." It was Maeve's turn to narrow her eyes at Kiki. "I know, you're wondering why the hell I know so much about Uncle Joey. But that's not the point here. I hear what you're saying. For a long time people–including Coulier–thought Alanis felt completely fucked over by him and yet someone still gave him a chance and found happiness with him."

Maeve tucked that random Uncle Joey kink Kiki was harboring away for another time and went back to her Steve and Annana theory. "Right. Steve wasn't a good fit for Annana, but that doesn't mean every woman on the planet should write him off. Maybe *she's* the one that's a bit off. That's what Heath said. He wouldn't go near her."

"That's a good point," Kiki said, setting the empty can next to the first one she'd set down. "Heath doesn't give off the vibes of being someone who's at all selective about his women, but Annana was off the table. That has to mean something."

"And we haven't heard Steve say one negative thing about her. That has to count for something, doesn't it?"

"I would say so," Kiki said, her hand reaching out to take over petting Hedy after Maeve stopped. "If anything, the song sounds more like what Heath would be like as a boyfriend."

This time Maeve raised her eyebrows at Kiki. "Been thinking about Heath as boyfriend material?"

"Never. He's a good shag, maybe. Though sometimes it's those smooth talkers who are the worst in the sack. All I'm saying is that Heath seems more the type to, as the song says, *'talk 'bout the women you've banged as you gloat, before shoving your snake-like tongue down my innocent throat.'* Who knows?

Maybe tomorrow you can get up the nerve to ask him about the song. They haven't canceled on us yet, have they?"

Maeve picked up her phone to check the home screen. "Nope. No texts or emails. I guess we're still on."

The guys had mentioned that they needed somewhere to park and serve for lunch on Wednesday, and Kiki offered the vacant lot next to Olive What She's Having as a joint promotion of sorts. More customers for both of them. They'd asked if the wine place wanted to get it on it too, though they hadn't heard back from them yet.

The vacant lot wasn't exactly Kiki's or Maeve's to offer, but while the bank battled with potential future property owners, Maeve and the owner of the building on the other side of the lot had been using it here and there when they needed the extra space. Not completely legal, but also not hurting anyone and no one had complained about it yet.

"Really? They must be hard up for sales. I thought for sure they would bail after the way today ended." She checked her phone. "I'd better head home. I have loads of work to do."

About a year ago, she'd casually mentioned she was taking on odd jobs here and there with accounting and doing some virtual assistant work. Kiki told her upfront that she wanted to do that full time and once she'd built up the clientele to do so, she would likely leave Olive What She's Having. Since then, they'd merely danced around the subject whenever it came up. Kiki hadn't offered any details of where she was at with it all, and Maeve didn't want to pry.

15

steve

He'd paced the empty lot next to Olive What She's Having for as long as he dared to under the cover of darkness. The last thing he needed was stalker charges on top of the terrible publicity from Annana's song and her recent TikTok.

He couldn't imagine what Maeve thought of him now. Well, actually, that was all he'd been doing that evening while he and Heath cleaned up the truck and prepped for the next day. In all the make-believe scenarios that occupied his mind, Maeve hated him, all future prospects would hate him, and he was doomed to walk the planet all alone for the rest of his life. He even saw himself as an old man at a retirement home where they had a mixer and played that song as they scooted around him with their tennis-ball-fitted walkers.

The worst current scenario running through his mind was that Maeve believed every word that had come out of Annana's mouth, and she desperately wanted out of their little arrangement before her good name and business were permanently marred by her connection to him.

But what really made him pace the lot with sweaty palms was the memory of the nasty glare he'd given her and how he'd grilled her about putting his face on the video. As if she had been the one who caused all his misery. She hadn't deserved any of it, and that, on top of his anger towards the customers, only fueled his worries that Annana's claim about what a piece of shit he was were valid.

No, he couldn't let that be Maeve's final assessment of him before she went to bed that night. Aside from the Annana TikTok debacle, Maeve had been the best thing to happen in his life for a long time. She was smart, had a great sense of humor, was creative, read books, was a fellow foodie, and so much more. Not to mention the coppery red hair and smattering of freckles on the bridge of her nose that sent his mind to very dirty places any time he stared too long.

More pacing.

They'd already severed ties on the marketing aspect of their partnership. That much was obvious and there weren't any hard feelings on either side when Steve said he and Heath didn't want any marketing, of any kind, for at least a few weeks while they tried to sort everything out and waited for the scandal to die down. People would hurry on to the next big thing if they just laid low and allowed celebrity gossip to take its natural course.

But for tomorrow—the Wednesday lunch service set up outside of Maeve's store—that was offered before their disastrous dinner service at the beach. He wasn't sure where they stood on that one. As much as Maeve intrigued him, he had to admit he still didn't know her very well. Was she the type to bail at the last minute? Would she not bail at all because she pitied him and couldn't muster the courage to pull the trigger on it and bring even more misery to his life?

It was all too much. He needed to know one way or the other, and he didn't want to resort to text messages or phone calls to do it. There was too much at stake to risk any sort of miscommunication. Face-to-face was the only way to go. When he'd first had his brilliant idea to pop up unannounced, he'd been confident and ready to rip off the bandage, regardless of how badly it might hurt.

Pacing outside her building, at night, he second-guessed himself. He should have called or texted to at least ask if it was okay to show up.

He pulled his phone out and found he had thirty-eight missed calls and seventy-two unread text messages. No doubt from random people he hadn't spoken to in months or years, all dying to know what the fuck was going on with him and Annana.

Nothing from Maeve, though. He shoved it back into his pocket. The steady stream of messages from everyone but her only made him feel worse and more stressed out than he already was.

A light came on in the building next to hers and acted as the catalyst he needed to get himself going. He quickly climbed up the steps leading up to her apartment and raised his hand to knock on the door.

Then he heard the music and Maeve's voice singing along. The exact words were muffled, but he got the distinct feeling it was melancholy and sorrowful, and he could only hope that he wasn't part of the reason she'd chosen that particular song or playlist.

Not sure if she'd hear his knock, he walked back down the steps and finally got up the nerve to text her. He dismissed all the unanswered calls, texts, and voicemails and brought up their text message chain. The last one was from yesterday during his meeting with Jackson. She'd asked if they could post the videos and he'd written back yes. Then she sent a gif of Matthew McConaughey saying "Alright, alright, alright" because during dinner they'd briefly discussed how the server looked a bit like McConaughey circa *Dazed and Confused*. A fan favorite for both of them.

Hey

He hated how quickly they'd gone from inside jokes to him sending something so short and simple. It was purposeful on his end; he wanted her to know there was still an out if she wanted to take it. She could pick up her phone, roll her eyes at the notification, and set it down again to go back to her quiet evening on the balcony overlooking the Atlantic.

The dots appeared, then disappeared, then reappeared.

Hey

That was all he needed. A small confirmation that she hadn't completely written him off, that she didn't hear and believe every word Annana said about him and chuck him in the "not worth my time" pile next to Jackson. Now it was on him to keep himself out. Still standing below her deck, listening to the mingling sounds of her music and the water–she'd stopped singing once he'd texted–Steve tapped out everything he should have said in the truck when he was too selfishly involved with his own problems.

He apologized for yelling, accusing, glaring, everything. Then he bounced on the balls of his feet as he waited for her response. Staring at the phone and willing the dots to pop up. He'd considered telling her he was there, but that didn't seem necessary anymore since he'd chickened out and apologized via text.

On the verge of losing faith that she would forgive him, he turned and looked up at the back deck just in time to see the cup of dirty water raining down on top of him.

It was August, but it was still after sunset and they were in Massachusetts, not California. The chilly water went straight to his bones and he let out a shrill, high-pitched, "Ah, fuck, that's cold!"

"Kiki?" Maeve called from up above. Her face popped over the railing and her concern turned to muffled laughter and a semi-suppressed smile as she said, "Steve, was that you just now? That shriek?"

"Just me down here." He'd already shown his humility with the previous texts of apologies, so he might as well own up to the girly scream, too. Maeve's failed attempts at suppressing her laughter only continued.

"Does this mean I'm forgiven, or is this your way of telling me to fuck off?"

Moments later, she was letting him into her apartment and handing him a kitchen towel at the door. "Watch out for Hedy. She's opportunistic; she'll make a break for it and then won't know what to do with herself out in the real world. You're not allergic, are you? She has a ton of fur." Maeve had a look of genuine concern that the cat hair could impede Steve's visit and he took that as another good sign.

"No allergies that I know of, aside from the gluten."

"Good." Maeve stood just inside the apartment with him. She'd already apologized for the paint water she'd thrown over the railing, so now it was on him to direct what was going to come next. His reason for standing under her deck so late at night, aside from the apology.

"I'll be quick; I know it's not fair for me to drop by like this," Steve said, still standing by the door since he didn't want to intrude any more than he already had.

At that, Maeve took a few steps into the living room and busied herself straightening the papers, laptop, pens, and highlighters that covered her coffee table. "No, no. It's fine. Really. Come in, have a seat. Can I get you anything?"

He gave a slight tug at his still wet tee that clung to his chest. "Do you happen to have a dry shirt? XL?"

"Actually, I do have a sweatshirt. It's from a fundraiser, so the sizes were mostly one-size fits all, meaning the smallest size they had was XL. I'll be right back."

While she disappeared into her room, Steve took in his surroundings. Everything was neat and organized, just like her store below, so that was no surprise. What did surprise him was all the artwork and various items covering all the walls. Nothing seemed to match in style, and yet it all somehow created a cohesive feeling in the room.

When she came back with a gray sweatshirt in hand, she found him looking at a painting on the wall.

Handing him the shirt, she gave a small, somewhat self-conscious laugh.

"You like that one?"

He did like that one. It was of Motif #1, but instead of buoys hanging off the side wall, it was covered with random objects: a sawzall, cell phones, locks, fishing poles, watches, and more.

"I've seen this painted a million times, but never like this. Is the artist a local?"

"I'm the artist. I painted it." Maeve gave the painting a last look before she stepped back to sit down on the couch.

"You are very talented." She'd told him the dirty water was from her latest watercolor painting, but he hadn't realized the extent of her artistic abilities. Steve leaned in closer to get a better look. This one was acrylic, and he could see each of the intricate brush strokes and colors that came together to make the scene. "The detail is amazing."

"Thanks. It's mostly just something I like to do for fun. A bit of stress relief."

"Where did you come up with all the items to hang from the wall?" He stood with the shirt in his hands, unable to pull himself away from the painting.

"I used to go magnet fishing with my parents. That's all the stuff we caught. And that woman and man at the end of the pier, fishing with their daughter? That's us. Magnet fishing."

Her voice almost faltered at the end and before he even asked, he had a feeling of what she was going to say.

"Do you still fish? With them?"

He could see the fake smile forming, and he wished she didn't feel the need to do that with him. Maybe if they somehow made it through the week and then some, she wouldn't feel like she had to hide what she was feeling.

"No. They both passed away before I moved. That's a Chesapeake Bay memory I superimposed up here. A way to move them up to Massachusetts with me."

"I'm sorry." His hands fumbled with the sweatshirt as he worked through something better to say.

"It's fine. It happened a while ago."

He gave a nod as words continued to elude him.

"My latest work is much lighter, something to hang over Hedy's food bowl." As if she'd been waiting for the right moment, Hedy made her grand entrance. The black ball of fluff trotted into the living room, took a quick look at Steve, dismissed him, and jumped up onto Maeve's lap to be petted.

"Speaking of Hedy... There's my beautiful, smart girl." The cat pushed its ass towards Maeve, demanding she scratch just above her tail. Then she jumped down again, completely ignored Steve, and was gone just as fast as she'd arrived.

Maeve politely focused on the retreating cat while he changed into the sweatshirt that smelled like her. He hoped her head was still turned when he tilted his own down towards the fabric to get a pull of that irresistible scent of sugary sweet vanilla.

"I think she likes me," Steve deadpanned before motioning towards the couch. "May I?"

"Yes, please. Have a seat." Maeve moved over on the couch to make room for him, even though there was already a cushion between them. "And yes, I think she does like you. Here you are, some strange man in the apartment, and she didn't hiss at you or anything."

"You think she'd hiss at Heath?" It was a stupid comment, but he couldn't help comparing himself to Heath, the man who exudes sex appeal with his mere existence. Also, he was nervous and had already spent entirely too much time over-thinking everything.

"Hard to say, but she certainly hated Jackson. She hissed at an old picture I found in a moving box. Too bad I didn't have her before we broke up. That would have been a nice red flag."

It was the perfect transition into the whole reason he was there. "Speaking of exes, can we talk about the angry, vengeful elephant in the room?"

Maeve laughed and a few of his muscles let go of the tension they'd held for the past few hours.

"Ah, yes. The ex. You mentioned a few things about her, but clearly some details were omitted. Or maybe I missed all your hints about who your ex actually was."

"Really? You weren't able to guess I'd dated an aspiring artist who'd found fame by trashing me in her Billboard Top 100 song?"

More laughter. More weight lifted.

"No, I did not. Clearly an oversight on my part. I didn't see that coming."

"Neither did I." Steve's hand rubbed at his chin as he worked out the best way to proceed.

"Have you talked to her since the song came out?" Maeve let the question hang for only a second before he could see in her face that her regret kicked in. "Oh, wow. That was so rude of me to pry. Forget I asked."

He raised his hand up between them. "No, please. It's a valid question." Then he pulled his phone out and checked the main screen. "I have over a hundred people trying to get in touch with me today, and they probably all have the same questions you do."

He made sure his phone was on silent and then he put it back in his pocket. "No, she and I haven't talked since we broke up. You can't tell from the song lyrics, but we only dated for a few months."

"What? It sounded like you guys were practically married. The whole 'you promised forever with your smile, but what you really meant was for a little while' line."

"Trust me. I know. Annana has the expertise of a fisherman when it comes to exaggerating. It's part of the reason I broke up with her. And yes, it was on a birthday, but not hers. It was her dog's gotcha day and honestly, I didn't know. She'd never mentioned it before." He forced himself to stop talking. No matter how he said his rebuttals, they always came out whiny and petty.

There was silence between them as Maeve took in the new information.

The mere mention that they'd only been dating a few months seemed to put Maeve firmly on his side, so he didn't feel compelled to defend each line of the song. Best to move on and hope for the best.

"I'm here partially to give my side of the story with Annana, but the main reason I'm here is because of how I acted in the truck."

"You already apologized in the text."

"I know, but I really wanted to apologize in person for the way I treated you. That's not me, and you never deserve to be spoken to like that, from anyone."

She took a quick sip of her water and he could see what looked like tears forming at the corners of her eyes. She blinked a few times and then he was no longer certain if they'd been there at all.

"Thanks, Steve. I appreciate it. Really."

There were cues people used to let someone know when a visit was over. Standing up and moving towards the door, mentioning how lovely it was to see them, or commenting on how late it was getting, were all subtle and polite hints for the other person to kindly leave, immediately.

Since he wasn't getting any of that from Maeve, he moved on to his final reason for visiting and asked, "Have you heard anything from Chasity or Jackson? Are they put-off by the negative attention?"

He had mixed feelings about the wedding. He and Heath could use the work, and Jackson was ready and willing to pay primo pricing for the last-minute catering. On the other hand, Steve was also eager for Jackson to leave already and head back south, away from Maeve. Forever.

He took her in as she sat with him on the couch. She'd changed into comfortable clothes of fleece pants and a long-sleeved shirt. Her hair was in a messy bun with little bits falling out here and there, just begging for him to reach out and tuck them back into place. Or maybe grab a fistful as he–

"No, but Jackson and Chasity haven't said much to me at all aside from when they stopped by the shop that first day."

"Good." She gave him a look, and he realized that wasn't quite what he'd meant to say. "I mean that they haven't canceled or reached out or anything. I drove the truck over tonight on the off chance that you'd accept my apology for being an asshole, and that we could continue our cooking lessons to prepare for Friday?"

He stood up and offered his hand, hoping he wasn't making a colossal mistake, and yet feeling almost certain that he wasn't.

16
maeve

As she sat on the couch looking up at Steve with his hand outstretched to hers, she couldn't help but regret not taking a shower when she'd gotten home earlier that day. Not that she smelled or anything–at least not that she was aware of–but because she could have better contemplated the whole Steve and Jackson situation.

The shower had always been Maeve's best thinking spot. All of her finest decisions and ideas had come about when she had scalding hot water pouring over every inch of her body.

Getting a cat and naming her Hedy after the fabulously clever Hedy Lamarr? That was a shower idea.

Getting trashed on the plane to the Mediterranean after Jackson texted he wasn't going? Not a shower idea–it ended horribly, and she was still in the midst of a five-year ban with the airline carrier.

Opening up her own olive oil tasting shop and moving to New England without her bastard ex fiancé? Shower idea.

Posting videos to TikTok without scrutinizing them for Steve's face in various objects in the video? Not a shower idea.

The morning after her dinner with Steve, she'd been in the shower–occasionally allowing herself to remember how their lips accidentally met–when she had the brilliant idea to keep it strictly professional with Steve. He was in an awful place after whatever heartbreak he'd had, and she was calling him from restaurant bathrooms, asking him to pretend to love and adore her. Disaster was written all over it.

Her confidence in her shower decision to resist Steve at all costs proved to be the right call as the day went on and every-thing imploded around them. Another example and rein-forcement of the idea that shower decisions were solid, well-thought-out decisions that had merit. They were worthy of her attention and required strict adhesion long after the shower was over.

If only her body would get on board. She hadn't techni-cally done anything that crossed the lines of friendship with Steve, but they were getting close. Like earlier in the day when she'd stood behind Steve to get footage from his perspective, but really it had been an excuse for her to press her body to his under the pretense of work so she could expe-rience it without putting herself out there or risking any nega-tive consequences. Just two people cooking and documenting said cooking.

And now, with Steve in her apartment, she was letting things slip into dangerous territory. Again. They both were. Because regardless of his very recent and traumatic breakup with Annana, Steve wasn't exactly keeping his distance from her. He'd enjoyed their flirting in the food truck and she was certain that when she'd turned around again just now in her apartment, she caught him taking a quick sniff of her sweat-shirt. A sweatshirt that conveniently smelled like her because she'd spritzed it quickly in the back room when she went to get it.

Sitting on the couch with Steve awaiting her decision, she threw out her previous shower promise to just say "no" and she reached out to take his hand in hers. She let him lead her outside and down to his food truck. The sounds of the ocean crashing against the rocky beaches that made up the outer edge of the harbor, and the feel of the mild New England summer-night air worked against them as it created the perfect romantic backdrop for their impromptu cooking lesson.

He climbed into the back of the truck first and turned to help her up as well. And then, as if he knew she needed just one more little subtle nudge to fully get her nether regions to wake the fuck up from their recent dormancy, he had the absolute audacity to stand in the truck doorway. No, standing wasn't anywhere close to what he did. There was a particular swagger and confidence in the way he leaned to the side with one arm raised above him, gripping the frame. If she'd given him a t-shirt instead of some bulky sweatshirt with a cartoon polar bear on the front, it really would have been a show. She might have tackled him right then and had her way with him on the truck floor. Why not? Heath was a neat freak; she was certain it was immaculate.

Instead, she took a deep breath, reached up for his offered hand once again, and joined him in the familiar, tight quarters in the back of the truck. If she didn't know any better, she would have thought it had been his plan all along–lure her back into the confined space they'd shared earlier in the day under the guise of practicing for the event.

Her theory was confirmed when he donned an apron and then turned to place one on her as well, his arms casually going around her waist to tie it for her. How thoughtful. As he leaned in, some of his silky hair draped down near her face and she gave up fighting. She'd been doing a sucky job at resisting, anyway. Instead, she closed her eyes and took it all in: the feel of his confident hands working a knot behind her, the feel of his arm muscles through her sweatshirt, and the masculine smell that was all him.

As if the mood wasn't already set with the dim lighting in the truck and the overall ambiance of a warm August night on the water, he got out his phone and tapped a few times until the sounds of jazz music filled the small back area of the truck.

"A little Stevie Ray Vaughan, one of my go-tos for cooking," he said, setting his phone up on a shelf. They filled the shelves with ingredients and inventory during service, but everything had to be cleared off whenever they drove, so his phone sat by itself on the barren ledge. She hadn't even thought to bring hers; it was still up at the apartment.

A combination of disappointment and admiration went through Maeve as Steve kept it professional during his cooking demonstration. Unfortunately for her–or perhaps once again by design from him because he's crafty as fuck when it comes to subtle seduction?–the sight of him working so passionately was the biggest turn on of them all. His confidence and focus as he maneuvered the spatula, flipped fish in the pan, and added ingredients here and there without even measuring. Seriously, what kind of sorcery was that to just throw in ingredients without measuring anything? To top it off, it was all done in a way that looked effortless in action while painstakingly meticulous in presentation.

"You ready to give it a try?"

She'd cooked with him earlier in the day, but that had been mostly her following his directions to "flip that for me," or "turn that burner down to simmer and stir the sauce." But now, in the dead of the night, they weren't in any rush as he gave her specific pointers on how to cook their two signature dishes so that each batch was just like the last one. Consistency was key, according to Steve.

"It's easier if you turn the pan like this," he said, coming up behind her and reaching around her body to slide the panhandle to the other side. "That way, you don't accidentally bump it with your other arm when you're reaching for ingredients."

"Speaking from experience?" She tried, she really, really tried to keep her attention on the hot stove and the food in front of her, but he was still standing right behind her, his warm breath coming in quick bursts over her neck so that it was alternating heat from him and then cool from the night air.

Without thinking, she let her body lean back ever so slightly so that it rested against his.

"Unfortunately, I am," he answered, his voice faltering ever so slightly, giving her the unofficial green light that he was feeling everything she was.

"I once flung an entire pan of chicken and spicy lemon sauce all down my front during a lunch rush. Surprisingly, dealing with the aftermath of impatient customers was more painful than the burn," he said with a chuckle, remembering some random day before he'd met Maeve.

Steve cleared his throat. "Looks like you're ready to flip. Remember how I showed you earlier?"

"I think so." She'd had every intention of flipping the fish, but she couldn't make it happen. His face was over her shoulder, and she couldn't resist turning her head a few degrees towards his.

"Whenever you're ready." His voice was almost a whisper, but she heard him clearly as his lips moved against her cheek before dragging down and pressing against hers. Steve's hands found her hips. In one fluid motion, he pulled and turned her to face him, then his firm hands were up and cupping her jaw as they deepened what was most definitely an on-purpose kiss.

His lips were softer than she remembered, and a stark contrast to the sharp angles that made up the rest of his face. While she'd let herself imagine what it would be like to actually kiss Steve, the reality of it far exceeded her imagination. It was slow and sensual even though it felt like it had been building for years and she'd expected a frenzy of hands and lips and tongues.

His eyes were still closed when he pulled away from the kiss while tilting his head forward so his forehead rested against hers. His hands were still on her jaw while his thumbs caressed her cheeks. Such a slight gesture, but that combined with the gentle nuzzling of his nose against hers, and she felt like she might melt. The urge to continue with their kissing and exploration of what could happen beyond that was incredibly strong, but so was the urge to simply continue to exist in that one moment, his thumbs caressing and lips so close but not closing the gap, for the rest of time. It was their own version of Keats's "Ode to the Grecian Urn."

"We shouldn't," he said before pressing his lips firmly together. Was that regret? Remorse? A way to physically prevent himself from doing what he'd just announced they should not be doing?

"No, I guess we shouldn't," she agreed with equal, nominal amounts of confidence. Her mind went back to all the reasons she'd told herself before she should steer clear of anything romantic with Steve. Nothing she could recall at the moment, but she was almost positive a shower had been involved.

He reached around her to turn the burner off and to remove the un-turned and now overcooked fish from the heat while she did her best to move out of his way. In the tiny space, it only led to them knocking into each other once again.

She'd heard what he said loud and clear, but she also felt in his knee-jerk reaction to her touch how desperate he was to continue. They wanted this, consequences be damned. So when their bodies collided in front of the stove, and she found her mouth right next to his neck, she let instinct take over as her lips brushed against the soft skin below the stubble of his day-old facial hair.

To her delight, he actually growled in response. As if he'd been holding back before as the perfect gentleman and she'd just unleashed the beast that had been begging to escape and wreak havoc on anything in his path.

Soft and sweet and sensual were gone. They'd done that already.

In a tangle of arms and legs, they pulled off their aprons, and he guided her through the tiny bit of truck real estate until her back was against the only flat wall surface: the back door.

In their fumble towards the door and with their focus on what naughty things they were about to get into, neither expected the thump her head would make at impact or that it would even impact at all. Her mind had been a fuzzy lump of mush, only able to think such things as *hmmm, kissing good, more kissing, muscular arms, hmmmm sandalwood*, and so on.

He pulled away again and his face softened, his hand cupping her cheek again as he said, "Shit, are you okay?" She gave a quick nod, but his eyes continued to search hers, boring deeply into them.

Satisfied that she wasn't hurt, his head dipped down to her neck and her eyes rolled back into her head as he licked and kissed the sensitive skin. That tongue, the one she'd watched so closely when he'd licked the ChapStick, her Chapstick from his lips that first night, that same tongue was finally working the delicate spot right below her ear. And this time, there would be no stopping.

Too many lines had been crossed for them to second-guess anything now. The flirting from the past two days, the way they'd both torn down their protective walls and confronted, together, the things that had destroyed them in the past. He was so new to her, but somehow he'd imprinted himself so thoroughly already it seemed impossible she hadn't known him just a few days earlier.

He let his hard body fall forward to press into hers, his left hand on the wall above her head, holding himself up, while his right gripped her ass and pulled her leg up to wrap around his waist. In this new position, she could feel his hard cock pressing up between her legs and she moaned as she dug her nails into his back, her hands having traveled under his shirt to feel the hard muscles beneath.

"We should take this back up to your place."

"Yes," she agreed. She nodded for added effect, as if that was needed. He smiled and planted a sweet but sloppy kiss on her lips before double-checking that everything in the truck was turned off.

Unfortunately, the universe had different plans for Maeve. As soon as Steve opened the truck door, they were met with an annoyed-looking Jackson, his hand raised and ready to knock.

Steve backed away from Maeve and they simultaneously did this throat-clearing thing people sometimes do to reset the tone of a conversation.

She tried to nonchalantly fix her hair and adjust her clothing, which she knew was frumpled just enough to look like they'd been dry humping, but mentally she was thoroughly unprepared to see anyone besides Steve that night. She knew she looked and acted awkward as fuck as she messed with her hair and then crossed her arms over her braless chest.

"Jackson, hey," Steve said, as if he wasn't still sporting wood from almost nailing Jackson's ex. "We were just doing a few practice runs on some dishes for Friday. Unless you're here to tell us otherwise..."

Jackson gave a quick glance at Steve before looking over his shoulder at Maeve. It wasn't until she broke their eye contact he looked back at Steve and said, "Because of the whole Annana thing? No, we're still on. Chasity's dead-set on your truck now. Thinks our wedding is going to somehow end up on Page Six or something."

"She's excited about my public humiliation?" Steve asked.

The edge in his voice wasn't lost on Jackson or Maeve. And did he puff out his chest a bit at Jackson, or was that just her imagination? Maybe residual testosterone? Was that how that worked with guys?

"She's excited to get married to me," Jackson clarified as he puffed his chest back at Steve. It didn't have the effect he'd wanted it to since Steve towered over Jackson with the extra height from standing in the truck.

Growing weary of Steve's reluctance to back down, Jackson glanced out into the street and then back to the happy couple in the truck. "But, uh, the reason I'm here… I need to talk to Maeve for a few minutes. Alone."

This was it. The moment she'd been waiting for since she landed in Italy. For the longest time, she'd been embarrassed at how sure she'd been that Jackson would show up, eventually. She actually stuck to her itinerary, so sure that at any minute he'd realize what a colossal mistake he'd made and would just show up, apologize for getting cold feet, and then they would carry on as if it had never happened. A funny story to tell the kids one day. By the last day of her trip, she couldn't believe she'd ever been so naïve to think that was a possibility. But now, it was finally happening. There he was, three years too late, looking like a teenager about to ask someone to prom.

Back then, she'd wanted a reconciliation with him, a shag-filled reunion, to be exact. It was safe to say enough time had passed that she no longer had fantasies like that anymore.

The feel of Steve's lips lingered on various parts of her body, but she had to admit she was dying to know what Jackson had to say. Was he there to finally apologize? Something he hadn't actually done yet since most of their conversations were about everything she'd done wrong that had driven him to his actions. Was he there to beg her to come back to him? She'd turn him down, of course. But the thrill of him begging and her rejecting him was beyond appealing.

"Now's not a good time," Steve said with pure delight in his voice.

With her right hand, the one that wasn't in Jackson's view, she reached down and gave Steve's hand a few squeezes: long, short, long, long, long. Morse code for "no" if Steve knew it.

He did not. Nor did he pick up on her tense stance as he continued to go back and forth with Jackson.

"It would only take–" Jackson argued at the same time Maeve said, "We could probably–" But they were both shut down by Steve before they could even finish their sentences.

"We're right in the middle of a cooking lesson. We can't leave anything unattended here for even a minute. Now's not a good time."

At that, Jackson gave a curt nod and then he was fucking gone, leaving Maeve more confused than ever.

17

steve

"What the hell was that?" Maeve hissed at him once the door to the truck was closed and they were once again alone.

Steve stepped back, thoroughly confused as to how they'd gone from about to have the best sex of his life, to Maeve looking like she was ready to slap him in the face. And not in a good way.

"I was helping you out. You know he's bad news, Maeve."

"No, you turned into a jealous asshole who ignored what I wanted. Literally talking over me when I tried to voice my opinion."

Steve bristled at the accusation. That wasn't what he'd meant to do.

"He ghosted you at the airport–"

"He didn't ghost me. He texted he wasn't coming."

"It doesn't matter." Steve could feel his frustration bubbling up as he watched this amazing woman defend that jackass. "He comes up here to get married to someone else, hires your new fiancé as his caterer essentially meaning you are now part of this whole wedding fiasco on Friday, and tonight he shows up without Chasity so he can have a private conversation with you. It's wildly inappropriate behavior for someone about to get married."

While he felt like he was losing control of the situation, Maeve portrayed the opposite as she calmly said, "You think you're better than he is, but after tonight, I'm wondering if Annana was a bit more on the nose about your relationship than I was giving her credit for."

There it was. Maeve, someone he'd felt deeply connected to, threw in his face the biggest hurt and insecurity of his adult life.

Neither broke eye contact as the heavy words sat like boulders between them. She was probably waiting for him to respond, to fight back and defend himself. When he didn't, she looked even more disgusted and left the truck with a slam of the back door.

"Well?" Heath asked when Steve got back to their apartment. "Everything cool? Is Maeve okay to help with cooking?" Heath and Steve knew it would be easier for Maeve to take orders while Heath and Steve cooked, but then Heath's charming self wouldn't be working the crowd and both men knew that was a major factor in them getting the gig. They also really needed more Yelp reviews, and unfortunately most of the people that left reviews did so to mention how much they loved Heath along with how delicious the food was.

"I don't know," Steve said. He sat down on the couch, exhausted. It was late, and he'd had to clean the truck for a second time that day after he'd left Maeve's.

From behind him came a woman's voice. "Can we order... Oh, I thought your roommate wasn't coming home tonight." A woman wearing nothing but one of Heath's t-shirts stood in front of Heath's bedroom door.

Heath shot a look at Steve. "It was fifty-fifty, love. Since he's here now, you'd better head out. Some things came up with work."

The woman—Steve didn't yet know her name and questioned if Heath even remembered it since he didn't bother to introduce them—was no longer smiling.

"What?" she asked in disbelief.

"I need to call it a night. We'll do it again soon though. I'll text you." Heath stood up and took her hand, brought it up to his mouth and gave it a kiss, bringing a smile to her face once again.

While they were in Heath's bedroom, probably getting her back into her own clothes so that she didn't take off with Heath's favorite Pearl Jam shirt, Steve's mind ran through what had happened with Jackson and Maeve. He couldn't figure out what she could possibly want with him. When they'd first talked, Maeve said her only goal was to win the breakup with her own engagement. Not winning per se, but not losing either. More of a tie, really. That was it. And she'd done that.

When he'd stated the obvious during dinner, that Jackson had intentionally followed her to the bathroom to corner her, she'd blown it off. They'd continued to innocently flirt. How stupid he had been, thinking that there could be something between him and Maeve when they were both so damaged and still reeling from their past breakups.

"Alright, spill it," Heath said once he'd escorted his date out of their apartment. "Why are you here and not shagging the lovely Maeve Morrison? Did you muck it up like you did with Annana?"

Steve shot him a disgusted look.

"Whoa. Easy. I'm taking the piss. What the hell happened tonight?"

"I'm sorry. I had a shitty night is all. Jackson showed up."

Heath huffed out a laugh. "That dude is unreal. I almost feel guilty catering a wedding we know is only going to fail."

Steve nodded in agreement to it all. He'd felt the same way about catering the wedding, but who was he to say who should and shouldn't be married? Jackson mentioning Chasity's belief that his infamy will somehow spread into popularity or interest for themselves only confirmed what he'd already suspected: they were perfect for each other as far as he could tell.

"There's something between Maeve and me. I know it. It's been there since we met. And in the truck tonight, before the jackass showed up, it was palpable–this energy between us. When I was teaching her cooking techniques…" He made a few incoherent gestures with his hands before clarifying. "Things started to get… Physical…"

Heath shot up from the couch and towered over Steve. "Tell me you guys did not bump uglies in the truck. So unsanitary. We'll have to get it professionally cleaned."

"Do I look like I got laid tonight?" He meant it as a rhetorical question, but he'd forgotten he was still wearing her shirt, which was probably sending mixed messages.

"Is that her shirt?"

Steve nodded and then let his head fall back onto the couch. It was suddenly too heavy for him, and he needed some sort of relief from the weight of everything.

Heath exaggerated giving Steve a once over and said, "No, I guess you don't look like someone who got laid. You're way too mopey." Satisfied that they wouldn't need to bleach the entire truck, he sat back down.

"We kissed and were about to go back up to her place when Jackson showed up wanting private counsel with Maeve. Again."

Heath clapped his hands and rubbed them together in anticipation. "Excellent. What did he say to her? I'm dying to know where this wanker's head is at. My money is on him thinking he can show up and get one last shag with her before he settles down with his new wife."

"You can't be serious." Steve's palms got clammy as it sank in. Maybe he was the asshole for stepping in, or rather overstepping, and blocking Jackson's attempts. He'd only wanted to protect her from him dragging the sordid affair out any longer. Maeve had been ready to move on during dinner. Hell, they'd kissed, and she'd practically drooled when he pulled out the Heath move of licking her Chapstick off his lips.

"What? I'm not allowed to get personal amusement from watching this all play out?"

"Not that. Though that is a bit fucked up. I don't get why everyone cares what he has to say. What does it matter? It's not going to change anything."

"Says who? You?"

"Yes, and anyone else who's been through an ex resurfacing."

"So if Annana called you right now and wanted to talk, you wouldn't talk to her? You wouldn't want to hear what she has to say about why she threw you under the bus?" Heath mimicked driving with his hands on ten and two, his mouth creating a motor sound for effect.

"Thump, thump," he said as his hands raised up a few inches and then slammed back down when he finished driving his invisible bus over a make-believe Steve. Before Steve could continue, Heath held up a finger, then put his bus in reverse and put his arm on the couch as he threw the pretend bus in reverse to take yet another pass over the body with more thumping sound effects.

"Exactly. Annana showing up would only be her reversing for another ride over my dead body. No, I don't care what she has to say. She's ruined everything. Besides, it would only be to benefit her. She'd just be looking for more material for her next song."

"Fine. That was a poor example."

"It's not. It's the same with Jackson. He wants absolution

so he can start his marriage with a clean slate, or he wants some sort of reassurance that he's the shit and Maeve's not over him. It's bull shit either way and it's at Maeve's expense."

"And are you here, unshagged, because you told her that?"

"She didn't give me a chance. I told Jackson she was busy cooking with me and didn't have time to talk." He said the next part with considerably less confidence. The more he thought about it on the way home, the more he was convinced that she was right. "After he left, she said I was ignoring what she wanted, and that Annana was probably right about everything she said about me."

"Damn…"

His palms reached the perspiration point where he had to wipe them on his pants. It was bad when Heath, the jokester of the two, found zero humor in a situation.

"Yeah… Damn."

Heath left it alone for less than a minute. "Then what did you say? After she said the bit about Annana, what did you say?"

"I didn't say anything. I was in shock about the whole thing. We were minutes away from being in her bedroom. It was too drastic a swing in the other direction for me. I froze."

Heath winced.

"That's not helpful."

"Even I can't sugarcoat this one. You didn't say anything… You know Lori has a single roommate if you're interested…" he said, pointing to the door where his lady friend Lori had previously exited.

Steve wasn't interested. Even after the knife to the heart with the Annana comment, there was still only one person he wanted to talk to that night, and it wasn't Heath or Lori's single roommate.

He laid in bed, tossing and turning; he had the sinking

feeling Heath was right. Were he to post the scenario to Reddit with the infamous "Am I the Asshole" tagline, he was sure the answer would be a resounding "Yes, you asshole."

He spent the rest of the night trying to figure out the right words to fix it and when the best time to talk to her would be. The words refused to come to him, but he figured the perfect time to talk would be after their lunch service outside the store. He needed to get it cleared up sooner rather than later, but he also needed a little more time to make sure he didn't muck it up again.

wednesday

18
maeve

"You're really going to sit here eating leftover takeout rather than buy something from the food truck?" Kiki asked, popping her head into the tiny back office where Maeve was holed up with the unsexiest book she could find: Don't Know Much About History by Kenneth C. Davis. She'd bought it years ago for her flight to the Mediterranean, but the drinks and her overwhelming dread of a future without Jackson in her life prevented her from getting beyond page three.

In her office, she wasn't fairing much better as she reread the same paragraph a half dozen times.

"Yes, I am. It's leftover egg rolls and garlic shrimp–also known as culinary heaven."

Kiki took the response as an invitation to engage further. She reached out to snatch the book from her.

"Don't you have work to do?" Maeve asked.

"What are you reading?" She skimmed over the page Maeve had blankly stared at. "Oh, no, no, no… It is not that dire that you need to resort to this."

Maeve furrowed her brow. "I'm not resorting to anything. It's a history book. I think it's interesting."

Kiki, a lover of smutty romance novels and a frequent visitor to her friend Sam's smutty book review website, scoffed at the non-fiction in her hand. "Did you see this part here where the author recommends another book called Cod? That's it; that's the entire book. A couple hundred pages about that one fish."

Maeve put her fork down and extended her hand. "Give me my book back. I'll be out when I'm done eating."

"I was born and raised in Gloucester; my whole family fishes, and I still would never read an entire book about cod."

"Wait..." Maeve could feel that there was something in her memory about cod. As odd as that sounded, the book was familiar to her.

"What?" Kiki asked. "Am I offending your taste in literature too much? More like saving you from yourself if you ask me. Though I suspect you're still thinking about Steve and Jackson while you're reading about..." She looked back at the book again. "Christopher Columbus? That's kinky, Maeve, and not in a good way. You are one sick puppy." Kiki shook her head in mock disgust.

"Ew, Keek," she said reflexively, still keeping her brain on what connection she had with the book entirely about cod.

"Oh my god..." she said when it finally dawned on her. "Let me see that book title, the one about cod."

"Seriously?" When it was clear that Maeve was indeed dead serious, Kiki reluctantly handed the book back to her. "There, top of the page," she said, pointing to a few lines.

"Kiki, what are the odds that the book I randomly picked up mentions one of Steve's favorite books?"

"About as slim as Annana finding Steve's reflection in Anne's sunglasses."

"One of our first conversations was about buying books and he mentioned this exact book, a cod biography by some guy named Kurlansky."

A look of confusion replaced Kiki's look of awe. "He said

his favorite book was a cod biography and you still want him to put his penis inside you?"

"Kiki…"

"It's a valid question."

Even with the book revelation, which felt oddly like some sort of sign from above, she still wasn't sure where she landed when it came to Steve. At least, her heart was confused about that part, her body was still very much on board and holding a grudge that it hadn't happened already.

"I don't know…"

Kiki rolled her eyes. "Please, with the way you two were eyeing each other in the truck yesterday. Didn't you notice I hauled ass out of your guys' way? There were so many sparks flying between you two I was ducking and dodging smoldering embers on my way out." She looked down at the floor and then back up again, adding in a low, traumatized voice, "Almost didn't make it."

Maeve put down her book and took one last bite before chucking the rest into the trash.

"Lucky for me you survived," Maeve said, preferring to play along rather than detail out what had happened the night before.

"Speaking of Steve. The man-bun hotty has been staring at you through the window since I walked in here."

"Really?" Maeve practically shrieked as she whirled around in her office chair and caught Heath and Steve leaning on the food truck order window and looking in her direction. At once they straightened, knocked into each other as they both turned to walk away and accidentally turned towards each other, and then finally disappeared into the back of the truck.

"You weren't supposed to look," Kiki said.

Maeve swirled in her chair to face her. "Something happened between us last night, after you left." Before Kiki could ask for details, she added, "We'd better get back out there. It was slow earlier, but hopefully things will pick up."

The two women walked back out to find a couple browsing their olive oil bread dip kits. After greeting the customers, Kiki followed Maeve behind the counter and grilled her there in a lowered voice.

"Spill it. About the thing."

"Steve showed up to make sure we didn't have second thoughts about having them on the lot today. He also apologized for the way he spoke to me after dinner service."

"Yes," Kiki said. "Good man. I told you."

"Once that was settled, he wanted to teach me how to properly make some of their dinner items for the wedding. But then, when we were in the back of the truck with Stevie Ray Vaughan playing in the background–"

"That explains our sudden change from instrumental pop to jazz playing in the storefront today."

Maeve blushed. "I'd never heard it before. I like it. Very soothing." She looked around the storefront as if assessing how the music fit in with their products and layout. "Anyway, we were good, and it was strictly professional in the truck until he came up behind me to show me some techniques... Then we kissed and... Things... And then Jackson showed up."

Kiki made a face of pure disgust. "Ugh, that man's timing is the worst."

"It really is. Jackson said he needed to talk to me and Steve morphed into this jackass controlling boyfriend. He said we were too busy to talk, and then he cut both me and Jackson off when we tried to say anything."

Kiki's eyebrows raised. "Steve did that?"

Maeve gave a slow confirmation with a nod of her head.

"Damn... He comes off as more laid back than that."

Maeve drummed her fingers on the counter, thinking

about the two different versions of Steve that she knew. "I don't know anymore."

"Then what happened? I'm assuming Jackson left, and you guys talked."

Maeve gave in and glanced out the side window. She couldn't see Steve from where she was standing, but her eyes were still drawn in that direction.

"I confronted him about it, called him a jealous asshole, and he said he was trying to protect me from myself."

Maeve's head hurt from the messiness of the whole thing. She saw and understood all the different angles and perspectives, but somehow it wasn't any clearer. Worse yet, an intense feeling of guilt was rising into her chest and threatening to crush her heart. Steve misguidedly tried to do the right thing, and she'd returned the favor by throwing the most hateful thing she could think of in his face.

But why didn't he fight back? Because deep down he agreed and didn't have it in him to keep denying it? Because he really was a good guy and didn't have it in him to keep trying to convince her?

Before she could finish her recap of the previous night, a customer waved their hand for assistance and saved Maeve from her inner thoughts. Mixed feelings about Steve lingered as she talked about the different infusion options Olive What She's Having offered. There was even a brief moment when she swore she smelled lemons, the same scent that was on his hands when they were passionately holding her face and neck, his fingers gently then desperately caressing her skin.

When the foot traffic died down, they resumed their conversation with Maeve explaining what she'd said to Steve and how she'd stormed off. Kiki restocked the areas hit hardest by the latest rush, and tidied up the bottles. She had an eye for minor details and was good at keeping the store looking pristine. They both firmly believed presentation and tangibility of the products were the keys to big sales. Make it look grand-opening ready and get the product into their hands, and the customers were sure to leave with a purchase.

Once Maeve finished, Kiki paused her efforts to perfectly align every bottle on the garlic infused shelf and said, "I know Steve has some stuff going on with his ex and that's interfering with whatever you guys have going on here, but I think the biggest obstacle–the one that you can actually do something about–is Jackson."

Maeve re-adjusted the new bacon infused olive oils displayed on the center table. It was counterproductive because the original table had been crushing it in sales and couldn't possibly be improved, but she needed something to busy herself with before she made the grave mistake of going out to talk to Steve without knowing what she should say.

"Maeve?" She walked over to the display table. "Did you hear what I said?"

Maeve relinquished the bottles. "Yeah, I heard you. You're right. I should see what he wants myself. Be done with it once and for all." She pulled out her phone and tapped a quick message asking Jackson to come by at half-past three, after the food truck would be done and gone for the day.

She looked around the store. As someone who enjoyed avoiding stress by focusing all her attention on work, the place looked immaculate. It was even to where she needed to step back before she overdid it, like with the bacon infused oils display.

"Enough about my mess," Maeve said, forcing herself away from any product so her full attention was on her bestie, Kiki Carlson. "Tell me more about how Carlson Accounting is taking Galway by storm."

On top of everything happening with Maeve's love life, Kiki had dropped a bomb on her when they were opening up the store: She was giving her two-weeks' notice. For the past year she'd slowly accumulated customers, other small businesses in and around Galway, for her accounting services at Carlson Accounting and she no longer had time to put in the store hours at Olive What She's Having.

19

steve

"Shit, now I look like a creepy stalker," Steve said to Heath as they stood in the back of the truck, hiding like a couple of stalkers who were just caught stalking.

"You're making things worse the longer you draw this out." The conversation paused as they emerged from the back to take a quick order. "If you'd have gone in when we got here and apologized, everything would have been fine."

"Or she could come to the truck and apologize to me for the whole Annana comment." While he was fairly certain he'd been an asshole for cock blocking Jackson against her wishes, he was also fairly certain he hadn't deserved that much vitriol in response to it.

"Get over it, mate. A mean girl said mean things about you in a song and on social media. It's over. No one cares anymore. Look…" He gestured to the lack of customers outside their truck not 24 hours after the video had gone viral. "No one cares but you."

He did care. He cared a lot. It was like that play he read in high school where Daniel Day Lewis would rather die than sign his name to something that wasn't true. Steve had the strongest urge right then to shout that same line to Heath about it being his good name that she'd drug through the mud and how he would never get another one.

On the other hand, what Heath said was spot on. People were mildly curious when they thought they could somehow get closer to the famous singer Annana through her slightly infamous ex. Shutting up the truck early and refusing to talk to anyone about it had sent the message that it wasn't going to happen. People had already moved on to whatever actual problems they had in their lives and had left Steve's problems behind them. He was a mere blip in their memory that likely wouldn't last more than a few weeks, if that.

They silently worked through a few more spurts of customers where they were either really busy or completely dead, on and off like that throughout the few hours they were there. It was like a variation of Newton's Laws of Motion: a food truck with a long line tends to continue to have a long line; a food truck with no line tends to continue to have no line.

Finally, a little before three when they were closing up and moving their focus to prepping for Friday's wedding, Steve said, "Can you drive back without me? I'm going to stay and smooth things over with Maeve."

"Gladly. 'Cause I'm calling out Friday if this isn't sorted. No way am I working the counter while you two bicker at the stove all night."

Once the truck was closed up and on its way, Steve ducked into the wine store across the street to pick up an "I'm sorry I was an asshole" bottle of wine. Surprisingly, when he told the salesperson that was what he wanted, she had an array of lovely reds and whites to choose from. They also conveniently had an assortment of fresh flowers for people who liked wine and flowers on the table for dinner. Not quite what he'd be using it all for, but helpful nonetheless.

As Steve walked across the street, he noticed a familiar car parked nearby. Jackson jumped out and made his way across the street as well, putting the two on intersecting paths, destined to end in a fiery crash if they both continued on their current course.

Jackson eyed up the flowers and wine in Steve's hand and shook his head in disgust. He got right to the point. "You need to back the fuck off, man. I'm going in to talk to Maeve," he said as he started again on his path towards Steve and the store.

"The hell you are."

Steve was acutely aware his current behavior was the exact thing he was on his way to Maeve to apologize for, but he couldn't stop himself. He'd seen how upset and confused and hurt Maeve was that first day. Jackson had no right being there, harassing her, and she was too nice to tell him to fuck off. Steve would do it for her and then explain everything afterwards. They were a mere few days from Jackson being married and out of their lives for good so that he and Maeve could get back to whatever was happening between them.

That last part drove him the most. There was something about Maeve's interest in talking to Jackson that made him nervous to where he maybe wasn't thinking straight. It wasn't rational how often his mind drifted to thoughts of her, how his body seemed to crave hers, to where he felt like a teenager again, ready to dry hump her in the back of the truck. But it wasn't just lust and carnal attraction, though that was certainly intense. It was everything about her: her drive to open her own business and run it like the rockstar she was, her mostly laid-back demeanor that allowed for a lack of vengeance and anger towards Chasity and Jackson, and a million other things he couldn't quite pinpoint or verbalize. It wasn't love since it was still so soon and they were in a bit of a row, but it could be if only they had a chance to get there.

So he kept walking towards Jackson even while the little angel on his shoulder dropped to its knees and pleaded for him to stop. Surely Maeve, someone who once panic-dialed him from the bathroom and begged him to continue to be her pretend fiancé, could understand the desperate measures people go through when they feel they're on the verge of losing something important.

Steve increased his pace and turned with his flower-filled hand raised in front of Jackson, a sort of floral old-school traffic cop. Jackson plowed forward, using the force of his weight to push Steve back a few staggering steps. Once he got over the shock of what a brick wall Jackson could be, Steve dug his heels down, stood his ground, and surprised himself when he bared his teeth.

"You don't want to get into this with me, man," Jackson said, exuding frat boy vibes as he rolled up his sleeves and made a big to-do of taking off his watch and placing it safely in his pocket.

"You're right; I don't. So why don't you go back to Chasity and leave Maeve alone."

Jackson stepped towards Steve so that their faces and upper bodies were almost touching. "You think I'm the problem? No one wrote a song about me being a dick. You're lucky I walked away last night; I'm not feeling as generous today. Back. Off."

In a perfect world where fate wasn't messing with Steve at every turn, that would have been the end of it. Jackson would have continued to be an imbecile, but Steve would have backed down. Maeve would have popped out of her store to see them both standing in the street just a few feet away from her and there would have been a happy ending for all the relevant parties–everyone but Jackson.

But luck (or fate) hadn't been on Steve's side in months.

When Jackson took another step forwards and bumped into Steve, the momentum knocked Steve back and his foot landed on a giant river rock dropped by some negligent tourist. He lost his balance and his elbow flew straight into Jackson's nose. A direct hit.

The blood gushed almost immediately and tough-guy Jackson doubled over with his hands covering his face.

"Fuck, you broke my nose, asshole," Jackson said in a muffled, off-sounding voice from behind his hands.

"You broke his nose?" Maeve must have heard the commotion from inside her store because suddenly she was in the street with them, demanding answers from Steve and moving to comfort and help Jackson. "Steve, what the hell were you thinking?"

Steve felt like an utter ass with his hands full of wine and flowers, untouched, while Jackson was still bent over and covered in his own blood.

"It was my elbow; I didn't hit him."

Maeve turned from Jackson just long enough to glare at Steve and say, "I told him to meet me here."

"Oh, god, it hurts so bad, Maeve," Jackson moaned.

"My elbow hit him. By accident." He repeated, grasping at the only straw he had, which was that Maeve was only mad because she hadn't heard him the first time. But clearly she had since his words once again fell on deaf ears. It felt like the battle was already over and he was clearly on the losing side. What's worse, he sounded like his father, a man known for his pathetic excuses for why the world was out to get him and it was everyone's fault but his own.

Steve's brain flip-flopped in his head to where he didn't know what was what anymore and he didn't trust his own judgment. Was he to blame even if the hit itself had been accidental? Was he fighting the wrong battle, trying to step in to save someone who'd already insisted she didn't need saving?

"Let's get you into the store," Maeve said to Jackson, ignoring the other man in the street.

Steve watched as Jackson leaned hard into his injury. His legs weren't hurt, but he made a big to-do of hobbling over to

Olive What She's Having, savoring every bit of his victory over Steve.

Assuming that was the end of everything, he waited until he was the only one left outside, then he placed the wine and flowers at Maeve's door and ordered an Uber.

It had felt like he was making progress on the East Coast with his new life and career, but he was still a fucking mess of a human. Considering Maeve had just escorted a mess of man into her shop, it was probably best she didn't have another waiting his turn in line. He didn't have any ideas about what would happen next with the wedding or their catering arrangements, but he was certain that the best thing he could do for Maeve was to let her go. It was what she wanted, and that was what a good guy would do, honor her wishes.

20

annana

Annana effortlessly rolled a quarter over her knuckles. As a child she'd wanted to be a surgeon and had spent an entire summer learning how to roll coins over her fingers to increase dexterity.

Now, instead of saving lives, she was ruining them according to a small percentage of comments on her TikTok duet video. With her left hand, she scrolled the comments while her right hand worked the quarter. Occasionally she leaned forward and took a sip of the vodka and Sprite on the balcony table. Overall, it was a lovely way to spend the morning.

She wasn't meant to be a surgeon, and even though she thought she could transfer all that finger dexterity into playing the guitar, that hadn't worked out as planned, either. All she had left was her new persona as the wounded woman who inspired other wounded people to fight back against their jackass boyfriends and spouses.

The quarter rolled off her knuckle and made a ringing sound as it settled on the glass top of the table.

She reread one of the comments and a few of the replies below it which emphatically agreed with the original statement: Steve's TikTok video was a desperate cry for her attention. He wanted her back.

"Holly!" she called back into the apartment. "Holly! Get out here! Now!" Her new assistant responded best to shouting and a strong sense of urgency.

"I'm here. What is it? What's wrong?" the panting woman asked as she clutched bags of groceries Annana forgot she'd asked her to get.

"This. Look at this. How did we miss this?"

Holly took the phone and her eyes searched the screen to see what had sent Annana into a tizzy.

Exasperated by her continued incompetence, Annana took the phone back and said, "Steve wants to get back together. That's why he did the video. He wanted me to see it."

Holly licked her lips, eyed up the half-empty vodka bottle on the table, and said, "Um, maybe... Or maybe it was just a coincidence? Maybe?"

The woman was meek. No wonder she could only find a job as an assistant. Annana smiled at the thought. For years she'd pushed those ideas down and pretended to be someone she wasn't. Her single was her first attempt at being her more authentic self, and it was a raging success. There was no turning back now.

"You don't think Steve wants me back?"

As she suspected, Holly backed down almost immediately. "No, nothing like that..."

They stared at each other. Holly unsure of what to say next, and Annana enjoying her discomfort.

"Book us a flight to Boston. Earliest available." She took another pull from her drink.

"I thought... I mean... Weren't you going to spend the day writing?"

She had to get a new assistant. It was almost too painful to listen to this woman who was miraculously walking around without a backbone.

"I'll write on the plane."

She wasn't going to write on the plane. Annana was going to continue her buzz at the airport bar and on the flight over as she planned out her next move. What she needed was a good backstory for Steve about why she wanted to see him again after she'd said all those nasty things on her TikTok. She couldn't tell him he was her muse or that she'd guessed he wanted her back based on some random TikTok comment. She needed to concoct some storyline about her song being artistic license and that they still had a future together despite everything they'd been through, and she'd only now just realized it.

When it came down to it, there were two likely outcomes for when she saw him again. One scenario involved a delightful reunion where he apologized for being the absolute worst and they'd go back to LA to continue building her music career. She'd have to tamper down her negative comments some, but she might be capable of doing that if she thought it would keep Steve around and help further her career. Whether she liked it or not, he was her creative spark and she was drowning without him. She was on the verge of hitting her expiration date. The TikTok video had helped, but it wasn't enough to keep her in the spotlight indefinitely. Nothing was. She needed consistent new content and Steve was the key to making that happen. At least, until she could find another source of inspiration, but at the moment, she was borderline desperate.

The other outcome for her hypothetical reunion wasn't nearly as desirable. She finished her drink and played out the other scenario in her mind. She could get to Galway Harbor and find out her trip was all for nought and the TikTok people had misread the entire situation of him trying to get her attention and win her back. It wouldn't devastate her; there was chemistry between the two, but it was more of a temporary good time than anything long-term between them. She was prepared for him to parrot back what Holly said about it being a coincidence. And that would be okay. He would either be her muse at her side, or she'd use his rejection to inspire her next song. Either way, she'd get the jumpstart her music career needed.

She'd had writer's block since "I Really, Really Hope You Die" first hit the charts. Getting dumped by Steve again could be the cure she'd been looking for.

21

maeve

Maeve noticed that Jackson, Mr. Tough Guy himself, was limping from a nose injury and was even relying on her to help carry his weight as they walked into her store and to the back office.

Kiki popped her head in once they were settled. "Damn. Steve did that?" she asked when she had a good look at his face. His nose bleed had mostly stopped since he'd pinched the bridge of his nose and Maeve had given him a towel to hold against it. The center of his face was red and swollen. While Maeve sat in a daze at the whole situation, Kiki went to work pulling up WebMD on the computer to see if it was broken.

"He sucker punched me." Jackson winced as Kiki gently pressed on the swollen skin.

"Sorry," Kiki said while continuing her torture. "The site says I need to hear if there's a cracking sound when I press down. Hush up for a minute." The office was eerily quiet as Kiki worked and they all strained to hear and sort of crunching of cartilage in Jackson's nose.

Finally, he pulled away, and Kiki's hands dropped. "I don't think it's broken, but swing by an ER just to be sure.

Especially with the wedding coming up. Best to get it all cleared up tonight."

"This is the guy you're going to marry?" Jackson asked Maeve.

Kiki rolled her eyes at Jackson's blatant dismissal of her and excused herself. She shut the door behind her.

"He has good intentions," she said in his defense, refusing to fully believe or accept that of the two of them, Steve was the bad guy. She wasn't thrilled with his continued attempts to keep Jackson from her, but she believed he'd done it more out of a misplaced desire to protect her from Jackson than from any sort of jealousy or unchecked anger issue.

"I know what his intentions were," he said before giving her the rundown of how he'd shown up to talk to her, as she herself had requested, and her overbearing fiancé had shown up at the same time threatening to kick his ass if he didn't back off his woman.

It was amazing to watch, really. Seeing his eyes bore into her own as he lied. He explained, including explicit details, though she never asked for such clarification, what Steve had done to him, completely unprovoked to boot.

When Maeve had stepped outside to see what was going on, she'd first noticed Steve standing there with flowers in one hand and a bottle of wine in the other. There was no way he took a swing at Jackson while his hands were full. There was no way he would have taken a swing at him in general. She was pretty certain of that. Unfortunately, she hadn't fully put those pieces together until she'd already dismissed Steve and was helping Jackson inside.

Once she was inside with him, three years having passed since they'd last sat down and had a proper conversation, she finally had all the clarity she'd been looking for: Jackson was a horrible person.

She couldn't say with complete confidence whether he

was a true narcissist, but there was something lacking, for sure: honesty or empathy, perhaps.

Thinking that she was taking in every word he was saying, Jackson continued to talk while she thought back to the bad times they'd had together. The ones she'd put out of her mind during and after their relationship, but listening to him lie to her face, she couldn't block out the past anymore.

Like the way she used to listen to audiobooks when she was doing chores around the apartment but had to stop because of him. He'd want to say something to her and she wouldn't hear him at first or she'd need to pull out her phone and tap a few buttons to pause her story to hear what he had to say. He'd sigh and say something like, "Forget it. I'm clearly bothering you."

Her brow furrowed as she worked out the memory in her mind. She saw his face again and heard in his voice how annoyed he'd been that he couldn't talk to her, that it was such a big to-do for her to pause her audiobook. Back then, she understood it, felt guilty even about how she was walking around essentially ignoring him and was being rude by having her earbuds in.

After it had happened a few times, she'd stopped listening to audiobooks when she was cleaning bathrooms, folding laundry, or doing any other of the chores he refused to help with. It had gotten to where she couldn't pay attention to the story, anyway. She was always waiting for him to need something or get annoyed with her about it, so she just stopped. And then the craziest thing happened. Once she'd stopped, he'd stopped needing anything. She would just do her work in silence on the off-chance that he would want to have a conversation or ask her something.

"Maeve? Are you even listening?"

Crap, she'd done it again. Ironically, she didn't even have earbuds in, but she'd missed what he said, anyway. His face looked exactly the same and the irritation in his voice was obvious.

"What's that?" she asked. Years ago, she would have apologized. It would have been an almost knee-jerk reaction to take the blame for missing what he'd said and to beg for his forgiveness.

"I said you need to get over what happened between us."

She heard it that time, crystal clear, though she could hardly believe it.

"You think I had Steve attack you because you left me at the airport three years ago?" She almost laughed to hear it said out loud. The whole thing was so absurd and yet there he was, stone-faced as he was saying it to her.

"No, I know you'd never ask that of anyone." He reached for her hands and before she realized what was happening, they were in his. The roles had reversed, and she was the broken thing while he was the one fixing and consoling what he thought was hurt.

"He hit me to keep us apart. Even though we're just friends now and I'm getting married in a few days. And I know you know all about his past with Annana. The entire country knows he's an asshole. Clearly, the only reason you'd ever be with a jerk like that is because you lost all your self-esteem after our breakup. You never got over it and now you're settling."

He continued to hold her hands throughout his speech, leaving Maeve beyond speechless. Was it possible that the conversation about her self-esteem was what he'd been trying to say to her all along? That even if Steve hadn't hit him (or whatever happened between them) that she and Jackson would have still ended up in the same position with him saying mostly the same thing?

"Chasity is a life coach. Did you know that? I bet she'd be willing to take you on as a client. Maybe even give you a friends and family discount."

At that, she laughed; it was a barking sort of laugh that made her snatch her hands back so she could clap them over her mouth. He responded in kind by giving her a warning look that he was about to get shitty with her.

"Sorry. I laugh when I'm uncomfortable." She loathed saying the word sorry to him, but she also could not get him out of her office fast enough. If saying sorry would appease him and send him on his way, it was a price she was willing to pay.

His face turned from anger to exhaustion. "Yeah, I remember. That's something else Chasity could help you with, if you gave her a chance."

"That would be nice," she managed.

He fished one of Chasity's cards from his wallet, and she took it. Under his critical gaze, she placed it on her desk and gave him her best, reassuring smile. The one she always pulled out for Jackson, the one which confirmed she'd heard what he'd said and she was happily in complete agreement with him.

He nodded. "Good. I'll let her know you'll be in touch."

Maeve continued to smile back. Why wasn't he leaving? He'd said his piece and potentially landed a new client for Chasity (as far as he knew) and yet he wasn't going anywhere.

"One of the reasons I stopped by last night was to talk to you about wedding favors. Chasity saw a final mock-up of the place settings with our wedding favor, a CD of all our favorite songs, and she thinks something's missing."

Kiki had suggested a few years back that they create and advertise bottles of olive oil as event and party favors. They hadn't had many takers yet, but it was hardly a hardship to have the image and sales button on the website, so they'd kept it up as an option, anyway. Since they didn't have a ton of extra room for inventory that didn't sell on the regular, they always ordered the smaller favor bottles and labels as needed whenever the rare order came through.

"Oh, yeah. Those we have to order weeks in advance. I... We couldn't have anything like that ready by Friday."

He gave a sad smile in return. "This is what I'm talking about. This..." He raised one arm and motioned towards the storefront beyond her office door. "Everything you have here is good. Really, you did good. But the Maeve I knew wouldn't turn something like this down. Not that quickly, without even trying. You've lost your drive."

Ah, yes. The Maeve he knew had been so desperate to please others that she almost killed herself trying to do just that. She wouldn't have batted an eye at the request. Rather, she would have accepted–once again taking on more than she could reasonably handle–all while showing nothing but ease and composure on the outside, even though she was flailing in open water on the inside.

"It's not that–"

"I've already talked to Miles about it, and he said he'll get everything squared away for you. All the materials and anything else you need." At that, he put his hands on the arms of his chair, getting ready to hoist himself up and out of her office.

That was the Jackson she knew. The one who didn't take no for an answer and felt the world should all clamber at his feet to help and serve him. She had to admit that when she was by his side, it had been an attractive trait, something she admired and shamelessly benefited from herself. Being on the other side now, she could see it for what it really was, and she couldn't be more repulsed by him.

Once Jackson was gone–on his way to the ER to decrease any bruising and swelling, and to get a second opinion from someone with experience beyond a quick skimming of WebMD–she and Kiki finished out their shifts, then closed up shop to get down to it in Maeve's apartment.

"His story isn't adding up," Kiki said as she plopped down on Maeve's couch. Hedy climbed into her lap and settled in for a quick nap while they talked. Kiki's fingers gently massaging as she pet her soft fur.

"He's full of shit. I'm well aware. It's funny, though. I remember I used to get full-on defensive any time my friends said something like that about Jackson." She sat down on the sofa as well, one leg bent underneath her so that she was facing Kiki and leaning back against the armrest. "I guess I always knew that something was off, but I never wanted to hear it."

"Sometimes we can't see it until we're ready."

Maeve detailed out to Kiki the little things that had happened between her and Jackson when they'd started to get serious, like the audiobook problem and how Jackson's needs and interests had always come before her own. How he'd spin it so that all his needs were met, but she was still seen as the selfish one. Then she told her what Jackson had said in the back office about her low self-esteem because of their breakup and how Chasity could help with that. She held up the card for Kiki to see. Proof of the insanity.

Kiki's hand froze and Hedy, suddenly alert once she was no longer being petted, nudged it with her nose to encourage Kiki to continue.

"And you're taking her up on that offer?"

"Fuck no. I made it seem like a possibility to get him out of here. I heard what he had to say. It's nothing I want to hear. I'm done."

Maeve took a sip of the wine Steve had left at her door before adding, "I'm done- ish."

"Done-ish isn't a thing." Kiki sipped her water. She had a "shit-ton" of work to do when she got home and she said she needed a clear head.

Maeve's face felt hot from shame, though she wasn't sure yet if it was warranted. "They want wedding favors from us and I caved. But for good reason, and it's a good sale," she added when she saw Kiki's reaction.

"Let me guess, you're spending your day off tomorrow assembling favors?"

"Not the whole day…" She felt a wave of flashbacks of all the times she'd defended herself to her friends as the conversation took on an edge that wasn't entirely unfamiliar to her. She'd had that same sort of conversation with many of her closest friends back in Maryland: they would gently suggest that perhaps she and Jackson were not a good fit, Maeve would get defensive, the subject was dropped with an awkward pause until someone changed the conversation topic to something more innocuous like the weather or whatever show they were binging.

"Look, I know he sucks at life and I owe him absolutely nothing. But I'd be lying if I said each time I saw him, I didn't feel a hell of a lot better about us splitting up. Even right now, talking about it with you, I'm having these memories and insights about what life was really like with him. And while what's happening right now isn't terribly enjoyable, it is profoundly enlightening and I want it all. I buried too much of it before and I need it all out in the open now."

Kiki nodded. "Yeah, okay. I can understand that."

Maeve searched for any signs of Kiki placating her, but they weren't there, and Kiki wasn't one to hold back, anyway. There would be no mollifying from Keek, only the truth.

"Besides, he already has Miles hunting down all the materials except the oil and seasoning packets, so all I have to do is fill the bottles, plop on a label and tie a nice ribbon around the neck with a pre-made card and a packet of seasoning. I can easily do that. I'm even happy to do that since, thanks to some negotiating on my part with Miles, they're paying double what we normally charge."

Kiki's eyes widened at the price tag of the favors. Because they weren't supplying the bottles or the printed labels, the commission was all the more impressive. A broad smile formed. "Holy shit. Way to stick it to them."

For the first time since she didn't know when, she'd had a candid conversation with a friend about Jackson. Fuck, it felt good. Tearing open the old scar had hurt initially, but this time, she'd do it right. Let it heal properly so it would finally fade away for good.

Now she just needed to figure out what to do about Steve. The poor guy had bought wine and flowers, and she'd followed her initial, incorrect assumption that he'd actually hit Jackson in some attempt to keep them apart. Had taken the argument they'd had the night before to the next level by resorting to violence. By the time she'd put all the pieces together, it had been too late. She was escorting the dick-parading-as-a-man back to her store and Steve's face had registered heartbreak.

Maybe what they really needed was some time apart to figure out what they wanted and sort through their past shit on their own. He could deal with his Annana aftermath while she continued to sort through the many epiphanies she was having about how mentally abusive her ex had been.

Steve could take the day off to think about if he still wanted to give her wine and flowers, or if he was through with her and wanted to find someone who didn't assume the worst about him each time something came up.

thursday

22

steve

Steve woke up the day before the wedding to a few last-minute requests from Chasity: get the truck washed and waxed the day of, make sure the truck was thoroughly cleaned of any traces of peanuts and gluten, and get in touch with Annana to see if she would make an appearance at the wedding.

"Shut up..." was all Heath could say in response when Steve relayed the message. "I can't believe she's still on that."

Neither could Steve. What bride wanted a celebrity singer to crash their wedding with a song titled "I Really, Really Hope You Die"?

"Oh, man. That one has really lost the plot. But then he's just as bad, so I guess they're the perfect match."

Heath checked the time on his phone and grabbed his car keys. "Lori helped me crunch some numbers last night. She's coming with me to pick up all the non-perishable stuff."

Steve's mug froze before it reached his mouth, and his eyes followed Heath as he gathered everything he needed for his date.

"What? It's not a big deal," he insisted. "She happens to be off work and offered to help out."

"It's the biggest deal," Steve said. "It's a day date and you don't do day dates. They're too similar to something actual couples would do, and you refuse to let any woman into that uncharted territory."

Heath made a look of being offended and was about to go off about it, but then his eyes caught on something beyond Steve and he said, "Ah, fuck. It's back."

"What's back?" he asked, turning to see what could be up on the third floor outside their window, aside from a bird.

There, on the other side of the glass looking in in much the same way a child would look into a holiday shopping display window, was a squirrel. He was sitting on his two back legs and munching on a nut while he watched the Heath and Steve show in the kitchen.

"The squirrel?"

"Yes, the bloody squirrel. It's back."

Steve waited a beat for an explanation. As far as he knew, Heath didn't have any illogical fears of squirrels or any other animal.

"I think it's okay," Heath said. "Before you moved in, I went through and made sure everything was closed up, but if that fucker comes inside again, mark it on the calendar and touch nothing. Don't open or close any windows, vents, or anything else like that. I'm going to figure out how he's getting in here." Heath pointed at the squirrel and in a raised voice he added, "You hear that? Don't fuck with me. I will end you."

"The calendar?"

Steve turned to the fridge and there was a brand new calendar hanging on the door, right where the other one had been.

"The calendar, Steve." Heath's hand was on the doorknob, but he stayed to spell it out for his daft friend. "I thought I had it under control, so I trashed the old one. But the bugger's been at that window the past few weeks now, so I got us a new 'squirrel came inside' calendar. I thought I told you about that?"

"No."

"Well, now you know. Also, I forgot to pick up our business cards. Can you swing by and grab them while you're out today? Lori and I will be on the other side of town most of the day."

They'd ordered new business cards from the local printer weeks ago and they both kept forgetting to pick them up. After they'd gotten yet another call from the print shop, Heath had promised they'd be by to pick them up that day.

"Mark the came inside calendar. Pick up the business cards. I can do that."

"Cheers." Heath gave a quick nod and left.

Steve sat on the couch wondering if it would be too weird for him to text Maeve that she'd been right about the calendar. In another dimension where Jackson didn't exist, he would insist on taking her out to dinner. Somewhere nice. And when she asked what the occasion was, he would reveal how right she'd been about Heath's calendar. She would laugh, the deep, all-encompassing laugh of someone who didn't have a care in the world. And he would fall a little harder for her because he was the biggest sucker for that laugh. He'd do just about anything to hear it.

Instead, he was living in a bizarro world where Heath was out with his girlfriend while Steve was left to tend to the came inside calendar. It was an even sadder concept when it didn't involve any sex at all.

Luckily, the squirrel was gone by the time he'd finished his pity party on the couch. He said a silent prayer of thanks that he didn't have to mark the calendar–he still couldn't get his original assumptions about it out of his head–and he grabbed his wallet and keys and left for a walk to the print shop to get their cards. The fresh air might help him think and figure a way out of his latest fuck-up.

His mind-clearing walk lasted a few steps before Steve heard the familiar voice that had haunted him for months.

"Get in, loser. We're fixing our relationship."

The voice was distinct, and so was the quote. Annana was a die-hard *Mean Girls* fan and her hands-down favorite character was Regina; another red flag that he probably should have noticed since he was the one who ended up on the other side of the mean girl attack from her. Right before he'd ended it, she'd had it playing in the background non-stop at her apartment. He was surprised and even a little let down that she hadn't waited until October 3rd to show up.

"Oh, come on. That was funny," she said when he stood there, feet glued to the concrete, staring back at her with his mouth hanging open and collecting flies.

"That's it? That's what you say to me after all of this?" He was the one giving her crazy eyes now; he could feel it. But what other appropriate response was there?

Still sitting behind the wheel of what was likely her rental car, Annana gave a fake pout in response, her hands sliding up and down the wheel.

"You're still mad?"

If he'd learned anything the past week, it was not to engage; just walk away. He should have walked away from Jackson every damn time. He probably should have walked away when Maeve first suggested her crazy scheme, and he definitely should have walked away from Annana the first time he met her.

After he'd turned and walked about a block, he felt her presence again. Sure enough, she was slowly driving a few feet behind him in her electric car rental. Damn, those things were whisper quiet.

"What do you want, Annana?" It came out as exasperated because he was. He'd stayed up half the night, almost texting Maeve and then deleting anything he'd written. He was in no mood for whatever Annana wanted. Inspiration for a new song, he assumed.

"I want to talk, obviously. And so do you." She was half hanging out the driver side window now with the car parked in the middle of the road and her hazards on. He could hear her own song playing on the car radio.

"Can you..." He pointed to her car dash, and he let the words hang there, hoping that she could fill in the blanks and realize maybe he didn't want to hear her fucking song right now.

"Oh, right." She gave a soft chuckle and switched off the music. "That."

As if that had been nothing but a minor misunderstanding that had had no negative consequences whatsoever.

She eased the car to the side and parked in one of the many open spots along the sidewalk. Reluctantly, and against all better judgment, he crossed the street and got in so they could have a chat. He suddenly understood with perfect clarity why Maeve had wanted to talk to Jackson. He really had been a jerk to try to stop her.

"I went to an AA meeting last night, and this guy Ron was talking about this one time when his girlfriend started acting out and doing some really crazy shit." Annana's eyes got wide with excitement. "Like, I know you think I did some crazy shit, but this woman has me beat hands down. So anyway, Ron gets all deep and is like, 'And then I realized she was just doing that to get my attention. Because I was revolving my life around alcohol instead of her.'"

Annana paused and looked at him expectantly. Her big revelation finally released out into the world, and she was waiting for his response. Except he had no idea what she was getting at.

"Are you..." He wasn't sure how to word it. He'd seen her have a few drinks here and there, but nothing beyond that as far as he knew. "Are you in recovery? When did this all happen?"

Annana threw her head back in laughter and it reminded Steve of every movie villain that ever existed.

"No, I'm not an alcoholic. You know me better than that, Steven. I was there with my aunt. She hates going alone. But anyway, back to my Ron story…"

Steve tried to think back to what she'd said about the Ron story, but he was more preoccupied with how Annana had shown up out of the blue, didn't seem to be at all aware that they were broken up and not on good terms, and he was also slightly concerned about her use of Ron's name since anonymous was in the meeting's title. He wondered if the poor guy (or his girlfriend) might make a future appearance in one of her upcoming songs.

He shook his head slightly to show he was at a loss for whatever response she'd expected.

"It's us!" Annana declared, her one hand reaching out to affectionately rub his shoulder.

The touch was not expected nor welcome, and Steve couldn't believe he'd gotten in the car and put himself in what was clearly a disaster of a situation. Would he never learn?

He pulled back and narrowed his eyes. She dropped her hand.

"I still don't get it," he said.

"You're Ron's girlfriend! That TikTok video was your way of getting my attention. So, you've got it, and here I am." She squealed with delight and clasped her hands together.

"Steven!" she said when he stared blankly back at her. That was not his name, but she hated that his name only had one syllable, making it difficult for her to put emphasis on it during conversation.

"Say something. You must have known I would come out here when you didn't respond to my duet."

"No, no, no, no… "

His mind raced with everything that could go wrong with this one meeting. Had she bugged the car? Was she recording live and everyone was waiting to hear what the asshole ex boyfriend Reeve would do wrong next? His neck twisted well beyond comfort as he searched the car to see if anything seemed out of place, seeking out any potential flashing red recording lights.

"No, what?" she asked in a playful voice. "What are you looking for?"

"No, that's not what happened. I didn't even post that video."

Annana laughed. "Oh, okay. You just happened to be in a TikTok video that used my song, and you didn't want me to find out it was you?"

The sarcasm was thick and Steve could feel a solid panic attack ready to bubble over. It was the closed-in space that was doing it for him. Sure, he was often in the food truck working a stressful job, but he never felt trapped there. In the tiny car with Annana and his future in her seemingly unstable hands, he felt more than trapped. The walls were surely closing in on him, and this was it.

"Really," Steve said, surprising himself even when he heard it. "I moved across the country." He almost added the words "to get away from you and that damn earworm of a song," but even with the pounding heart in his throat he could still think semi-clearly, at least enough to know that complete candor would not be the way to go with Annana.

"And I bought a food truck with Heath," he said, emphasizing the fact that he wasn't moving back for a very long time.

"Who's Heath?" Her head cocked, and she looked like she was struggling to put a face to the name.

Steve didn't bother to tell her that Heath was a friend whom she'd met multiple times back in LA. He had a point to make and there could be no misunderstanding with superfluous information like how she'd already had multiple conversations with Heath but she was too self-centered to bother to remember them.

"I moved and bought the food truck," Steve continued, "because you and I were over. I called it off, but your song carved it in stone." He pushed the button to turn the music back on. Just as he'd thought, she hadn't been playing the radio. She had her own song set to play on repeat. The car filled with Annana's words.

I really, really hope you die

I can't lie,

I wouldn't cry

Leave me alone and never call

Your heart of stone hits like a wall

"See?" he asked, happily turning the music off again once he'd made his point. "I moved on. How could I not when all I heard was your song for the past few months, telling me how horrible of a person I am and how much you hated our relationship?"

Annana sighed. Now she was the one who was exasperated. "Well, yeah. But you know I exaggerated a little here and there. Art and all; you know how it is."

He nodded his vague understanding of the music industry.

"You flew out here to get back together?" There was a sense of caution in his voice that he couldn't hide. He was down-right terrified of all the terrible ways everything could go down in the next few minutes. She really didn't seem to have any clue. Still. And she'd changed in the months since their breakup. He couldn't tell if it was the fame or what, but this person was not the person he'd dated last fall.

"Yes, Steven. I can see my devotion to work was a problem in our relationship, and you were just trying to get my attention in the only way you knew how to. And I forgive you for that."

He felt his jaw drop open, but he successfully refrained from saying what was on the tip of his tongue. Now was not the time to point fingers about who was guilty or innocent in the demise of their relationship. And yet he couldn't help but nudge a little in that direction when she once again looked back at him with expectant eyes.

"You're admitting that you were the bad guy in our relationship?"

Her shoulders slumped at the shame of it all. "Yes, Steven. I am. I'm sorry I didn't realize how much attention you need. You felt neglected and I am very sorry you felt that way."

The car fell silent. She waited for a response, and he waited for an actual apology. It was plain to see how mismatched they were and how they had never really known each other at all.

"And the song…" he prompted.

Annana cocked her head to the side, and for the first time, her smile twitched as it faltered.

"It was artistic license. I told you that." Was that sincerity in her eyes? He couldn't tell. He couldn't say anything for sure about this woman. For all he knew, she really was in AA and this was some sort of attempt at the latter steps which involved making amends. He nodded slowly to accept her version of amends and glanced at his watch. He didn't have time for this.

"Now you…" she prompted.

"Now me? You want me to apologize?"

"It takes two to tango, Steven."

He could feel himself loosening up. Finally, he understood why she was there and how he could get rid of her.

"I'm sorry I was so needy." He couldn't come up with anything genuine, so he stole a version of hers. It was working. Her expression softened, and he felt at the bottom of his soul that she had no ill intentions towards him anymore. "I'm also sorry I broke up with you, on your dog's gotcha day, at your favorite restaurant."

That last one was only half true. It was dick move, but in his mind he maintained that he couldn't take another day as her boyfriend, and it was just bad timing—nothing as malicious as what her song led people to believe.

"But we're still not getting back together. I'm engaged now. It's too late for us."

Her fake smile remained, and her words came out through gritted teeth. "What do you mean, you're engaged? We haven't even been broken up that long."

Before he could explain, she launched into a myriad of questions about whether it was that whore waitress he used to work with or if it was anyone else she knew. Where did they meet? Did he cheat on her?

At that question, he saw the fire behind her eyes and a pit formed at the bottom of his stomach. *Fuck, fuck, fuck.* Everything he feared was happening. There would be another song and with this one, she wouldn't hold back.

"Whoa, whoa..." He mimicked Chris Pratt interacting with his velociraptors where one wrong move would lead to talons ripping through his throat.

"It's no one you know. She lives out here. We met after I moved. After I'd given up on us getting back together since your song so clearly stated that was the last thing you wanted to do."

At that, some of the rage fell from her face, and was replaced by what looked like despondency. It was a wide swing, but still not quite in the right direction. Sure, the next song might not be about his demise, but it could still be about what an ass he was, set to a more melancholy beat. Her artistic license pulling a Thelma and Louise as it drove his reputation off a cliff with her catchy chorus.

He didn't believe she loved him that much, or even at all

when it came down to it. They had very little in common and he was sure he annoyed her 99% of the time they were together. The sadness wasn't from losing him; it came from her wounded pride.

Since the problem was her ego, all he needed to do was boost it. Steve needed to offer some sort of self-sacrifice that wouldn't destroy him, while still satisfying her intense need for approval.

He needed to beg her to appear at the wedding he was catering. Maybe even grovel about how having her sing her hit song would really be the highlight of the wedding.

No! No, no, no, no! his mind screamed in denial. There had to be another way. And yet, there wasn't. She was an egomaniac. The warning signs were all there earlier in the relationship and they were still there as he sat in her car with her hateful song on standby, waiting to play again once he got out.

Steve cleared his throat. He had to. The words inching their way up were choking him.

"Listen, Annana…" Her eyes lifted and widened with hope. "I'm catering a wedding tomorrow…"

23

maeve

Once the term "narcissist" entered her mind, she'd spent a considerable amount of time online and on Reddit finding out everything she could about narcissistic ex-lovers. It wasn't good.

The information helped explain why Jackson was desperate to continue to get himself in front of her, even when he had no interest in being with her. According to all the articles and the super-helpful folks over in the Reddit universe, Jackson's only concern was that she still be hung up on him.

He'd probably come up to her store expecting her to break down in tears at meeting his new bride-to-be. Had likely planned it out for months how he would drop that little bomb on her and how much joy it would bring him to see her collapse in self-pity over losing him for good.

Jackson had never even considered the possibility of Maeve moving on and turning down his attempts to speak with her. Hiring Steve as his caterer gave Jackson more opportunities to put himself in proximity to her, and it made sure that she witnessed the wedding she could have had with him.

This was what went through Maeve's mind as she sorted through all the supplies Miles had dropped off.

The best way for Jackson to continue to get himself front and center in Maeve's mind? Request bottles of olive oil as wedding favors for each of his guests. It was glaringly obvious why he did it, but she kept reminding herself of all the positives: it was a large sale and an easy way to get her bottles in front of a bunch of people outside of the Galway Harbor vicinity.

It annoyed the hell out of her to tie each tag to the bottle and carefully attach a packet of the homemade seasoning she used in her classes. Even their song, "You Belong With Me" by Taylor Swift, felt like an obnoxious dig at her where she was the other woman, and Chasity was the one Jackson should have picked all along.

A few bottles in, though, those thoughts faded as she thought instead about Steve. She replayed their brief encounters–her class, their fake dinner date, recording videos during prep and lunch service, the shared jokes, the cooking lesson in the back of the truck, the nasty look she'd shot him outside her shop as she catered to Jackson's bloody nose–it was all quite the roller coaster given how briefly they'd known each other.

"You're thinking about Steve," Kiki accused.

Maeve looked up from her corner table to find Kiki staring back at her. The store had a few customers helping themselves to different flavors of olive oil and balsamic vinegar. They set up the shop like a wine bar so that customers could release a small amount into a glass and sample at will without having to rely on Maeve or an employee to serve them.

She set another finished wedding favor in the box on the floor by her feet. Ten down, one hundred and forty more to go. Just a little intimate wedding. She couldn't imagine what a big wedding would have looked like for them.

"What makes you say that?" she asked as she pulled out a

fresh bottle and gathered the ribbon, tag, and seasoning packet she needed to assemble each favor.

"Your humming. When you first started, you were humming 'We Are Never Ever Getting Back Together' with this vengeful little smirk on your face." The corners of Kiki's mouth twisted up into a wicked smile and Maeve momentarily wondered if she'd really been humming that hateful song with such a malicious smile on her face. It certainly seemed plausible, given her current feelings about Jackson.

"That was the first few bottles. The next time I walked by, I could hear 'Fearless,' and your nasty vengeful smile turned into this far-off look of longing." Kiki sang out a few verses of the song as she playfully did a few dance moves that ended in her pointing accusatory fingers at Maeve.

Busted.

This was why Maeve had decided to assemble everything in the store rather than upstairs in her apartment. Her heart hurt thinking about Kiki's last day and how quiet the store would be without her presence. It was the end of an era and she had an aching suspicion that they would drift apart once they weren't seeing each other thirty to forty hours each week. The night before, she'd even contemplated if she could convince Kiki to stay with more money or some sort of partnership in the shop.

"And, I'm pretty sure you were picturing yourself getting all kinds of freaky with the food truck guy," she half whispered so the customers wouldn't hear.

Completely busted.

"I'm almost positive you moaned at one point."

"I did not!" Maeve argued even though she probably had, and her bright red face confirmed it as a possibility. Her capacity to lose herself in her thoughts and daydreams was astonishing. She really needed to get it under control. Moaning in the shop while there were customers? Unacceptable.

Kiki sat on the other stool at the high top table where Maeve was working. Their only customers were serious olive oil shoppers, so they had at least thirty minutes before they'd be ready to check out. She grabbed some materials and helped with the assembly.

"Do you think I would have married Jackson?" Maeve asked. "Would have gone through with it without realizing what a colossal mistake I was making? Sometimes I think there's no way, and other times I'm certain I would have." Maeve ran a finger over the twisty calligraphy letters that formed Chasity's name and imagined her own in its place. The tag itself was lovely, and she approved of their choice of wedding favors. It could have been her.

"Not a chance. Look at the way you just adjusted that bow and tag." Kiki picked up the bottle Maeve had finished and put off to the side. "Look at it."

It was pristine and identical in every way to the others that she'd assembled. Maeve measured out each ribbon and cut them all at a 45-degree angle. The tag fell to the left of the label so that the eye first went to the tag before the bottle's title. She meticulously placed the bag behind the tag so it looked almost like a border around the tag.

"This piece-of-art wedding favor is what you do for an ex that you loved with all your heart and lost to another woman?"

"It's a piece of art because it's an extension of my business. I'm a perfectionist when it comes to Olive What She's Having."

Kiki scoffed. "Yes, you are. But that's not the point. The reason these bottles are the portrait of perfection is because you aren't petty as fuck right now and subtly messing with their shit. And the reason for that is because you don't care. He's not the one that got away, which means he was never the one."

Maeve's assembly line ground to a complete halt.

"I'm serious. He's got you thinking that he pulled the plug on the whole thing, but I know his type. He only left because he could tell that he was losing you. Rather than let you dump him, he jumped the gun and beat you to it."

"I wasn't going to leave him." She went back to assembling favors once Kiki's explanation dissolved into hypothetical theories with zero evidence to back them up. The *Ancient Aliens* guy with the cray hair wouldn't even have believed her explanation.

"Yes, you were."

"You weren't even there–"

"I don't have to be. I was there afterwards and I've heard all the stories."

The customers crowded around the checkout counter, and Maeve hopped off her stool to ring them up. It was another substantial purchase. She felt a rush of gratitude that even though her personal life was a disaster, her professional life was thoroughly intact. Three packed-up cases of mostly balsamic vinegar and a small box of seasoning later, and Maeve was back at the high top with Kiki. She'd made good progress, but it was clear which favors Kiki made versus which ones Maeve had assembled.

"You went to the Mediterranean without Jackson," Kiki said, as if Maeve could have possibly forgotten that bit of information from her past.

"And I almost killed myself guzzling the watered-down wine they serve on the plane. I still can't fly Mediterranean Air for another year and nine months." A few taps on her phone and Maeve held up her calendar showing the exact day she could start booking flights again.

"That was a jarring life change," Kiki said. "It wasn't about Jackson leaving you; it was about you learning to be on your own."

She shrugged, but she was warming to the idea that it wasn't about love. Maybe her self-destruction had resulted from Jackson sweeping out a false sense of security out from under her feet.

The bell dinged, and another group piled into the store.

"I'll get this one." Kiki was out of her seat before Maeve had time to react. "You stay here and think about it."

Maeve absently watched as Kiki worked with the next group. She was good with her run-down of the various oil and vinegar samples they offered, the explanation of how the sampling worked, and her laid-back but still professional demeanor as she casually immersed herself in their group. Kiki had an eye for identifying the customers who wanted an almost one-on-one experience with an employee, even though they didn't sign up for a formal tasting.

She was a natural in the shop. Since Maeve had hired her, perhaps Kiki had a valid point. Maeve wasn't as terrible at judging character as she thought she was.

24

steve

"Annana stopped by while you guys were out earlier. She's probably singing at the wedding," Steve casually threw out as he and Heath went over the details for the service the next day.

Heath's finger paused over the calculator app on his phone, just hovering over the equal sign in perpetuity.

"OMG! I love Annana!" Lori squealed from the couch. She'd come back to the apartment with Heath and then busied herself watching reality television in the living room while they squared away everything for the biggest sales day of their brief career. "Can I come? No offense, Steve, but 'I Really, Really Hope You Die' speaks to me. Annana and I would be besties if we ever met. I'm sure of it," she said before a gasp from the TV recaptured her attention.

What the actual fuck!? Steve mouthed to Heath.

"Hey, hon?"

Steve's head pulled back in surprise at the word "hon" coming out of Heath's mouth.

"Can you run out to the truck and grab the wedding contract? I left it in a folder on the dash."

Once it was the two of them again, they spoke quickly.

"Your girlfriend adores Annana," Steve hissed, even though she was out of the apartment and unable to hear their conversation.

"Majority of the country adores Annana. Am I not supposed to get laid because of your bad choices?"

"She's a bad choice!" he argued, pointing in the general direction of where they'd parked the truck.

"Speaking of bad choices, your ex tracked you down from across the country. She's singing at the wedding."

Lori came back in and set the contract down on the table before laying back down on the couch, unaware of the tension between the guys.

"I said she might be singing tomorrow." Steve had too many regrets to count at this point, but Annana at the wedding wasn't the worst of them. He'd passed Annana's information off to Chasity, so now it was up to them to figure out the specifics and if it was something they actually wanted to do. For all he knew, Annana could be expecting some big payout they couldn't afford, or she could refuse to sing if the couple didn't kiss her ass enough. There was no way to read whatever game she was playing.

Heath rolled his eyes, and they went back to their planning. Serving 150 customers as close to concurrently as they could was immensely different from their typical truck service, and fucking it up wasn't an option. They couldn't afford the bad publicity that would come from ruining someone's wedding.

Lori was still there that evening when they ordered another round of takeout for dinner after making what they hoped were the final adjustments to their plans for the next day. They had their timing mapped out down to the minute, created a list of prep-work set up and the order it had to be done in, and they triple-checked their current inventory against a list of everything they needed to pick up before the wedding.

When 7:30 hit, Steve was ready to dig into his now cold gluten-free fried chicken and cornbread while watching some *Jeopardy*. Alone.

"Don't you guys want to go out, or maybe hang out in your room?" Steve threw out on the off-chance the idea hadn't occurred to Lori or Heath.

They were snuggled up on the larger couch while Steve was relegated to the love seat. Nothing about Lori appealed to him, but he was beyond jealous watching her and Heath live out what was essentially one of his dream dates with Maeve: vegging out with takeout food while watching *Jeopardy*. Lazily lounging on the couch after a long day and finding comfort and solace with your person.

"Nah, we're good here. Right?"

"I just want to be with you," Lori cooed back before engaging in a kiss that was sensual enough to have Steve turning to give them privacy.

And yet they still didn't leave. She'd practically initiated sex, and then they stopped and just went right back to their food and the G-rated programming Steve had chosen for the night.

Awesome.

"Besides," Lori added, "I love *Jeopardy*. I'm super good at it."

"Perfect!" Heath said. "My boy Steve here loves to get all competitive with it. Maybe you can humble him a bit." He gave Steve a wink and a wicked grin, while Lori clapped her hands in delight.

Rightfully so. She kept him on his toes throughout, but he had a distinct advantage with three categories in his favor: In Cod We Trust–general trivia about cod; Thrill Me, Author–all answers were author's names of best-sellers in the thriller/suspense genre; and Word Origins–a look at the roots of language.

Heath acted as the official judge for which one of them

dinged in (slammed their hand on the coffee table) first, and he kept the scores. That alone would have been enough for Steve to assume his low score resulted from bias on Heath's part, but even without that, Steve was just having an off night with no one to blame but himself.

Nothing had gone the way it was supposed to the past few days, and half the questions reminded him of Maeve, which only reminded him once more how nothing was going the way it was supposed to the past few days. Because mostly, it was his cluster-fuck of a relationship with Maeve that was not going as planned.

"And so it's come to this…" Heath paused the show so he could draw out the tension between the two. "Lori, our sexiest contestant tonight, has a well-earned $5,400, while Steve, the most loathed man in America, leads, but just barely, at $8,000."

Steve rolled his eyes which only encouraged Heath to carry on with his horrendous impersonation of a television announcer.

"You already know the category for Final Jeopardy is 'World Geography.' Now it's time to make your wagers. I'll hum the theme song."

"Please don't," Steve said, but Heath's humming thoroughly drowned out his plea.

Once they'd secretly scribbled down their wagers, Heath hit play again, and the host revealed the final answer: "The only city in the world to straddle two different continents."

Istanbul. Usually, his knowledge of world geography was lacking. One week prior, he wouldn't have any idea. He only knew the answer now because he vividly remembered the radiant smile on Maeve's face as she reminisced about visiting Istanbul for an entire day during her trip. She'd commented on how anticlimactic it was driving over the bridge into Asia, but how she was still glad that she'd done it. Another item off her bucket list.

This was a sign. The entire night was a sign. Jackson was obviously horrible, and he'd made a mistake or two himself. What Maeve deserved was more than flowers and a bottle of wine. Ugh, how cliche and unoriginal. He cringed just thinking about how he'd gone to her store the day before to apologize bearing gifts he'd casually picked up on the way to see her. An after-thought, really.

Why had he thought that was good enough for Maeve? She deserved more than that–

"Hello, Steve…"

Steve snapped out of it and found the host shaking everyone's hand on TV while Heath and Lori looked at him as if he were a ghost.

"You were catatonic there, mate. We already checked the answers. You won with your pussy wager of $500."

Lori shrugged her shoulders. "I couldn't remember if it was Constantinople or Istanbul. I guessed wrong."

Heath pulled her into his lap, causing her to shriek with delight. "Still a worthy adversary. Wouldn't you say, Steve?"

He nodded in agreement, but all he could think about was how it should have been him and Maeve on the couch that night, and what he could do to make things right with her.

friday

25

steve

He'd made it all of ten minutes in the bookstore before an associate approached him.

"Excuse me, sir, I'm going to ask that you refrain from doing any sort of social media influencer activities in our store."

Steve looked up from the table he was at. He'd grabbed books from the various displays and was making a large stack of them on the empty corner of a table. So far, he had a dozen books he was arranging and rearranging. It was a fair assumption he was pulling some sort of stunt that he then intended to film.

"Oh, it's you..." The associate's expression faltered as she appeared to debate bending the rules for Steve.

He used every ounce of self-control to not roll his eyes. He'd asked Annana to please lie low until the wedding so he wouldn't have to deal with any renewed interest in his pathetic love life.

She hadn't.

A few hours after he'd gotten out of her car, he saw a post on one of the community groups with a picture of her decked out in designer clothing, wearing a pair of barely tinted sunglasses as she had dinner with Jackson and Chasity at one of the most popular restaurants in the area. He'd smirked when he noticed the slight bruising and discoloration still visible under Jackson's eyes, even with the obvious attempt to cover it up with makeup.

"Yeah, it's me, but I'm not filming anything–"

Before he could finish, another associate came up behind the first and said, "No, absolutely no filming in the store. A woman scaled one of our bookshelves last month and sent it crashing to the ground. Our liability insurance can't handle another incident."

When she caught sight of whom she was reprimanding, she said, "Oh, it's you. You still can't film anything."

"I'm not filming anything. I'm not even on TikTok. I'm just buying a stack of books for my fiancée." His mind wasn't quick enough to figure out if he should continue their relationship lie in perpetuity, so he'd blurted out the first thing that came to his mind, which was to refer to Maeve as his fiancée.

A force of a habit? A Freudian slip? Who could say for sure, but it flowed so easily off his tongue and at this point he'd almost convinced himself it could one day be a possibility. Though he'd probably be able to believe it more if they'd spoken since the elbow-to-Jackson's-nose incident.

The first associate crossed her arms. "You're buying your fiancée a dozen books?"

The second eyed up his stack and crossed her arms as well. "You have a fiancée?"

He scowled at the second and answered the first. "Twenty books, actually."

They looked at each other. The second one shrugged and walked off.

"Fine. Let us know if you need any assistance." She turned to leave him and then called over her shoulder, "Don't wreck the place, please."

He had no intention of doing that. It wasn't completely out of context given the mess he was currently making, but he would clean all of that up once he was finished. Like Shakespeare once said, there was a method to his madness, and the mess was essential for what he was trying to create: a tower of twenty books that would simultaneously act as the fantasy first meeting Maeve never got, and the apology that she absolutely deserved.

He had no idea what kinds of books she liked to read. There were two large bookcases in her apartment and he'd had every intention of nonchalantly pursuing them the night he'd been there, but then other things had distracted him.

Maeve had mentioned she had a friend who reviewed romance novels, so he grabbed a few of those from the current hot reads table. Given her abundance of knowledge about the Mediterranean area, he assumed she was interested in other cultures and history, so he hit up the historical fiction and world literature tables as well. To cover all his bases, he continued to pull two or three books from all the remaining tables and displays as he assembled his final tower of twenty titles.

His initial idea had come from his uncle, a high school English teacher. During some holiday dinner, he'd told everyone about a poetry day in the library where he had his students use book spines to create a poem.

Steve imagined himself doing the same, except instead of a poem, he would craft the ultimate apology. It was perfect in theory only. In reality, most titles lacked the articles and conjunctions he needed to make an apology that flowed rather than chopped and clunked along.

Realizing it wasn't working as planned, he improvised. He wrote out his apology on a piece of paper while inserting the titles of the books throughout. It was the bit of wiggle room he needed since he was on borrowed time as it was.

Heath was skeptical he'd be able to pull it off at all, but he was rooting for him. Especially since he would be in tight quarters with both of them in a few scant hours and didn't want to deal with the awkwardness of ex-lovers who were mid-spat.

Steve gave himself a two o'clock deadline to have his selection paid for and for him to be on his way to Olive What She's Having. They still had a lot to do to make sure they were set for the wedding, and he didn't want to leave Heath hanging. He promised he wouldn't.

The alarm went off on his phone at 1:50, and he stepped back to admire his work.

It looked… Well, it looked like an abomination. A mish-mash of random books from all different genres. Nothing flowed, the colors all clashed, and reading the titles on their own, it made little sense. It would have to do, though. He was officially out of time.

After he'd paid for his books and was almost to the store door, he heard the not-so-subtle sales associate say to the other, "What a disaster. Who would marry Reeve? What is she thinking?"

"Some women settle, I guess," the other responded.

With a clang of the bells, he was out the door and only mildly shaken by what they'd said. Regardless, he started the next part of his plan and began walking the two blocks to Maeve's store, his mind reciting his planned speech over and over in his mind.

He'd carried the books to the check-out desk using multiple trips from the table to the counter. He'd gotten them to the shop using the shopping bags they'd provided him. So what made him think he could then breeze through the shop doors balancing twenty stacked books in his arms? Foresight was usually a strength of his, but it had completely aban-doned him as he stood there on the front sidewalk staring at his stack of books and absently fumbling with his hair.

"Steve?"

And then he couldn't think clearly about anything because Maeve was standing on the sidewalk in front of him. A knowing smile on her face. As if they had been lovers for years and even though the last time they'd interacted he'd accidentally assaulted her ex and she'd given him the stinkiest stink eye known to man, she knew without counting that there were twenty books stacked on the sidewalk and that they were all for her.

He went to hand her the note, only to find it wasn't in his hand anymore. He'd poured his heart out onto that sheet of paper, but he hadn't the slightest idea where he'd put it. The weather was a scorching ninety degrees, so the note was crumpled and quite moist from his sweaty hands, but the words had been perfect; not something he could recreate on the spot.

He gave up uselessly patting his empty pockets and looked back up at the woman standing in front of him. She really was stunning with her coppery red hair catching the sunlight just right so that it highlighted all the variations of blonde, brown, red, and everything in between.

"I wanted to see you before the wedding tonight." The brilliant, suave speech he'd rehearsed in his mind on the way over? Gone. She had that effect on him. That ability to make his mind go to mush with a single smile or touch or word.

"Are these for me?"

There was hope in her voice that made him want to respond in ridiculous ways. Yes, these books, my life, the world… It's all for you, he wanted to shout.

Instead, he took a tentative step closer to her and said, "Twenty books. All for you."

They were in two stacks on the sidewalk. He really wished he could find his note. As they stood, the spines read from left column to right column:

Things We Never Got Over

X

How to Fake it in Hollywood
Twisted Hate
Blindsided
Trust
The Change
The Moment I Met You
Easy Beauty
Last Resort
The Deal
Mistakes Were Made
Sorry, Bro
Drunk on Love
Tomorrow, and Tomorrow, and Tomorrow
Take My Hand
I'm So Not Over You
All This Could Be Different
Hook, Line, and Sinker
Cod: A Biography of the Fish That Changed the World

It wasn't terrible, per se, but there were some mixed messages like with the *Sorry, Bro* title, and if he could just find the damned note, he could explain everything. She deserved that, and so much more.

Maeve stooped down, lifted the cover of one of the top books, and revealed a sheet of paper that had been sticking out ever so slightly. It looked like someone had found it in the trash and then shoved it inside the book in a failed attempt to smooth it out.

"Is this note for me?" She carefully opened it the same way one would handle a priceless work of art.

"Oh, thank god. Yes, that's for you. Along with the books. It's all for you."

The sun beat down on them and Steve felt sweat on his brow as he ran his fingers through his hair and waited for Maeve to read what was essentially his Hail Mary.

26

maeve

She'd been sitting at a table going over some final numbers with Kiki, all the information she'd need to know once Keek left for good, when she'd noticed Steve out front on the sidewalk, off to the side.

He'd had a note in his hand that he read, his lips moving as he did, in between periodically looking up to the sky for some elusive word or maybe some answer from above. He was nervous. She watched as he tucked the note under the cover of one of the books before shaking out his hands to release all the tension, as he closed his eyes and gently shook his head. His long hair swished this way and that before he put it up into a bun and then let it back down again. Finally, Kiki gave her a hit on her arm and said she'd better get out there and put him out of his misery.

The butterflies were back. The ones that showed up every time he was around, the ones that first started when he'd shown up for dinner looking all sharp and throwing around his charm. Things had gotten confusing with Jackson being around and messing with her head and heart, but she'd since come back to her senses.

She probably should have said something to that point

before reading the note; put the poor guy at ease. But once she had the paper in her hands, she couldn't think of anything beyond what he'd written in impressively neat handwriting on paper that appeared to have been handled a few dozen times with folding and refolding.

He'd gone through the trouble (and cost) of attempting to recreate what she said would be the perfect meet-cute. She needed to know what was on the weathered paper.

Maeve,
There were
Things We Never Got Over
from our
X.
Mine thrived learning
How To Fake it in Hollywood.
Yours thrived on
Twisted Hate.
When the relationships ended, we were both
Blindsided
with a loss of
Trust.
For me
The Change
happened
The Moment I Met You.
It wasn't only your
Easy Beauty,
and you definitely weren't a
Last Resort,
and it wasn't just because of
The Deal
we had…
But,
Mistakes Were Made,
and

Sorry, Bro
won't cut it.
Please know that I am
Falling
and will apologize today, and
Tomorrow, and Tomorrow, and Tomorrow
until I convince you to
Take My Hand.
Because
I'm So Not Over You.
All This Could Be Different
if we just let ourselves fall
Hook, Line, and Sinker.
Yours if you'll have me,
Steve

p.s. I had Cod in there a few times, but I couldn't make it work. I kept it in the stack because it's a brilliant book and I know you'll love it.

Maeve's eyes looked back through the note and saw faint lines here and there, left over from an eraser. *Cod* had indeed made it temporarily onto the list. A few times.

She looked up beyond the paper and found him staring back at her. His head lowered as if he still wasn't sure if he was good enough, or if this was good enough for her. Black hair hung down and covered his eyes, but not enough that she couldn't see the flurry of emotions coming from them: hope, desperation, longing. All of it radiated off of him as he patiently waited for her response.

When she'd first stepped outside, she'd expected them to talk a little, perhaps make up with a sensual kiss before they went to do all the things they needed to do to prepare for the damn wedding.

Standing there with him, a stack of twenty books between them, a heart-felt note in her hand, and his tongue licking his lips in a way that should be criminal, talking was the last thing she wanted to do. Unless it was filthy bedroom talk.

She carefully folded the note and placed it back in the novel where she'd found it. Then she stood back up and curled her pointer finger to make the universal "come here" motion.

Steve stepped forward between the stacks of books. "I'm so sorry. I will never–"

Then Maeve had him by the collar and was pulling him against her so hard that she stumbled backwards a step and hit her back against the store window.

After that, she couldn't say. The only sensation she was aware of was his stubbly skin against hers as he passionately kissed her. His hands cupped her face and even though it was crazy hot outside, there was still something so soothing about the warmth of his skin against hers.

She couldn't say if she was cognizant of it happening or not, but at some point she found her legs were slightly parted and his thigh had conveniently nestled in between them, hitting her in just–

Knock, knock, knock

Steve pulled away, and they both turned to find Kiki on the other side of the store window, a half dozen customers standing behind her.

"Your apartment is a few steps that way," Kiki called through the glass as she pointed towards the outside staircase.

The heat from the weather, the heat from his body, the heat from hers, along with all the embarrassment she felt, sent boiling blood to her face as she gave Kiki and the customers an apologetic look.

"Right, sorry," Steve said.

"Apologies," Maeve said before adding for good measure, "Oh, that's our top selling extra virgin! You'll love it. Highly recommend it." She motioned to the older gentleman in their small audience who was holding a bottle of her favorite oil.

He didn't shout back through the glass or make any sort of motion in response.

"We should," Steve said, pulling lightly at the tie on Maeve's apron to show the direction in which they should head.

"Yup," Maeve agreed.

"I'll get the books and take care of the customers," Kiki called. "Go!" she added with a shooing motion when they still stood stupefied on the front sidewalk.

27

steve

The awkward walk up the stairs after being busted by Kiki and friends had almost killed the moment, but when they were alone again in her apartment, he felt his body tingling with the anticipation of touching, licking, stroking, and doing all sorts of ill-mannered things to the sweet, sweet woman in front of him.

"Finally," he said in a low grumbly voice as she locked the door behind them and he tugged at her apron strings, relieving her of the first layer of clothing that separated her body from his.

Maeve's dress had two thin straps holding it up. He ran his thumb across the bare skin of her back before looping it under a strap and easing it off her shoulder. Before he could repeat the process on the other side, she let out a soft sigh and her shoulder, the one he'd just caressed, inched up ever so slightly, as if demanding more attention before he moved on.

While he was more than happy to oblige by dipping his head down to kiss every single freckle that covered her shoulder, he also reminded himself to take it down a few hundred notches. To ignore his animal instincts. Pushing her up against the wall and lifting her dress to take her from behind was not a stellar follow up to the book-gift apology he'd made on the sidewalk–regardless of how much his dick told him otherwise.

No, that was not what Maeve needed. There would be plenty of time for that in the future. For now, Maeve deserved deep kisses, hands that massaged as they gripped, and at least an orgasm or two, before he'd even let himself consider his own gratification.

He was ready to slowly devour every inch of her perfectly soft skin when Maeve turned to face him and said, "I'm sorry… For what I said… About the song, and for not coming out to see you for lunch."

Her hand went up to his face and cupped his jaw as her eyes searched his to see how her apology landed. Another example of how she was the product of her relationship with Jackson, focusing more on Steve than on herself.

He'd felt so deserving of the Annana comment he'd forgotten all about it, but he appreciated that she hadn't.

For reasons unknown to even him, he leaned in and gave her a soft kiss on each eyebrow before lowering his mouth to plant a reassuring kiss on her lips, his settling in so easily to hers he almost forgot how new it all still was.

"Let's talk about that later," he said when he pulled himself away from lips that unbelievably tasted faintly similar to her sugary sweet scent. Pulling his phone out of his back pocket, he checked the time and silenced it before tossing it onto the couch.

"We have just under two hours before I have to meet up with Heath, and I have every minute of that time booked."

"You do?" she asked, her voice breathy and her eyes wide in anticipation.

"All of them," he confirmed. His fingers twisted in her hair, luxuriating in the feel of it and the knowledge that he could after holding back for so long. "Where's Hedy?" he asked, remembering the one potential obstacle to their union that had previously slipped his mind.

"On a play date at a neighbor's house."

There was a victory in not having to deal with potential clawing and meowing at the door while they were making their own primal sounds in the bedroom. But what really got him was the basic human kindness under all of it. The light she left on for the cat who was scared of the dark, the portrait of the cat she was painting to hang above the food dish, and the play date for company since Maeve was working all day in the shop and at the wedding.

Even with her ambition, Maeve wasn't one to step on others or neglect them on her way up the ladder. She was not Annana. He was not attracted to people like Annana. That had all been a fluke, not a reinforcing example of his true identity.

He fought the urge to attack her and have his way with her on the hard, unforgiving parquet flooring. Jackson would have done something like that. Satisfied his most basic needs while overlooking hers. He was not Jackson; now was a good time to remind her of that.

Steve leaned in and her back rested against the door. His body firmly against hers. The movement caused her thumb to slip dangerously close to his mouth. His tongue couldn't resist the tiniest of tastes before he lost control and nipped at her thumb.

She responded with a wicked grin. "Let's go into the bedroom," she said, tugging his hand so he would follow her. It was laughable to think she'd need to use any force or persuasion. He'd follow her to hell if he had to.

A playful shove from Maeve had him seated on her bed, the soft pink down comforter pillowing up around him. She climbed onto his lap, straddling him as she combed her fingers through his hair.

"You have gorgeous hair." Her nails on his scalp provided

a sort of massage, tamping down his sense of urgency and leading them into something more sensual than what they'd started in the back of the truck. When he eased the second dress strap over her shoulder, she maneuvered her arms out so he could unzip and undress her.

"Stunning," he said in between sweet kisses on the soft skin of her breasts. "You're perfect."

Her hips moved rhythmically over his still-clothed cock, a nice warm-up for what was to come, and she continued to massage his scalp and twist her fingers in his long hair. Hair he'd almost cut to make him less recognizable. What a mistake that would have been. There had been so many mistakes before Maeve.

His mouth teased her nipples with flicks of his tongue and gentle pinches. She gasped and buried her face in his hair, and he could feel her knees squeezing against his hips each time he licked or sucked. Her warm breath on his ear, he could hear every whimper and sigh. Then she pulled herself upright again and let her head fall back in pure contentment.

Wearing nothing but panties and a smile, she was utterly magnificent, and he allowed himself a quick moment to take a mental picture of it. The way he could see every shade in her hair when the sun's rays from the window hit it just right; the scatter of freckles that he now knew covered most of her body, her glistening nipples—still peaked and moist from his mouth—and the look of adoration in her hooded eyes.

"What are you thinking?" she asked as she tucked a bit of hair behind his ear and continued to rub her now wet panties over him. Even with his jeans on, it was like a gentle massage. That combined with her fingers on his scalp and her mouth periodically on his... He hadn't felt that loved or appreciated in a very long time.

"I'm committing to memory how beautiful you are, how perfect this moment is."

Still unable to take a compliment, she wrinkled her nose.

He caressed her cheek. "So beautiful, in all ways," he said, as his hand slid to the back of her neck and pulled her in for another kiss.

Closed lipped at first, and he could sense her taking him in as well, as she inhaled his scent and ran her fingers over his neck, back, and arms before deepening their kiss to explore that area as well.

When her mouth was on his, he was fully immersed. The other stuff faded away into the background. It was a feeling of weightlessness that he'd thought he'd lost for the indefinite future. Annana outing him to the world and then showing up in person had once been unthinkable. As if either action would be the catalyst to some drastic change where he was no longer the same person he'd been before. It had felt like Annana, using her perfect pitch voice to tell the world he was shit, would somehow irrevocably make him a shit person.

But there he was, in Maeve's apartment, kissing the woman who understood him most. The one who knew what an absolute geek he was about how cod changed the world, who knew he once threw flaming porn magazines from his bedroom window, and the one who knew that he was mostly awkward with occasional bouts of cool which only occurred through some rare form of osmosis from hanging out with Heath.

But she didn't want Heath, and she certainly didn't want that asshole of an ex. She wanted him. Her fingers were clawing through his hair because she wanted all of him, and she was greedy for it. The whole thing made his dick throb with his own want and greed for her.

Steve's hand slid up her thigh and he rubbed his thumb over her drenched panties.

"Is this because of me?" he asked in a husky voice.

She gasped at the contact and breathed, "Yes." He continued to stroke and tease with his thumb and she said, "I can't get our night in the truck out of my mind. How it could have ended."

He slid his thumb underneath the thin fabric to feel it for himself, and her head dropped to his shoulder. The perfect position for him to ask, "Do you think about me when you touch yourself?"

She whimpered and nodded her head as he worked the spot right next to her clit.

"Do you use a vibrator?" he whispered before he allowed his inner animal to come out with a quick nip of her ear. He gave a gentle pull before releasing the soft skin and kissing her neck.

"Yes…"

"Can I watch you use it?" He pulled his hand away and her head shot up.

At the risk of breaking the sound barrier, Maeve got up and returned with a purple, already-pulsing vibrator and a condom. She tossed the condom to the side, along with her panties.

Steve got up off the bed and motioned for Maeve to lie down. There was a tinge of apprehension, but once the vibrator touched her, that melted away as she allowed herself to get lost in the moment.

A beat or two later—though it felt like an eternity for his impatient cock—he felt confident enough to replicate her technique. Maeve's eyes opened when he climbed onto the bed and took over with the vibrator. Then her head fell back and her eyes closed once again as he put his tongue to work alongside the toy.

She'd picked one side of her clit to move the moan-making toy up and down, so he did the same. His tongue worked the other side, so it didn't feel too neglected. And god, she tasted amazing. As much as she was moaning into the pillow, he was moaning into her wet pussy.

There was nothing sexier than knowing he was the one

making her head fall back and forcing incoherent sounds from those luscious pink lips. His cock was a cement block and his boxers were damp with pre-cum.

"Oh, fuck." Her toes curled and her fingers gripped his hair, holding on as if more than an orgasm was at stake.

He got up and put the vibrator in her hand. "Keep going. I want to watch."

As she worked her magic, Steve shed his clothes and rolled on the condom. Then he climbed on top of her and kissed her breasts and neck as he lined himself up.

"Can you feel that?" she asked, referring to the vibrator that was still between her legs and right above the tip of his dick.

"Mmm, it feels amazing. Gonna have to get one of those for myself," he half teased.

He rubbed the end of his cock between her swollen lips as they both enjoyed the added effects of the pulse sending sparks to every one of their nerve endings. Then he eased himself inside.

"Oh, god. Yes, just like that," she said once he ground his hips against her.

With each movement, his face lowered until the tips of their noses touched and his forehead was on hers. Their breathing came in shorter bursts as they looked into each other's eyes and raced toward the ultimate release at the end, then their lips were together again with a fumbling kiss, their attention fully focused on what was happening below.

"Don't stop."

"Never," he agreed.

"I'm going to come… Fuck, I'm coming…" He kissed her again, reveling in the moan she made, and then he buried his face in her neck and gorgeous hair as he rode through his own orgasm.

They laid together afterwards. Both naked with their skin still glistening with sweat, surrounded by the heady scent of sex. Exhausted from a week filled with months' worth of highs and lows. Before he fell asleep, he mustered the courage to tell her about Annana's upcoming appearance at the wedding, but Maeve wasn't concerned or even remotely interested, so he finally turned his brain off and drifted off.

28

maeve

She almost snickered in Jackson's face that evening when she noticed the touch of discoloration still visible under his eyes.

Snickering wasn't an option, though. Reddit, her bible for all things Jackson recently, had multiple entries about narcissists and humiliation. They didn't mix. It was like that time in her college chem class when the professor placed burning magnesium into a beaker of boiling water and it became a tiny sun, so fiery and bright that she'd had to look away. That was Jackson's reaction any time he felt the slightest bit of embarrassment or even the potential for it. Yet another Jacksonism she'd forgotten about in her quest to erase him from her memory.

"This isn't going to be too hard for you, is it?"

The sick bastard was hiding a smile behind his mask of concern. She could tell.

"I'm engaged now, too," she said, reminding him of Steve, the guy who'd (accidentally) clocked him a few days prior and who was standing directly behind her in the truck. He gave a polite wave to his employer-for-the-night, but Jackson was beyond caring about even the most basic of manners. Not surprising since he insisted on having Steve's ex sing a vitri-olic song about Steve at an event that he was working at.

"Sure you are," he said, bringing his attention back to Maeve.

Maeve was ready to throw down about it if need be–even if he was completely and unknowingly accurate in what he'd said–but she had a better idea when she noticed Jackson's mom on the other side of the beach.

"Bummer. Looks like Velicity needs you. Better go see what she wants. You know how she hates being made to wait."

Jackson's ears flamed bright red. More than once, he had confided to Maeve that he didn't particularly care for his mother. Their relationship was based solely on money and dependence, with Velicity using her bank account to keep Jackson tied to the ends of her marionette strings. One quick tug and he would come running. He had no choice.

A miniscule part of her brain and heart registered a modicum of sympathy for Jackson. She knew what it was like to be manipulated by someone, to be forced into dependency. She didn't wish that on anyone, not even him.

She watched him walk away and felt Steve's arms come around her from behind. Strong, confident arms that had already mastered the delicate art of comforting without constricting.

"Well done," he whispered in her ear.

Since she was going to be working in the truck, she had her hair up and Steve had easy access to that tiny little spot below her ear that he seemed to love. The one that made her squirm and moan when his bit of stubble tickled her. He planted a few quick kisses on the spot and said, "Can you help me with the fish?"

As if he needed to ask. There was something soothing about working side by side with him in the truck. The smell of lemons and garlic while music played from the speakers as they made easy conversation about any and everything that came to their minds.

The first day she'd filmed him in the truck, he'd confided in her about his most embarrassing moment–prior to the Annana song incident. Did she love him because he'd once chucked red-hot pornography out his window? No, that would be weird. But the ease he'd had telling her about it and the way he'd laughed it off had been beyond endearing. There was a trust in sharing the story and it was a raw portrayal of a younger Steve: mortified, but he came out stronger on the other side because of it. He could handle a bit of embarrassment. It was refreshing.

There, in the truck prepping for the event, Steve had a similar look on his face as he turned and said, "I need to tell you something, but I don't want you to think worse of me."

Maeve donned an apron and stood to his right, in front of one of the burners. A spot she'd already thought of as "her place."

"Worse than what's happened already? Is that possible?"

She reached out to give him a reassuring little pinch to his side, pulling out a hint of a smile. He didn't seem too serious, but any conversation that started with "I need to tell you something" was bound to give her a pause given how their week had been going so far.

"Okay. I'm going to hold you to that," he said, pinching her back and making her give a small squeal of delight.

Maeve may be the only person in the history of people who has ever enjoyed being tickled.

"Remember when I told you Heath had a calendar on his fridge of what days he…"

Maeve looked behind her to see if anyone else was in earshot. "Came inside a woman without a condom?" she said, filling in the blanks he'd left.

"Yeah. That."

Here it comes, she thought. It was actually him that had

the calendar, and he was just feeling her out to see how she'd react to something like that. Now he's going to tell her how he got someone pregnant and his stupid came-inside calender proved that it's his baby.

"It turns out it wasn't a calendar about that."

She let out a roaring laugh that turned a few heads of the people setting up the make-shift bar on the beach, a few meters out beyond the parking lot where their truck was stationed.

"I knew it!" Her hands were still empty since she hadn't started to cook yet, and she did a quick in-your-face style dance that involved a lot of accusatory finger pointing and hip shaking.

Steve, relieved to find that Maeve didn't judge his hasty misjudgement of his current best friend, smiled and shook his head as he continued to cook.

He gave her a few minutes of gloating before he asked, "Are you almost finished? I really could use some help here on the grill." When he took another peek at what moves she'd moved on to, Maeve caught him trying to hold back his laughter.

"Not yet."

He turned to fully face her. "Is that the Dougie?"

"Damn right. It's a classic."

Heath opened up the back door and climbed into the truck. "Alright, we're doing the Dougie. What's the occasion?" He slid by Steve and danced with Maeve. Each moving a little awkwardly given their tight quarters and propensity for banging hips and limbs against counters and equipment.

"Yeah, Steve, what's the occasion?" Maeve asked, giving Steve the opportunity to fess up to Heath.

"I told Maeve about your squirrel calendar. How each time the bugger came inside the apartment, you marked it down so you could try to figure out how it was getting in."

Heath stopped. "What? Hardly seems worthy of the Dougie."

Maeve stopped, too. "No, I was rubbing it in his face about how Steve was wrong about the calendar. He told me it was your sex-themed, came-inside calendar…"

Heath stared at her, utterly at a loss about what she was trying to tell him.

"You know, you mark on the calendar when you come inside a woman… Without a condom… I had your back. I told him there was no way that's what that meant."

Heath turned to look at Steve, then back at Maeve, and then back at Steve.

"Why would I put that on the kitchen calendar?" Now it was Heath's turn to be judgmental. And rightfully so. Maeve had had the same question, and it turned out to be a valid one.

She crossed her arms in solidarity, ready to join in on the banter when Heath beat her to it.

"I keep that stuff on my digital calendar. You heathen."

The three of them bickered about calendars and all other topics as they prepared for what would surely be a disastrous wedding. They only hoped the attendees wouldn't associate the truck or the olive oil wedding favors with the ugliness of the event.

29

steve

They parked the truck at the edge of the beach parking lot. Before they got out, someone knocked on the door and they found Miles on the other side.

"Howdy there!" Miles said with the enthusiasm of someone who'd just snorted a large dose of coke. He held up a tee-shirt with Jackson's and Chasity's faces on the front along with the words *Chasity Belongs With Jackson*. "Aren't these fabulous?"

The guys stared back while Maeve politely took the shirts and spoke for the three of them when she said how excited they were to wear them. A round of small talk followed where the guys busied themselves in the closed-up truck while Maeve stayed outside and responded to everything Miles said with one-word answers until he finally got the hint.

"Holy crap, is that guy chatty," she said as she climbed into the back. When they turned to talk to her, she doubled over with laughter. "Have you seen yourselves in those shirts?" She grabbed onto a nearby shelf to stabilize herself, so overtaken by the absurdity of them in the shirts that she could barely keep herself up.

"There will be no filming tonight, Maeve. TikTok can never know," Heath said, pointing his spatula at her as a weak threat.

"Laugh it up," Steve said, tossing an oversized shirt at her head when she was bent down once more in laughter. "Here's yours. We'll avert our eyes so you can change." He'd said it merely to be polite. Heath's eyes stayed on his task at hand with prepping dipping sauce cups while Steve helped himself to a few glimpses of the lovely Maeve donning her new digs. She flipped him off when she caught him, but there was a playful smile on her face, even while putting on a tacky, over-sized shirt with Jackson's big dumb face on it.

After their brief shenanigans with the shirts, it was back to business for the three of them as they worked their asses off making sure everything was ready to go by the time their appetizer service was ready to begin.

A few minutes before the wedding started, Steve lifted the service window. He could see rustic looking benches filled with guests facing out towards the ocean. Jackson and Chasity, in semi-formal attire, stood just beyond the benches and recited their vows to each other. With the best speakers and sound system Velicity could buy, the guests, the catering crew in the truck, and most people in Galway Harbor could hear them.

"Chasity, three years ago, you stumbled into my office: coffee stain on your shirt, a broken heel, ten minutes late for an interview. And my first reaction was, who let this woman past the tenth floor?" Jackson said, starting his portion of the vows he'd clearly written himself. There was a distinct murmur of male laughter as his coworkers chuckled in the crowd. "But I'm so glad that they did, because timing is everything. We actually went to high school together, but I didn't recognize you or know that until we'd started working together and pulling late hours, talking over take out at the desk. After just a few weeks of working with you, Chasity, I could tell you knew how to respect and honor."

"Ah, fuck," muttered Heath as he stirred and added the last ingredients to the garlic lemon sauce. "I'm starting to feel dirty wearing this shirt and being a part of this shit. Serving this asshole who so clearly expects nothing short of absolute servitude from his wife."

Jackson went on and on with some nautical references thrown in about how their love swelled like a rising tide, and about how her love was an anchor that grounded him and pulled him out of his previous, toxic relationship, but Steve was more interested in Maeve. She was standing next to him at the grill, shaking and wiping her eyes with the sleeve of her shirt with one hand while turning chicken kabob appetizers with the other.

His hand went to the small of her back, providing a gentle massage, unsure if that was even remotely enough given the situation at hand. For anyone who had half the backstory of what was happening, it was clear that Maeve was the toxic past and Chasity was the one he'd left Maeve for.

"Did you know?" he asked. "That he called it off because of her?" He wasn't sure if she wanted to talk about it or not, but he figured he'd better ask in case she did.

Maeve's sleeve wiped away the last tear and her arm fell back to her side, revealing that she wasn't crying. She was laughing. Laughing so hard that she'd shed tears.

"No," she managed between more bouts of laughter. "But I should have. This is all so… So Jackson." She shook her head in disbelief. "Twisting it all so that I'm the monster who held him back from his true potential. Blasting it out at his wedding to another woman while I cater the fucking event." She laughed some more, doubling over from the absurdity of it all.

He looked over to Heath who joked as he whispered, "She's crazy. You're addicted to crazy." Heath gave him a pained look, as if Steve's future looked bleak with yet another version of Annana.

Steve understood where Maeve was coming from. He'd had an overwhelming emotional relief himself when he could finally see beyond the gaslighting that had been blinding him. He knew Maeve wasn't crazy. She was right there with him in that blissful stage of not giving a fuck about her ex.

As the ceremony wrapped up, the three of them stocked a few tables with hors d'oeuvres for a cocktail hour before dinner would be served. The temporary bar was run separately and was already set up, so they didn't have to worry about drinks. Once they'd finished with the various appetizers, it was time to cook the main dishes. Guests had two dinner options and four sides to choose from, so they worked to finish the various meals and sides they'd painstakingly prepped earlier, while sneaking peeks at the photographer getting all the shots he needed of the couple, the bridal party, and the immediate family.

"There it is," Steve said, his head turned toward the beach. "They're doing the photo where Jackson's meathead frat boys carry the bride off while he looks all annoyed and jealous."

"It's a classic," Heath said. "Five bucks says they do some sort of serenade later and sing 'You've Lost That Loving Feeling.'"

"You're on," Steve said, shaking Heath's hand to solidify the deal. "Clearly they're going to do 'Let's Get Married' by Jagged Edge."

"Ugh, I hope not. I actually like that song," Maeve said. "Looks like that was the last shot. They're heading back to the tables. You're up, Heath."

Heath beat Steve out in creativity and presentation, so he plated the bride's and groom's dishes. With a sauce squeeze bottle, he did a few floral designs on the edges of the fancy-looking plastic plates to make them stand out from the rest. Chasity requested Heath serve them at their table while the guests themselves line up and "order" at the truck on a table-by-table basis. It was all so last minute they couldn't take pre-orders in advance, so they'd guessed how much they'd need of each dish and adjusted as they went. Not ideal, but even with a bit of waste, the hefty price tag the newlyweds were paying easily covered it.

After he served the bride and groom, Heath was back at the truck to help serve and flirt with the women, and some of the men, at the event. It wasn't stated in their contract that Heath was part of the entertainment, but it was certainly implied and he didn't take that sort of thing lightly.

As they fielded the brief rush of hungry patrons, Steve's mind drifted to thoughts about the gorgeous woman manning the grill with him. He and Maeve were finally on what felt like solid ground. To an extent, it was even better than the beginnings of other relationships he'd had where it was all still exciting and new, but also immensely uncertain how serious they were as a couple until they'd been dating for at least six months or so.

This was different. They'd already been through the gauntlet that week and had seen each other at their high and low points, but the excitement of the newness was still there while the agonizing thoughts about where this thing was going were nowhere to be found.

The only thing standing in their way now was strutting towards them across the sand. Annana's dark hair had blue streaks that hadn't been there yesterday, her nails had changed from hot pink to electric blue (to match her hair, of course) but instead of a blue dress to pull the whole thing together, she'd opted for white. Bright, blindingly pure white. Bridal white.

The line to the truck eventually dwindled to nothing as the guests had all been served and Steve and Heath were getting ready to tidy up before switching over to the two dessert options they offered for the night. The three of them stopped what they were doing when they saw Annana heading their way.

"Nice shirts," Annana said when she got to the window.

"And look at you, wearing white to a wedding. Can't say I'm surprised," Heath said. "Though I am surprised you came all the way out here only to have Steve reject you, and yet you're still here."

Steve fought the urge to slap Heath upside the head for repeatedly poking the already pissed off bear. When he'd first asked her to sing at the wedding, he'd reassured himself with the mantra: How bad could it be? So far, everything was pointing to very bad as she appeared to be hell-bent on pissing off the bride and now probably Steve as well after Heath's imbecilic comment.

Annana glanced around at her soundings, taking in the "here" Heath was referring to.

"It's Heath, right?"

That shut him up. They'd met at least half a dozen times on the west coast, so either Annana was truly that self-absorbed that she couldn't be bothered to acknowledge anyone outside of her immediate circle of friends and relatives, or she was determined to give it right back harder knowing Heath had his limits. Going against Annana was not a game that people won.

"I'm here as the main entertainment, or haven't you heard?" She gave an accusatory glance at Steve. How could he not have informed everyone he knew that she was performing tonight?

"Yes, we know. That is very generous of you. Very kind," Steve said with as little sarcasm as he could manage. "Can I get you something? We're switching over to desserts now, but we had a few extra main courses made up in the back here. Chicken or fish?" They'd made them up for the Today's Gluten-Free Specials crew to eat, but he'd sacrifice his meal to keep her content. Whatever it took, he was more than willing.

They were a few mere hours away from freedom; he'd give his right toe if she'd asked him for it. The thought didn't feel as hyperbolic as it should and a chill went through his body.

"Very generous of you," she said, throwing his condescending words back in his face. If he'd wondered whether there was still any bad blood between them, there was his answer. "Nothing for me. I don't eat from food trucks." She looked around the beach and then stepped back and looked into the parking lot beyond their truck. "Just waiting for my assistant..."

Annana walked out of view of the truck, and they began prepping the small dishes of bananas foster and brown sugar grilled peaches.

"She's interesting..." Maeve offered. In the background, they could clearly hear "All of Me" by John Legend. Maeve had the peaches on the grill, Heath assembled and mixed sauces, and Steve cut up bananas. They only took a minute and a half to cook and needed to be served immediately afterward, so that part was still mostly prep until the last second.

"She's awful," Steve said, unable to hold back. "What the fuck were we thinking?"

He'd meant it as a rhetorical question, but she bit her lip in concentrated thought. Then she adjusted the peaches and lost that look of intensity when she casually answered, "I was young and naïve. I don't know what happened with you." She flashed him a mischievous grin and he couldn't wait until the event was over and they could just exist together. A time where she could make a comment like that and he could respond in kind with a playful bite to her shoulder, or a light tackle to a bed where he'd make her take it back or suffer the dire consequences. Currently, with Heath's elbow bumping his own because they were on top of each other in the truck, he had to hold back his urges for at least a few more hours.

"I'm back, bitches!" Annana's horrid and yet lovely voice

interrupted their conversation. She had the kind of personality that made it hard for people to ignore her.

"Recognize the truck?" she continued. "That's right… I'm standing outside Reeve's–" Annana put her hand up to mouth and giggled as if she'd actually made a faux pas. "Sorry, I mean Steve's food truck, Today's Gluten Free Special, and, just as promised, I have a huge surprise for you all."

Her eyes went back to the people in the truck, who stood looking out the service window with their mouths hanging open, those awful shirts on full display. A woman who looked to be no older than a high school student held up a ring light with a phone to record Annana's video.

Then Bethany, the scorned woman at the food truck whose video had led to Steve's outing as Reeve, walked up to Annana. Her hair and make-up had been done, and she wore a sundress with strappy sandals. A distinct look from her business casual attire the other day, but not unrecognizable.

"You all remember Bethany?" Like the stealthy ninja that she was, Annana produced yet another phone seemingly from thin air since it didn't look like there was a stitch to spare on her skin-tight dress. A few taps to the screen and then she held up her phone to show the TikTok video Maeve and Kiki had posted. Steve and crew couldn't see the screen since they were mere background pawns at this stage in the live TikTok, but they could hear the familiar sounds of Heath's voice and Bethany's as they discussed what a wanker Dereck was.

Once the video ended, Annana's hand went behind her back, and the phone disappeared again. She held Bethany's hand. "That was difficult, wasn't it?"

The two rehashed that day and what had happened between her and Dereck, while Steve surveyed the wedding beyond them. For the most part, they were still going somewhat unnoticed as everyone focused on eating their dinner, getting more drinks, or dancing out on the makeshift dance floor that covered a decent portion of the only sandy beach in the area.

He couldn't tell if their oblivion was a good thing or not. Without the extra audience, aside from however many were watching the live stream, whatever horrible thing Annana was about to do didn't feel so devastating. But that also meant there was no one there to stop her if she took it too far.

"Dereck, come on out!" Like a fucking episode of *Jerry Springer*, Dereck came trotting around from the other side of the food truck and Annana stood between the two ex-lovers, an actress playing at being a judge or some demented form of a goddess. Bethany looked shocked. Unlike the people on those old daytime television shows, Steve could tell she wasn't faking her reaction. Annana had ambushed her, too.

30

maeve

Another epiphany popped into her mind: Annana and Jackson were actually the same horrible self-centered person.

She and Steve had spoken briefly about her reappearance and her upcoming performance at the wedding, but they hadn't expected this. Or rather, Steve hadn't expected this. He had the tendency to see only the good in people. While it somewhat bit him in the ass in this situation, it was the exact quality she was looking for in a man.

Maeve loved his Mr. Rogers "find the good" personality. Loved a lot of things about him. She only wished he knew that. Because regardless of how he saw everyone else in their best light possible, he sometimes only saw himself as that guy from that song or the teen who rained fireballs of nudes on a dinner party whose house almost burned down. He defined himself by his worst actions and how everyone else saw him.

Under the counter, his hand gripped hers and gave a quick squeeze. She read his mind: Shit's about to go down again, but we're in this together… Right? She squeezed back an emphatic yes! as she took in his sweaty palm and the uncertain look in his eyes.

After a quick confirming head nod, she turned her attention back to the live train wreck that was about to happen in front of the food truck.

To the utter horror of everyone except Annana and her featured guests, Dereck apologized for the various wrong doings he'd committed during their relationship and then got on his knees to beg Bethany to take him back.

Maeve's eyes narrowed in on Bethany's facial expressions. While they looked good and convincing, she was convinced they had staged it for the audience. When? Who could say? Who could say anything when Annana was involved? Her levels of deception and master planning for her own personal gain were unmatched by anyone Maeve knew.

"Okay, you lovebirds. I already talked to the bride and groom and they'd love for you to stay for the show and cake. Maybe you'll even catch the bouquet." Annana nudged Bethany's arm and the previously "broken up with no hope of reconciling" couple was suddenly downright giddy about catching a bundle of used flowers and potentially planning for a wedding of their own.

They walked off hand-in-hand towards the dance floor just as Chasity saddled up next to Annana.

"Annana, so happy you could make it on our special day," Chasity gushed as she gave an awkward look towards the camera. Then she gave the woman she'd met the day before a quick side hug as if they'd been besties for years. The memories were coming back now and Maeve could recall more than a few occasions where their field hockey coach had had to have the talk with Chasity about passing to others who had a better shot than she did. Chasity wasn't one to share the spotlight. Maeve couldn't put her finger on why in the hell Chasity would even entertain the idea of Annana upstaging her at her wedding.

Annana accepted the side hug and gave a small, curt smile in response. "You look gorgeous, Chasity." Annana spoke back to the phone as she added, "Stay tuned, everyone. This was just the beginning, and you don't want to miss the main event happening in thirty minutes." She made a motion with her hand and her assistant let the phone and the light drop to her side.

"I spoke with the DJ," Chasity said to Annana, whose smile was nowhere in sight once the live-stream had stopped. "We're going to do the cake and dessert, then you're on. Right at eight."

"I'll need to talk to the DJ," Annana said, walking off towards the DJ's table while her assistant and Chasity followed.

Maeve could hear her phone buzzing in the drawer and decided it was worth washing her hands again to see what was going on. She had almost a dozen text messages from Kiki who was likely closing down the shop for the night.

I'm watching on TikTok. Did you know she was live streaming all of this?

> I see you! Your hair is fabulous. But that shirt
> :(

> She found Bethany????

> She found Dereck????

> He wants her back????

> She took him back???

> WTF!

> People are going nuts in the comments.

> Half think she walks on water. Other half is
> only here to see her drown.

That white dress is too much.

Yes to all of this. Keep me posted on what you're seeing on your end.

It was encouraging to hear Annana's wave of online support was shifting.

"What's her angle?" Heath asked as he dumped brown sugar and butter into a skillet for the bananas foster. They'd already announced the cake cutting, so they needed to be ready to serve desserts in the next five to ten minutes. Of the 150 guests, they estimated at least half would want a dessert from the truck.

"I told you, I offered the gig as an ego boost. She's not here for me; it's all about her career now."

Steve looked to her for confirmation that he'd had no choice in mentioning the wedding to Annana, and she was happy to give it to him. Just like she'd helped Jackson with his injured nose and pretended as though she would consider using Chasity as a life coach. The thought almost made her dry heave, but it was a necessary lie, needed to defuse the situation. There was no chance of winning in a fight with Jackson or Annana. No point in fighting them, anyway. Aggressive engagement only prolonged their interest. Appeasement followed by detachment was the answer.

"You had to apologize, and you had to offer up something," she said. "She would have twisted the situation again if you didn't." She leaned in for a quick kiss on his cheek.

"Break it up, you two. Here they come." Heath motioned out to the beach where the party-goers were once again making their way towards the truck. The downfall of serving up a fantastic dinner? Most of them skipped out on the wedding cake in favor of the cooked up sweets in the truck. Maeve couldn't blame them. Grilled peaches and bananas foster always beat cake in her mind.

The dessert service went considerably faster than dinner given the easier prep and limited plating involved. Before they knew it, the speakers seemed to double in decibels with Annana's voice. Heath didn't even pause in his cleanup work, but it entranced Maeve and Steve.

There was Annana's assistant, shoulder to shoulder with the wedding videographer, as they both did their best to capture the moment. Him, over six-feet of solid muscle toting a commercial-grade camera, and her, five-foot-two on a good day with her light-ring and cell phone. If it came down to battling it out for the best shot, the assistant didn't have a chance.

"Hello, you lovely, lovely people," Annana said to her TikTok fans rather than anyone who was actually in front of her. Apparently, those were not lovely, lovely people. "I know this is a celebration of love between Jackson and Chasity." She pointed off stage to where the happy couple stood, looking up at the D-list celebrity who'd taken over their wedding for the next ten minutes or so. Beef, the wedding videographer, moved to get a shot of the newlyweds while the assistant kept her phone trained on Annana.

"But I'm sure you both didn't get to where you are now, without a little heartbreak along the way." Murmurs went through the crowd as they all acknowledged the truth bomb Annana had thrown their way: people rarely get married to the first person they date. Some heads turned towards the truck, either remembering that time long ago that Maeve had dated their sweet Jackson and apparently broken his heart, or perhaps they'd stumbled upon Annana's TikToks and knew Steve was actually Reeve.

The dance floor filled with women who'd long ago ditched their heels, bridesmaids who refused to set down their filled-to-brim glasses of wine, and former frat boys on the verge of landing on the ugly side of drunk: everyone gathered as they eagerly waited for the singing and dancing to commence. But it didn't come. Annana dragged on her speech as she explained how Reeve (or sometimes Steve or Steven having thoroughly confused even herself it seemed) had feigned gentlemanly behavior to get into her pants and to high-jack her burgeoning career, only to drop her like a bad habit once his mood changed. Once he thought he could no longer benefit from their union.

Yes, Maeve decided. Annana and Jackson were the same person. Except Maeve had had years to figure it out and somewhat recover prior to his resurgence. Steve had not had that luxury and the look on his face showed his prior attitude of nonchalance was on the verge of escaping again if Annana dug her blue fingernails too deep into his still-healing scar.

31
steve

Someone else may have been immune to it all. May even have found humor in it as they enjoyed the brief and random ride of having instant and fleeting notoriety for something as random as breaking up with a girlfriend who wasn't a good fit.

Steve wasn't someone else. He was a man who grew up praying he would not become his father. His high school research project was a thorough examination of nature versus nurture. Are people born assholes or do they become one because of outside influences? End result: no one knew. There was too much evidence going in both directions. Nature and nurture appeared to be so intricately intertwined that the only certainty he could find was that life was an unpredictable crap shoot. All he knew was that his father was blissfully unaware of how horrible a person he actually was, and Steve's fears of turning into him without even realizing–either through genetics or by just being around him throughout his most formative years–those fears were deep-rooted and painfully exposed throughout this whole ordeal.

And somehow, it was as if Annana knew that. Had some super power that let her into his deepest fears of being the secret asshole. The guy who had no idea everyone hated him and carried on with his life, being none the wiser about it, like his father.

Luckily, just when he'd started to let Annana's words get the best of him, again, he felt a pair of lips on his neck, reminding him he was more than the sum of that one horribly written song.

That sugary scent filled his nose. And while it was probably from a mixture of Maeve and the desserts Heath was still working to clean up a mere foot or two behind him, his body responded as if it was only Maeve, and as if they weren't in a food truck.

She kissed him again, and again, ending each one with the gentlest suck that caused his dick to twitch with each one. He was a neck guy. Who knew? There was just something about the teasing of it all and the anticipation that while it was only a few pecks on the neck, a lick here and there for good measure, it would eventually hit other parts of his body. How could he not react as he stood there, eyes closed, imagining all the things that were soon to come?

When she whispered in his ear, "Are you okay?" that was all he heard, despite Annana's incessant accusations coming from across the sandy beach.

Maeve's fingers gently scratched at the back of his neck, officially breaking the trance he'd been in watching Annana's way-too-long-for-a-wedding speech about their breakup. When he turned to ask if Heath could take over the cleaning for a bit, he found Heath already eying him up.

"Just go," he said with a mixture of amusement and annoyance, but mostly amusement."

"Thanks, man," Steve said, wanting to hug Heath for the offered escape, but also not wanting to poke him in his somewhat excited state. He settled on a hit to the arm, and Maeve planted a chaste kiss on Heath's cheek as her own thank you.

"Yeah, yeah… No big deal. It's pretty fucked up for either

of you to be serving these people after all of this, anyway." Heath said as they threw their aprons on the counter and hauled ass out of the back of the truck.

Steve jumped down first. When he turned for Maeve, he found her flying into his arms. Her legs wrapped around his waist and they kissed as if they hadn't just shagged a few hours earlier.

"I Really, Really Hope You Die" started up and instead of inciting panic or feelings of inadequacy, it led to nothing. Not a damn thing.

"Do you want to dance?" he asked, letting her feet slide down to the street.

"You dance?" There was anticipation in her question, and Steve couldn't wait to keep surprising her with all the things she didn't yet know about him. He backed towards the beach, his hand outstretched and waiting for hers.

Maeve's face lit up, her beauty unmarred by the hideous shirt she was wearing. When she took his hand, he raised it up and guided her into a spin under his arm before pulling her in close. Their one set of hands extended out to the side as per tradition, while his other hand rested on the small of her back, and hers caressed the base of his neck. The gentle scratch of her fingers soothing any hurt, but there was no hurt to soothe.

By all accounts, it shouldn't have been heaven, but it was. He'd gotten so lost in dancing with Maeve, he didn't even notice the groomsmen collecting Annana from the stage and hoisting her onto her shoulders like an athlete who'd just scored the winning point in some championship game.

Heath and Steve had correctly read the room in guessing that there would be some sort of serenade during the wedding, they just hadn't realized it would be for Steve during Annana's song.

"Oh my–" Maeve said.

Steve cut her off. "Don't stop dancing."

They'll never know how it all would have played out, because before Annana and crew could get close enough to the truck, the mic cut off and the song abruptly switched to a wedding fan favorite: The Electric Slide.

Jackson, unable to keep himself away from a situation which had the potential to hurt or embarrass Maeve, turned towards the DJ table, looking as though he was ready to raise hell for the DJ interfering with his plan.

Steve and Maeve stopped dancing. He saw the DJ put his hands up in surrender before pointing to the lovely bride, moving impressively fast over the sand in her long, intricately adorned white dress.

The groomsmen, a group of four well-dressed and confused-looking muscle-heads, lowered Annana to the sand. Her assistant, still holding her ring light and phone, looked for guidance on what to do next, but Jackson's and Annana's eyes were glued to the approaching, pissed off bride.

"Don't do something you're going to regret," Jackson warned Chasity.

"Like fuck the woman who's performing at our wedding?" she said as she lunged for Jackson.

Everything that came next happened within a matter of seconds, but it would live rent free in Steve's mind, in slow-motion, for the rest of his life.

While Jackson leaned back to avoid Chasity's angry fists, Annana lunged for Chasity with the other groomsmen intervening so that no one made physical contact. The assistant recorded while Annana demanded she stop and as she flailed in the arms of her drunk, suit-wearing captors.

"Jesus, do you hear how fucking insane you sound, Chassy? And on our wedding day?" He shook his head in disgust while Chasity writhed against the grip of the two groomsmen, desperate to break free.

The vein in his forehead pulsed. He'd ditched the linen suit coat earlier, and he'd rolled up his dress shirt sleeves. He looked eager to fight. It was deceptive because he'd be smiling, but Steve knew his type. The smile came from the anticipation of a brawl, not because he was actually pleased about anything.

"You son of a bitch. You're not going to gaslight me any–"

A swift backhand from Jackson stopped Chasity midsentence. The groomsmen not only released her, they took half-a-dozen enormous steps back from the situation. A situation that was still being broadcasted live to however many viewers Annana could amass.

Chasity's hand went to her already red cheek, and she backed away, too, her face turned down and away. A bridesmaid and Maeve rushed to her side, the bridesmaid offering her a cold bottle of beer to hold up against her cheek.

The onlookers–everyone at the wedding who watched in horror from the dancefloor and at their tables a few yards away, Dereck and Bethany, additional staff hired by the bride and groom to set up the tables and run the bar, and one lone bridesmaid who'd followed Chasity out there–they all stared, shocked into immobility as the showdown continued.

The only one not stepping back was Steve. His father had never hit his mother, but to him, the emotional abuse always felt as damaging as any physical abuse he could have thrown her way. He couldn't walk away from what he'd seen Jackson do.

Steve grabbed Jackson's shoulder and spun him around to find his eyes wide with rage and excitement.

"Don't start with me, asshole." Jackson pushed his sleeves up even further and took a small step forward. He inhaled deeply and drew his shoulders back, drawing him another inch or two higher. Intimidation was likely his oldest and only friend.

"Walk away, Jackson."

"From my wedding?" he laughed. "Get lost, dipshit, and don't expect a dime from me." With all the testosterone and hate flying through his veins, his voice was cool and filled with optimistic anticipation. Someone needed to pay for Jackson's current humiliation, and that someone was Steve and Maeve.

In what sounded like an afterthought, he added, "Take that cunt with you." His thumb over his shoulder signaling to Maeve, his wife, the bridesmaid, or perhaps all of them.

Without thinking, he wound up and punched Jackson in the nose. This time there was a distinct sound of crunching as the already injured cartilage finally gave way and collapsed under the force of Steve's amateurish, but effective, punch.

When Steve was nine, he pushed a kid from behind during a game of tag during fourth-grade recess. Memory had a way of skewing facts, and this was no exception. He no longer knew for sure if he'd pushed the kid on purpose or not, or if he'd done it maliciously or playfully. What he knew for certain was that the kid fell and broke his collarbone. The other kids and Mrs. Lipporn, his teacher at the time, had treated him differently for the rest of the year. Conversely, his horrible father had renewed interest in him for a few months, until it was clear the incident was an anomaly and his father went back to ignoring him and his mother.

The entire experience had been beyond traumatic for his little mind and heart, and his nine-year-old self had made a solemn vow that he would never, ever physically hurt someone again.

And yet he had zero regrets about slamming his fist into Jackson's nose. It was practically orgasmic to feel the bone and cartilage collapsing under the force of his knuckles. Since he'd never hit anyone before, he didn't know the right way to do it aside from keeping his thumb out of his fist so that he wouldn't break it.

Clearly, he'd not done it correctly because even though he'd had the intended effect of fucking up Jackson's nose, immediately following came a searing pain shooting from his knuckles through his arm.

The two grown men turned away from each other as they cursed, doubled over, and tended to their fresh wounds. Maeve and everyone else looked on with amazement. Annana was nowhere to be found. She must have slipped out during all the commotion.

Jackson gave a hollow laugh that made him wince. "And now I'm going to sue your ass for assault."

"Jackson, please–" Maeve made a move towards Jackson and it squeezed the life out of Steve's soul to see her still stuck under his hateful thumb.

"Enough, Jackson."

Everyone turned to see the bride, her knuckles white from clutching the bottle of bear. It wouldn't have surprised anyone if by sheer anger and willpower she'd been able to crush it with her one bare hand. The intensity on Chasity's face rivaled Jackson's as the showdown shifted from Steve and Jackson to the newly pronounced husband and wife.

"You and I will–" he said, but she cut him off.

"We're done." She took a nip of liquid courage, though it was debatable if she needed it or not. All week he'd judged her as vapid and shallow. That may have been a mistake.

Actual fear flickered in Jackson's eyes before he took a few timid steps towards her.

Chasity shook her head and said, "I warned you." Her eyes narrowed at him.

Jackson's giant Adam's apple plunged down and back up again as he swallowed and gulped for air.

He stopped in his tracks and his shoulders rose back up when he said, "Let's just get out–"

"No."

Jackson glanced at Maeve, balled his fists, released them, then walked up to Chasity. In a low voice that everyone could hear because the entire crowd was collectively holding their breathes, he said, "I'll see you back at the hotel."

Then he was gone.

Steve went to Maeve with renewed concern. He doubted Maeve's experience with Jackson was exactly what he'd witnessed on the beach with Chasity, but he also doubted it was very far off. Once again, he regretted not fighting harder to keep him away from her as soon as he'd sensed the bad vibes from Jackson.

Maeve was shaking. He took her hands in his and held her when she buried her face in his chest.

"We should go," Heath said gently to Steve before climbing into the truck.

The audience dispersed. Steve stood with Maeve, while Chasity and her bridesmaid spoke in hushed tones a few feet away.

"I'm so sorry," Maeve repeated, her tears soaking his shirt.

"No, you aren't responsible for Jackson's behavior."

Maeve shook her head and pulled away from him. "I drug you into this mess and now you're going to go into debt from this wedding and from legal fees. That *is* my fault. I forced you–"

"I made the choice to cater the wedding, and to hit him." That last part got a slight smile from her. He could almost see her reliving it in her mind, reveling in the glory of it all. Consequences be damned. It was exactly how he felt, too.

He and Heath would figure it out. They always did. Buying the truck and starting their business had had them living their own version of paycheck to paycheck since they'd started. It wasn't ideal, but it also put things into perspective in regard to money.

"For what it's worth, I wouldn't worry about it," Chasity said, inserting herself into their conversation. "He's not going to do anything. I won't let him."

Unfortunately, Chasity's white-knuckled hand was still

shaking when she said it, so it didn't come out as confident as Steve would have liked. Before he could ask for clarification as to why his nemesis was suddenly going to disappear into the sunset and leave him alone forever, Chasity's friend tugged on her hand, and after a sad wave goodbye, she made her way across the beach, her head resting on her friend's shoulder as they maneuvered through the random chairs and pieces of stage already being dismantled.

"Bloody hell," Heath said when Steve and Maeve climbed into the truck, "do I have a story for you guys."

32

maeve

Heath told them everything on the way home. It was one hell of a story.

As soon as Maeve and Steve had stepped out of the truck, Heath sought out Miles, the pseudo (according to Heath) wedding planner Jackson and Chasity had hired. He wanted to let Miles know they'd finished and that they were going to pack up and get the hell out of there.

He found the planner, but he could barely get a word in since Miles was knee deep in the cluster-fuck that was Chasity and Jackson's wedding. Even though he was surrounded by three of Chasity's family members who were all demanding Miles fix the disaster happening on stage with Annana's blubbering about Reeve, Miles quickly gave him the go-ahead to leave and pointed out a dumpster off near the community building where he could get rid of any waste from the night. Never one to pass up a free trash dump, Heath ignored the craziness on stage, gathered up what trash they'd created that night, and made a quick run to the dumpster.

Since it was an outside wedding, Jackson and Chasity had access to the bathrooms in the community building for their guests. When Heath got to the dumpsters, right near the bathrooms, he found a group of people in their formal wear arguing about whose fault it was that Chasity actually went through with marrying Jackson.

"It was a real-life Spiderman meme," Heath said as he drove. "Four guys in suits were all pointing at each other, making accusations. Heath changed his voice for each accusation and used his best American accent.

"You got drinks with them last night; you saw him get too close to Annana."

"You saw him grab her during an argument last year, and you said nothing."

"You knew he forced her to quit teaching. She loved that job."

"And so on," Heath said, making the universal sign with his hand that it continued on even though he wasn't going to list it all out. "I think they're all guilty."

Maeve remained quiet while Steve and Heath went back and forth about whose fault it was. Maybe if it ever came up later, she'd put in her two cents. But in the truck after the horrible night they'd already had, she didn't have it in her to explain to them how calculating Jackson was. How there'd probably already been at least one or two friends or relatives who'd spoken up and had been banned from the wedding or from her life altogether. Maeve herself had lost a few friends that way.

Heath dished out more tea and Maeve listened with mild interest about all the dirt thrown down on Jackson, the biggest being embezzlement through his job at a company Chasity's family owned and his serial cheating habits. She only half listened because flashbacks kept popping up in her mind with all the warning signs that it had probably been happening when they were dating, too.

"Are you okay?" Steve asked, his hand rubbing her knee and his eyes full of concern.

She smiled back at him. "Yes. I'm good now. With you."

His hard angles, his sandalwood scent, his masculine scruff against her jawline when he nuzzled her. That was all the comfort she needed. The brawl that night and all the events of the week had more than slammed the door on any unresolved feelings or questions she still had about Jackson. That was her past. Steve was her future.

33

steve

"It's finally just us," he said, his face buried in her hair since she'd practically raced into his arms as soon as he'd led her back to his room. Nuzzled right in, as if that had always been her place. Maybe it had been, and they just needed to meet each other to figure it out.

His fingers went through her hair while his other hand rubbed her back. Maeve didn't say a word, just clung to him. He got the sense that she was taking him in as well. He could feel her deeply inhaling, savoring his scent as much as he was savoring hers.

Maeve pulled herself back just far enough to peer up at him with those gorgeous brown eyes.

"Was that the infamous 'came inside' calendar I saw out in the kitchen?"

They still had enough emotional baggage to overflow any airline overhead compartment, but humor was a good sign.

"The one and only. Looking to get your own mark on it?"

She shook her head and wrinkled her nose, her freckles scrunching on the bridge. "Too late. I'm officially off the market."

"Damn right you are," he said, leaning down to finally put

his lips to hers once more. He was like an addict with how often he daydreamed about it, and with the way his body craved it at all times.

"Mind if I stay the night?" she whispered between kisses, as if she was unsure what his answer might be. She deepened their kiss and her hands moved around his body with want, need, and urgency.

Twice in one day? He hadn't done that in a while, but surely his exhausted body could rally. His body's reaction to her nails at the nape of his neck assured him he could.

After they'd become reacquainted in the bedroom and then extensively covered where they stood on the subject of their exes–they were both beyond tired of talking about it and ready to move on–Maeve found his battered copy of *Cod* on the nightstand.

"Holy crap. How many times have you read this?" she asked, her voice showing nothing but pure awe. She flipped through the worn pages, little sticky notes sticking out here and there throughout the novel.

"I told you; it's one of my favorites."

"Do you read it every night?" That time, the awe dropped and made room for skepticism and possibly even some apprehension. Rightfully so. It was a good book, but it wasn't that good.

He chuckled and kissed her bare shoulder as she read through some of his scribbles on the sticky notes and on the pages themselves.

"I've read it a few times over the past decade or so. I only picked it up again recently because you just got your own copy. In case you want to discuss it, I want to have it fresh in my mind." Some animalistic urge took over him and his sweet kisses on her shoulder turned into playful bites. She looked so freaking hot holding up his abused copy of *Cod*. A third round might not be in the cards for him, but he craved her regardless and couldn't keep his hands or mouth off of her.

Maeve put the book down and turned to face him, her auburn hair fanned out over the pillow and in stark contrast against his light gray sheets. He could tell she was weighing her words carefully.

"I love my book stack present. At least half of those books I've had my eye on or I've read and loved enough that I was eventually going to buy my own copies. You picked out the perfect stack of books and crafted the sweetest apology ever. But…"

"But what?" He tucked a section of hair behind her ear. A cheap ploy to touch her as much as he could without being too creepy about it.

"I'm probably not going to be diving into *Cod* right away." She grimaced. "Don't hate me. I'll get to it. I will. It's your favorite and I'm excited to discuss it, really."

His heart melted. It had been more of a joke that he'd included it in the stack, not an actual expectation that *Cod* would be the book to win her over. She'd made that adorably clear the first time they met. A biography about fish wasn't her thing.

"I understand." Steve reached out again. He caressed her cheek, and when her hand reached up for his, he took it in his own for a brief second before turning to grab his phone off the nightstand. "I figured you might say that." With a few taps on his phone, he pulled up his ebook library for her to see. "I already downloaded all the other books. Just tell me where you want to start."

The phone fell off to the side as she threw herself on him and nuzzled into that spot on his chest that was quickly becoming her spot.

"Are you canceling my book club for one Mondays?" she asked. Despite her excitement about his extensive e-library and their future reading journey together, it was late, and they'd had one of the longest days of their lives with the emotional ups and downs they'd experienced. Her eyes were half closed before he even answered.

"Whatever you want. I'll join you, or you can still keep your night for yourself." He kissed the top of her head and took a pull of her vanilla cookie scent. "Whatever makes you happy. That's all I care about."

34

epilogue: maeve

"This singer briefly found fame with her hateful song, 'I Really, Really, Hope You Die,' before leaving the music industry for a career as a therapist."

They could barely hear Mayim Bialik. The ruckus that followed easily drowned out her and the Final Jeopardy! theme music.

Steve groaned about how he couldn't get away from Annana and how he couldn't believe that was the clue for the last question. She knew he never wagered much with categories like pop culture.

Heath questioned the validity of the clue as very few would call Annana an actual therapist. According to him, she played a therapist on a reality television show in a state that had flimsy licensure requirements and even flimsier ideas about morals and ethics.

Maeve broke out in a victory dance as she celebrated her win and taunted the guys. She'd bet everything she had and was already in the lead going into Final Jeopardy!

Lori offered faux condolences to Heath, who, in her opinion, was getting way too worked up over something that didn't affect him in the slightest. Then she joined in the victory dance even though she was in last place going into the last clue.

Maeve liked that about Lori. She didn't take things too seriously; she helped Heath not take (some) things too seriously, and she was fun to be around.

Unfortunately, the more Heath brought Lori along, the more Kiki had declined to join them. For a while Kiki would bring dates with her or guys that she was seeing–not quite boyfriends, but something close to it–whenever she hung out with Maeve and Steve, and Heath and Lori.

Slowly, so slowly that Maeve hadn't even realized it had been happening until Steve brought it up one day, Kiki had increased how often she declined their invites to dinners, hikes, fishing trips, and days out on the beach.

It had been almost a year since they'd worked together, and their group outings were becoming more and more infrequent, but she and Kiki always met up at least once a month for dinner at Cuppa Chowda.

When she'd casually brought up how Keek hadn't been around as much, Kiki broke down. Through tears she said that even though she was bringing dates with her, she and her date still felt like fifth wheels whenever they were out together. The four of them, Maeve, Steve, Heath, and Lori, were always together or texting in their group chat. There were unlimited inside jokes and referenced experiences that Kiki just wasn't a part of anymore. She wasn't mad, and she understood. She just didn't want to keep putting herself or her dates in the position of being on the outside looking in, even though they were all at the same dinner table.

As Maeve and Lori danced it up in the living room, Maeve had a pang of guilt knowing that this would become another inside joke of theirs. That time Annana was the winning Final Jeopardy! answer, and Bialik had referred to her as a therapist.

It should have been Kiki dancing with her, and it should have been Kiki who finally achieved girlfriend status with Heath.

That night, she couldn't focus on the book she was reading. After rereading the same page at least three times, she set it down on her nightstand and turned to face Steve.

Regardless of the temperature outside, he always slept shirtless. Heath had finally worn him down about hitting the gym with him, and Maeve could see the difference in his upper body. She noticed the way his muscles popped, especially the ones on his upper back that ran from his neck to his shoulders, each time he used his arms to brace himself during missionary. She was admiring his new physique in bed when Steve caught her.

"What's wrong?" he asked, not looking away from his book.

"Nothing's wrong. I'm admiring my sexy boyfriend."

He set his book down and turned his body towards her, propping himself up on one arm. Then he reached out to trace the furrowed line between her brows.

"This tells me something's wrong, and you barely read any of your book. Pretend I'm Annana, and talk to me," he joked.

She gave him a sorry-looking half-smile. Just another reminder of the joke Kiki wasn't in on.

"I miss Kiki."

Steve mumbled a sort of confirmation before adding, "She would have destroyed us tonight with all the science categories."

"That's why I miss her. I need a challenge."

Steve's relaxed expression turned to something akin to mischievous as he used both hands to relentlessly tickle Maeve into submission.

"Take it back," he ordered. "I won't stop until you admit I'm just as worthy a *Jeopardy* adversary as Kiki is."

It wasn't easy to say through the fits of laughter, but Maeve finally got out the lie.

Afterwards, as they were laying in comfortable silence with Steve on his back and Maeve curled into the crook of his arm with her head on his chest, he said, "You should go hang out, just the two of you. Take her up to New York next weekend."

"Really? Are you sure?" She and Steve had planned a weekend up in New York to do all the typical tourist things: museums, a show, restaurants, etc.

"I don't mind." He kissed the top of her head. "I'll miss you, but this is important, and you and I can go up again some other time. Maybe before Christmas so we can see all the lights."

"Yeah, maybe I will. She and I had always talked about going up there and doing nothing but walking tours and eating at hidden gem restaurants." As she thought about which areas of the city they should visit, she adjusted her leg slightly and was shocked to knock up against Steve, rock hard.

"Steve!" She gave him a playful swat to the chest.

"What?" he asked, laughing as he put his hand under the blankets and gave his dick a quick few tugs. "I have this gorgeous woman I love pressed up against me. You're wearing a threadbare old shirt so I can feel your nipples dragging over my chest and side every time you make the slightest movement. I'm not acting on it because we're having a serious conversation, but I'm a hetero man and this is how we react to hot, half-naked women in our beds."

She knocked his hand away and took over. "Then maybe we should put the serious conversation on hold." Pulling back the covers, she ran her tongue up his cock, reveling in Steve's moans and the feel of his muscular hands that tightened their grips each time she licked.

Almost a year later and she still couldn't get enough of

him, and she knew he felt the same way. She'd been cleaning the apartment the other day and found an engagement ring hidden in a back drawer. Maeve was going to be the woman who married that Reeve guy from the song, and she couldn't wait.

want more? of course you do!

Missed Sam's enemies to lovers rom-com?
Scan the above code to read it now!

Scan the code below to check out my website which includes bonus material!

www.ingramcontent.com/pod-product-compliance
Lightning Source LLC
Chambersburg PA
CBHW030923210726
48290CB00007B/2041